P9-BIG-719

DATE DUE

DEMCO 38-296

BELOW
THE
SUMMIT

BELOW
THE
SUMMIT

JOSEPH V. TORRES-METZGAR

Riverside Community College
Library
4800 Magnolia Avenue
Riverside, California 92506

AUG '94

2150 Shattuck Avenue
Berkeley, CA. 94704
USA

TONATIUH INTERNATIONAL INC.
PUBLISHERS OF CHICANO LITERATURE
berkeley, california   san antonio,   texas

First Printing   August 1976

COPYRIGHT © 1976 by JOSEPH V. TORRES-METZGAR

All rights reserved. No part of this book may be re-
produced in any form or by any means whatsoever
without permission in writing from the author and
the publisher.

Library of Congress
Catalogue Card Number   76-41036

ISBN   0-89229-005-6

This book is a work of fiction, and any similarity to specific persons, institutions, and iconographies, living or dead, is purely coincidental.

"And they proceeded from Beer to Nahaliel, and from Nahaliel to Bamoth; then from Bamoth to the valley in the Moabite country below the summit of Pisgah overlooking the desert."

Numbers 21: 19—20
The New English Bible

CHAPTER ONE

He was hurrying, accelerator to the floor, anxious to get home. A jaw-hanging stupor enveloped his body, a fatigue so heavy that his stomach was queasy and his head throbbed viciously and his eyes would not focus well. He knew he must be careful, must stay awake. The guideline down the center of the highway, and the piercing headlights of his old Ford pickup did not help as the steady hum of the engine soothed his body toward sleep. He became increasingly fearful of the stupor that dulled the senses so enticingly. He must not drop off to sleep. He must not. He began singing in throat-bursting shouts.

> "You'll take the high road
> And I'll take the low road
> And I'll be in Scotland afore yuh.
> But me and my true love
> We'll never meet again
> On the bonnie, bonnie banks
> Of Loch Lomond."

He repeated the stanza a hundred times almost, or so he thought. Even if the lyrics were so alien to his life in Texas he still liked the song. *His wife was waiting for him and she was lovely and she would lie close to him for the rest of his life. Yes, and he was grateful to the Lord for all that was provided him. He must not throw it all away in an instant of dozing stupidity.*

He began to worry about the jack rabbits, narrowly missing one earlier. He felt sorry for the poor stupid creatures. Never

1

swerve to avoid them. That would be suicidal. He had run over jack rabbits before and there was nothing one could do about it. *You just had to hold the wheel steady when it jerked slightly on impact,* he thought. *That is all you can do.*

The black silhouettes of hills against the moonlit sky told him he was not far from home. It would just be minutes. Soon he turned the little truck on a dirt road off the highway, and the wheels of the Ford bumped quick successive little thumps over the cattle guard. To the left the headlights peeled off the blackness from the trees and bushes that made up the edge of his private woods. He treasured the woods. They were so rare in this country, for one thing. For another, they provided a shelter and refuge for the harmless animals. He never allowed any hunter to enter the woods to stalk the wild creatures. He enjoyed watching the deer as they emerged from out of the thickets in early morning. They were wild and innocent and un-afraid here. Sometimes they would even brush against the side of his home. Other creatures also visited the vicinity of the house. A certain skunk often threw his family out of bed with that singular weapon that edged into the rooms at night. But he and his wife and their child did not mind and they laughed it off as a minor inconvenience.

The truck rolled over the rough-hewn bridge he had built over the deep but narrow arroyo that cut across the ranch. He stopped at the side of the house, climbed clumsily down from the high seat behind the steering wheel, and reached back to pull out a black leather case.

Glancing back at the highway which circled around a hill at least sixty feet above this neat little valley that was his domain, only the lights of a solitary car indicated any highway at all. If he had not known better from ten years of living in these hills, he would have experienced the frontier feeling of being cut off from any link to civilization. Yet, from time to time, he really did feel he was living on some last frontier, forgetting the high-way at such times and savoring the feeling of self-sufficiency and of living on the good earth. An old gentleman from Virginia had once written that yeoman farmers were God's chosen people, and Cross believed that deeply.

Robby Lee Cross stepped wearily up the two rock blocks that were the threshold of his home. The porch was screened to protect against mosquitoes that could eat you alive, or at least so said the local ranchers. This was a good house Cross had built. It was a rock house and it stood like a rock. It was sturdy and strong and made from the stone of his land. Cross believed it would stand forever. He often boasted to himself that not even a Texas tornado could hurt his home.

He walked through the porch and into the living room. Doors were never locked out here. Only migrant Yankees from Michigan and New York ever bolted a door. Out here there was nothing to fear.

"Marie!" he called.

In an instant a woman stepped into the light of the living room, moving gracefully to the man who called. She reached up his tall frame and took his head between her hands, kissing him.

"I'm awful tired," he announced.

"Go rest on the couch, Lee." She wrapped her arm around his waist and led him to the sofa. "Go on, lie down," feigning command. "Here, let me take off those boots."

"Thanks honey."

Kneeling, she pulled off his boots while his half-shut eyes followed the liquid movements of her body. Her long jetblack hair was lovely and it framed a strikingly beautiful face from which large dark eyes soothed and caressed the beholder. And the silky black hair flowed down over her shoulders along smooth pale arms to the tender curving line of her hips. Her voice was soft and she seemed to whisper even when raising it to call him from corral or woods.

"I'll get you some supper now."

She took the small black valise and disappeared behind the swinging door of the kitchen. "Business does not belong in the living room," she often told him.

He could hear her moving about in the kitchen now, and it seemed as if it were happening a long way off as he was falling into a deep, dead sleep. He felt a slight chill and he pulled up the rainbow-colored Mexican blanket that covered the couch. When the woman came through the swinging door she saw his heavy slumber, and she placed the food on the coffee table before the couch. Then she vanished into the back bedroom.

Cross lay in a nervous dream. He moaned and his eyelids twitched and his head moved from side to side. Suddenly his body jerked, wrenching him awake. He opened his eyes wide and felt his heart pounding madly.

Feeling he'd slept a long time, he didn't recognize the bare walls of his own home, gazing in wonder around the room, his eyes stopping at a picture of a solemn figure holding a bible. That man seemed so strange, so unrelated to anything. Cross lay back, closed his eyes, and then realized the unsmiling figure of the portrait was the Reverend Robby Lee Cross. Photographed several years ago when he decided to assume an independent ministry, his intentions had been, and were still, as serious as the guise of that hanging image on the wall.

He glanced at his watch. It was 10:30. Luckily he'd slept just twenty minutes, and could still listen to the revival hour. Taking a piece of cold chicken from the plate before him, he went into the kitchen, picked up the portable radio from the dinner table and walked out the back door to sit on the stoop and listen. Organ music, static, and a voice broke the stillness of the night.

"If yuh know the power o' God is heah tanight—Shout Amen!"

"AMEN!" responded the crowd.

"If yuh know God's creatin' miracles each an' ever' night—Shout Amen!"

"AMEN!" rejoined the crowd.

"If yuh know yuh cain talk ta the Lord God tanight—Shout Amen!"

"AMEN!"

The sounds of the organ broke in heavily and the clear sharp voice of the radio announcer explained that you were listening to Brother Billie's Miracle Revival Hour coming to you transcribed at the fairgrounds in Montgomery, Alabama. Then in rising and reverent tones, he introduced Brother Billie himself —the one and only! The organist struck a fanfare and the crowd applauded, shouting many hallelujahs and amens!

"Give JESUS a big hand!" the voice demanded. The crowd responded.

"Ain't God wonderful!" he exclaimed. The crowd cheered.

"Glory hallelujah! Praise the Lord!" he cried. The crowd rocked.

In solemn tones the preacher began his sermon.

"The Lord God come ta me yesterdee an' talked at me. Ah had went up ta a Colorado mountaintop ta seek the Lord.

An' yesterdee he come ta me.

Ever'day for seventeen days an' seventeen nights ah waited on God.

An' yesterdee he come ta me.

An' ah ast the Heavenly Father ta deliver me an' hep me ta touch his people in his name.

An' he give me a unusual gift.

This gift . . . . this gift of discerning spirits—that's what the Lord God give me!"

The preacher accelerated the flow of words. His voice began to assume a rasping, emotional pitch. It began to quiver, to growl, to screech. The forceful emotion was overpowering the crowd, intensified by the electric crackling words of the conductor. Shouts of hallelujah erupted among believers like the bursting sparks of tangled wires in a shorted circuit.

Senses flickered and hearts pounded.

". . . The angel of the Lord is talkin' ta me! The Holy Ghost descendin' 'pon me! Ah see through the eyes o' the Lord God! He's a-talkin' ta me now. . . ."

The lips of Robby Lee Cross were thin and tight and his brow was deeply furrowed as he listened to the radio. A vise-like sensation tightened hard around his head. He listened intently, not noticing the prickly feelings in his legs which were pulled up under him. The circulation was cut off from his lower limbs, but it made no impression on his brain. He was away— gone far off.

The radio preacher spewed out hell-fire in sobbing tones now. Growling, sobbing, screeching filled the air waves. Incoherent sounds were interspersed with assertions of "the bible says!"

"We's fixin' ta be saved! The Holy Ghost is a-huggin' yuh from the crown o' your haids ta the soles o' your feet. Ah speak of no sugar-coated, no bargain counter God! Ah speak for him ta all—ta all—from the guttermost ta the uttermost!

Ah be-LIEEEEEEEEEEEEEEEEVE in the Lord God of Josh-oo-way!

Ah be-LIEEEEEEEEEEFFFFFEEEVE in the old-fashioned jack-bible Jehovah!

Ah be-LIEEEEEEEEEEEEEEEEVE Jesus done saved us from hell fire on the cross o' cavalry!

Ah be-LIEEEEEEEEEEEEEEEEVE he'll save us again from atom's fire by the old rugged cross!"

Adam or atom, Calvary or cavalry—Cross was not sure. It made little difference.

The radio preacher sustained the level of emotion. And the believers screamed and sobbed in approval and frenzy. Then the conductor began, at first imperceptibly, to lower the nerve-jangling current. His crackling words seemed to moderate a little and he reduced the current more, and then more.

Testimonies were now to be heard. Organ music wafted in the background.

"Ah see visions, ah see names," drawled the preacher in anguished tones. "Now . . . now . . . ah see someone in the second . . . no . . . the third row behind the lady in the big white hat. Yes . . . yes, that's you! Yuh have some affliction. Your name is . . . is . . . your name is Hopper! That right? Your name is Sally Hopper!"

A startled cry and then a whimper.

"Come heah now, child," said the preacher. "Let me lay ma hands on yuh! Now sister Hopper, what's ailin' yuh?"

"Glory hallelujah!" came the answer. "Nuthin's hurtin' no more, Brother Billie. All 'causa you. Ah oncet laid ma hands on the ra-dee-o like yuh says one night an' ah was cured! Glory hallelujah!"

"Yes indeed, now it's comin' ta me," said the preacher. "Yuh lost your female organs through a operation, didn'tcha? An' yuh wanted a little baby sooooo bad. A little baby! An' yuh put your faith in the Lord an' listened ta ma preachin' an' next day yuh got pregnant, didn'tcha? Your husbin's mighty happy an' the doctor don't know what happened an' he cain't explain it, can he? Well, glory hallelujah! Ah have wrote it in ma heart. Thank yuh sister. Thank yuh!"

"Go ta Brother Billie," the woman shouted into the microphone, " 'cause no doctor cain't hep yuh none!"

"Now, what have we heah," said the preacher, addressing a new suppliant. "Yuh cain't talk none. Ah know, the Lord's a-tellin' me! Oh, look at yuh—you're bald as a billiard ball! You're paralyzed—ah know! Yuh got brain cancer—ah know! Yuh want God ta cure your cancer an' that pain in your kidney and make yuh walk again—ah know! Pitiful, pitiful, pitiful, pitiful!"

"Cain God do it?" asked the preacher.

"Yes" and "Yes" came the echoing response of the crowd.

"Yes, God's goin' ta do it an' he's a-goin' ta cure it all. God don't turn out no gingerbread cake half done! He'll do it right!"

A whimper and a sob. And the preacher invoked all his powers in alien guttural sounds: "Mahatma lahnda shackta lahna. . . ." And a scream burst forth and the clear voice of the

announcer broke in to report that Brother Billie had taken the
girl by the hand and lifted her to her feet from the stretcher and
she was walking and praising the Lord! Then the clear voice was
drowned out by the roar of the crowd. The organ attained glorious strains of victory and joy. For several minutes Cross heard
garbled words and blasting music and high-pitched shouts of
hallelujah!

Again the voice of the preacher, calling for silence and meditation. In a very slow, deliberate manner, Brother Billie began
to seal the evening's revival.

"The Holy Ghost worked through your 'umble servant again
tanight. The work was sensational. Jest like Jesus waited till
Lazarus was dead afore he come there ta his burying place, so
this happened heah tanight. He wanted ta be sensational—
SENSATIONAL! An' he was. An' his 'umble servant was.

Friends, accept these testimonies of ma special gifts from
God. If yuh need hep, write ta me tanight. Ah have decreed
miracles for millions!

An' friends, do yuh like the preachin' an' old-fashioned
bible teachin' ah bring ta yuh? Is this the kinda preachin' America needs? Ah preach the truth, the whole truth, an' nuthin' but
the truth! Ah heal folks with ma unusual gift from the Holy
Spirit. Ah ast yuh, is this 'umble servant a-doin' the work o'
God?

Friends, ah need hep ta continya this radio ministry. Write
ta me taday! Ah will pray ovah your letter. Ah pray someone
out there in radio land will send me a check for a hundred dollahs. Obey God and send that check or that crumpled ol' hun-
dred-dollah bill yuh got hid in that shoe in the closet. Won't
yuh hep God's work taday? God will hep yuh back. He'll even
put gold an' silver in your pocket. God is in the prayer-
answerin' business. Remembah!

Send your love gifts ta Brother Billie, Vale of Miracles, Box
999, Montgomery, Alabama."

A moment's pause.

"This is XDY, Ciudad Acuña, Coahuila, Mexico."

Cross snapped off the radio.

Awakened to reality by the stillness of the night, he felt his
legs numbing rapidly. Cross pulled them out from under him
and stood up as if his lower limbs were made of flexible rubber.
Holding on to the wall of the house, he shook out his legs.
Shaking them awake, a native would say.

Robby Lee often listened to broadcasts that originated from Mexican border towns. *These hell-fire preachers,* he thought, *probably transcribe their programs for broadcast from Ciudad Acuña and Monterrey and Juarez because it's cheaper to operate from the Mexican side. And they reach as many people in Texas and the Southwest as they would from this side. The Rio Grande border stretches far and wide and many little towns lie along it. It's easy and cheap for Brother Billie and the rest to use the Mexican side.*

Cross despised people like Brother Billie who were so presumptuous of God's favor. *They pretty near act like Christ incarnate, what with all their visions and inspirations and miracles and folderol and gobbleydygook. Twenty-twenty visions no less! And those healing powers! Their only faith is in the gullible. Their only gift is turning a quick dollar. They all believe they can open a ministry like a hamburger stand and sell meatless wares to the masses. And they do just that.* Robby Lee Cross felt a chill run down his back.

Yet, he believed they had a role to play and that was why he listened to their preaching. *They do arouse religious feeling and that is more than most broadcasters do. That's something anyway. Those so-called disc jockeys play only sex frenzies and talk hippie-beatnik nonsense. At least Brother Billie and the others were shrewd preachers. They did hit the right emotions hard. Why, even he had learned a little about preaching from them. He shouldn't put them down too much. In the long run they did good.*

Cross forgot about the revival and listened to the sounds of the night. It was peaceful and calm. The crickets were chattering more than usual. Altogether like that, they sounded almost like rattlers. He remembered the rattle he had cut off the tail of a big sidewinder once. He had brought it home and had rattled it playfully at the baby. Danny was only a year old then, but he giggled with big wide eyes and tried so hard to grab the rattle that he almost fell out of the high-fenced crib. He wanted it and he cried in anger when his father would not give it to him. In spite of Marie's displeasure, Cross decided to carve a thin wooden handle for the rattle and then he gave it to Danny. It didn't work out well, though. The baby chewed on it and it fell apart. After that, Marie wouldn't speak to him. He finally had to search all over Geneva Gap for a baby's rattle that sounded like the jiggling tail of a sidewinding serpent, until he found one made of plastic. Danny recognized the difference but the boy accepted it anyway. Now, several years later, the boy still had the rattle. Cross chuckled and shook his head and ran his hand like a comb back through his hair.

Business was not good this week. He could sell his goods only in the evening since he was too busy during the day with other things. Of course, the cutlery was quality merchandise and it really sold itself. But he had been unable to visit enough prospective buyers lately. His college classes took most of the day and then he had to check with the radio station about his own weekly broadcasts. Women's committees from the many churches in Geneva Gap often invited him to speak at afternoon luncheons or at a coffee and gossip gathering. He was constantly on the run, yet he seldom earned much money. He didn't spend much either. He and his family lived frugally and they even managed a bank account. But he just had to concentrate more on his sales job. It was his only real source of income. Yes, the ranch produced a few garden foods, some vegetables and fruit, and the goat gave milk generously. But he always had to add to their diet by buying food from the big chain store in town. Sometimes he wondered if he was being irresponsible with those college courses and all, since he wasn't even working for a degree. He would talk to Marie about it in the morning. It was always so hard to speak to her about such things. "I don't know anything about such business," she would say, and "You do what you think is best." She had the damnedest way of looking at things.

Suddenly Cross straightened up and listened intently. The two mares in the corral were trotting around and neighing in alarm. Predators sometimes dared to come this close from the mountainside. He had often thought of having a dog to guard the few livestock, but he always decided against it. A dog would only scare away the harmless creatures of the woods. And besides, a dog messed about in filth and God knows what all. And his son might catch some disease from the foot-loose creature. So now he had to see for himself what was causing the horses to spook.

He opened the screen door of the kitchen, unhooking a flashlight from a nail hanger, and walked to the corral. The horses whinnied nervously and reared up, kicking against the posts. There was a growl, a big cat, a cougar, maybe.

"It's a big one all right," he said aloud. "It must be in that cottonwood back there."

Cross owned no gun. He disliked weapons, so he had to use whatever he could find to protect his home. Picking up two fist-size rocks, he walked slowly around the corral to the big cotton-wood. The wild beast shuffled slightly in the lower branches that formed a bridge to the sloping mountainside. Cross was near the tree but out of range of a sudden lunge. He stood still for a moment then flashed the light directly into the limbs of the cottonwood. In a startling instant a black shadow leaped down with a menacing growl, peering with yellow shining eyes at his challenger. Cross was already swinging his arm hard, sending a rock hurtling against the taut muscle of the black wolf. The beast had lunged in attack, but the strike of the rock swung the predator around and forced its hind quarters to dip to the ground. Then in an instant the wolf jumped away and was gone in the night.

Cross leaned against the fence and breathed heavily.

"It darn near got me," he whispered. He was sure it was a lobo. It was strange for such a predator to be in the area and on the prowl alone, but it was a large black wolf. He was convinced of that. He had to keep a sharp lookout from now on.

Cross walked back to the house and leaned against it, closing his eyes for a minute and breathing heavily. He let the cool breeze fan him as his listened to the lonely sounds of the night. Entering the house, he turned off the lights and felt his way to the back bedroom. He glanced at the crib and saw little Danny, sound asleep. Then he took off his clothes and rolled into bed. He caressed the nude curves of María Dolores. Soon she turned on her side to face him. And they embraced.

CHAPTER TWO

At dawn the birds in the woods whistled and warbled, as they did each day in spring and early summer. Cross heard them even before he had fully awakened. The birds seemed to alarm him to awaken and arise, for the sun would soon be flashing its warm rays across the cool damp valley. They called to him, and in the cool half-light of the morning they made him feel good and fresh and alive.

Cross cherished this early hour of the day, the time when no one was afoot or aloft except the animals and the birds and himself. He enjoyed walking about on his land on such a morning before the sun appeared over the hills. It was peaceful at such a time and cool and clean and almost a paradise. But always it was gone too soon.

He heard his wife in the kitchen making tinny noises with pans, and he smelled fried bacon. He slipped a robe over his naked body as he arose and entered the bathroom.

At table they did not speak. They never did at such time. In fixed-eyed silence Cross ate an egg and several strips of bacon, along with two cups of strong, rich coffee. His belly felt warm and good, and his whole being felt strong, anxious to begin the long day. He hurried now, picking up his black leather case, whispering a short farewell to Marie while kissing her lightly on the lips. She said, almost pleading, "Come home early!" and he was gone in the old Ford pickup up the dusty road and onto the highway.

She didn't move after the Ford disappeared but remained standing on the doorstep watching the highway, thinking. One car and then another and another raced around the hill on the

11

highway above the valley. The town attracted them each day before the sun appeared, for Geneva Gap was a hundred miles away and they should not be late for their business. Marie wondered about the lives of those intense tight-lipped young, old, and middle-aged women whose heads and shoulders appeared from the windows of the speeding vehicles. They seemed to be committed to an important race which they dared not lose. They were intent on their driving, looking neither to the left nor the right. *They know where they are going,* thought Marie, *but what of their babies, or maybe they do not have babies. These strong-eyed women are the level-headed kind people admire so much.*

She took one more look at the highway then turned and entered the house. The curving lines of her young body could be seen underneath the light house dress she wore. Her body was shapely and round in the right places and her man sometimes joked that she had filled out well since the birth of the baby. This playfulness caused her face to redden every time. He had thought her scrawny before, but now, to him, she possessed all the warmth and softness and curving sensuality of a real woman. Marie knew it and felt it.

They made love very well together. Like last night. Marie was sleeping when she first felt his large hands move softly over her naked body. She lay still for a time, enjoying the trembling moving hands as they awakened her from a heavy drowsiness, then to a demanding passion. she had turned to him and embraced him and she had placed her mouth to his and for a long while their mouths did not part but rather turned this way and that as if better to draw the life and the love from each other. And he had moved tenderly as her body writhed under the strokes of his love. She had heard him sigh in ecstasy and she felt her body emit fluids of passion. It was smoothly moist and warm as their bodies touched and slipped and undulated in a warm sea of pure sensuality and union.

"Mi alma . . . mi vida . . . mi amor," she had whispered instinctively.

Then, as if in fear of losing their chance at absolute oneness, they had stroked wildly, hungrily, and had groaned long . . . with lips parted, with nostrils burning, with hearts pounding, with eyes showing white.

Marie remembered all of this now and she knew once again that Lee loved her deeply. She was content.

But she was especially happy today, because the doctor from Geneva Gap had stopped by yesterday to tell her that she was pregnant. She had thrown back her head at the news, a wide ecstatic smile on her face, lifting her arms straight up towards some heaven where such dreams are made. Throughout the day she had bubbled with happiness, occasionally tittering to herself at the thought of surprising Lee with the glorious message. When should she tell him? She had wanted to break the news last night, but Lee had fallen asleep and then later their love-making had sealed the night. Tonight must be the night. Of course, tonight.

She was in the rear bedroom now and she hovered lovingly over the first flower of their love. Danny was breathing evenly, asleep in the large crib. She smiled over him and stroked his silky reddish-blond hair and saw his large eyes twitch slightly under the long-lashed lids. He is a beautiful baby. Nearly everyone said it was true, and she knew such people were not merely saying so to be kind. He was a beautiful boy. He had a strong body with fine sturdy legs. He would be tall and strong and beautiful like the David of Michelangelo. And like the king of the Scriptures he would be wise and just and beloved. She had wanted the boy to be christened David. Now, she smiled at her hopes for this first-born son. I guess I am like any other mother, she thought. And she was glad there would be another.

The woman now peered out the window towards the mountain, that towering presence she called Sun Mountain. Already the first rays of the sun had lighted the pinnacle. It was always so. Sun Mountain caught the first bright light of dawn and the last fading light of dusk.

Marie loved her mountain. It towered over the snug valley and their ranch home with great authority, shielding them from the searing sand-laden winds of the desert stretches, and cast a long shadow over the valley through the early morning, protecting them from the singeing rays of the sun for a good portion of the long day. Living at the foot of Sun Mountain, Marie felt protected. Spanish swords stood guard over the ranch from its slopes. Some Texans called the thick-trunked, nine-foot yuccas the Spanish dagger plant, but Marie preferred to call them Spanish swords since the stiff, clustered leaves were long and in a raised attitude like the high-lifted swords of knights guarding and honoring their liege. Yes, Marie loved her Sun Mountain. It was her special providence which so beautified the valley.

From the window she could also see her gardens. The flowers looked especially colorful and fresh in the morning. The blue morning glories clung gracefully to the small lattices and were already open in the early coolness of the dawn. The century plants stood tall and proud with tufts of pastel-shaded blooms reaching skyward. The oleander bushes were also blooming, while the roses competed for Marie's favor with pleasing fragrances but in a losing cause, for the petals were drying and falling to the ground. Roses live such a short life, she thought, and they give me such pleasure. It seems the good and the beautiful leave us so soon.

The vegetable garden was doing well. She nursed the sprouts toward becoming those large succulent foods her family so prized. She had an ally in protecting the garden from aphids and other insects that sucked and chewed at the greens. Her loving ladybugs flitted about the sprouts, consuming insects, and Marie coddled them tenderly. Occasionally, a ladybug would light on her arm as she labored in the garden, and she would talk to it in loving tones and purr softly as it crawled through the fine silky hair of her forearm. She treasured the ladybugs for their kindnesses in her garden. They were true ladies. And she was careful not to crush them underfoot as she stepped lightly through the rows of burgeoning plants.

Both gardens demanded much of her time and so much of their water, yet they provided sustenance and beauty for her loved ones and this pleased her.

She heard the boy turn in his sleep and she looked to his bed. She entered the kitchen, took a pail, and left for the small barn by the corral. Marie disliked the job of milking the goat. It was an ornery creature and often kicked back as Marie squeezed the bloated udders. It was a dirty animal with its stiff fur of brown and yellow-stained white and it had long ugly cracked toenails that it used to great effect in its backswings against its tormentors.

"Now you be good, Hippie," she said sternly as she entered the barn and saw the goat stop abruptly in its interminable cud-chewing and look challengingly at her with its amorphous yellow-green eyes. Lee had named the creature. Hippie really was a sloppy animal, anyway, and boasted a long stringy goatee that often picked up the many different thorns of the desert shrubs.

Marie now took an armful of sweet-smelling alfalfa from a

storage room in the barn and placed it in the feed bin to bribe old Hippie. A side dish of barley would be even more welcome, so she added it. As the goat chewed its favorite feed, Marie sat on a low stool near the pinkish udders to drain its milk. For once Hippie seemed quite patient, and she was able to fill a large bucket of warm bubbling milk.

In the house Danny had awakened and was calling Mamá when Marie entered the back door, struggling a little with the well-filled pail. "Momentito!" she called, and she hurried to prepare his breakfast.

Danny didn't wait. He entered the kitchen like a fawn on staggering, unsure legs and puffy, half-lidded eyes, walking a zigzag path, because he was not fully awake yet and his sturdy legs refused to walk in a straight line. He dropped onto a chair at the table and rested his tired head by the chin on his flat-lying arms on the table's edge.

"¿Qué pasa, hijito? You tired?"

The boy smiled at the fuzzy figure he saw through his misty eyes, the figure he knew as his mother from the consoling words and reassuring tones of her love. She reached over to him and brushed back his hair with the full palm of her hand. He liked that she did it so often. Now she placed the hot cooked cereal before him and he looked down at it and it stared back at him. A round smiling face as always was there in the bowl, a face of strawberry jelly lines that stared gaily up at the boy. Danny laughed in the rolling, uninhibited way that pleased his mother and he took his spoon and began to eat hungrily. As always when he saw his little friend in the bowl, he was awake and happy.

The morning went well for Marie and the boy. She had cleaned house hurriedly and then had gone outdoors to work in the gardens. It was already hot in the yard and she tied a bandanna around her head, but soon the sun beat unmercifully hot on her head. Marie owned a large Mexican sombrero but she dared not free it from its dark corner in the large closet. *Lee would tan my hide if he saw me wear such headgear.*

Her husband disliked anything "Mexican." He never said such a thing in so many words, but she knew it anyway.

Like the use of my real name, she thought as she moved slowly along the rows of sprouting vegetables and hoed away the life-strangling weeds. Her name was actually María Dolores, christened as such by her parents in honor of Our Lady of the

Seven Sorrows. Soon after her marriage to Lee he had demanded she no longer pronounce the rolling r's of her name in
the Spanish manner, especially when friends and acquaintances
asked for her Christian name. But it was hard for her to do as
Lee wanted. So it was that Lee decided María Dolores was too
long a name and too foreign-sounding—too Mexican—to please
the ears and sensibilities of true-blooded Texans. Although she
knew all about Texan customs, Lee explained to her that West
Texans were a friendly folk who liked to address persons by
their Christian names and even to simplify given names by ab-
breviating them to what they considered "a right friendly cut."
Her real name just didn't fit. María Dolores had claimed that
she understood. And so it was that she came to be known
simply as Marie, with soft "French" accents. But to herself she
would always be María Dolores, with rolling r's.

She didn't speak Spanish in Lee's presence either, except on
special occasions. Even then Lee preferred his own language, she
knew that. But last night as always, almost instinctively, she had
whispered softly to him in her native words of love that she had
said only to him: "Mi alma . . . mi vida . . . mi amor." She never
failed to whisper them, for they expressed exactly what she felt,
and Lee knew it and he allowed it at such times.

She remembered now, as she irrigated the rows of plants,
that Lee had once used words from that language he considered
so foreign to his land and his kind. It had been their wedding
night and she had trembled wide-eyed in a chill—a strange chill
for it had been a warm spring night and the moon had been
full-faced, reflecting a bright warm light on the landscape. Her
trembling had caused her voice to waver and break, and her precise English had degenerated into stutterings and hesitations.
She had been sitting on the bed in a filmy nightgown and the
moonglow coming through the unshaded windows of the motel
seemed to spotlight her feelings. Lee had been kind and understanding.

She remembered what he had said that night. In Spanish,
Lee had whispered that they were to be joined physically as
they had long been united spiritually. It was good that the two
loves—one sensual, one spiritual—be combined in two people
who were so devoted to each other and whose love was now
sealed forever in marriage.

"No tengas miedo," he had said.

And she had lost her fear and they had made love for the

first time and it had gone well as it had most of the time, or so she imagined, ever since that night long ago.

María Dolores crossed the arroyo bridge and joined Danny in the little opening to the woods where the branches of the closely bunched trees made a wide-spreading parasol. The boy played here every day when she worked in the gardens under the scorching sun. María Dolores sat down on the cold hard ground next to the boy and as always was surprised at the coolness of this spot. Danny was busily digging into the ground which was moist underneath the surface and good for building small sod houses. His rattle lay on a pile of freshly dug earth nearby. María Dolores smiled at Danny and caressed him, and then looking away off into the sun-glaring distance, she resumed her thinking.

She had feared other things on that night, their wedding night, long ago. Lee had not guessed those fears, she was sure. She remembered Ol' Dan'l Cross. He had raved and cursed at their plans for marriage from the first time they were mentioned, and he never slackened his vile words against them until his death. She had heard his vulgar abusive language from Lee's truck outside the Cross home in Geneva Gap that night, the night their plans were first broached to the old man. Lee had tried to quiet him, but that had simply made Ol' Dan'l shout the more.

"Ma son marryin' up with a Mexican," she had heard him say over and over again between the abusive four-letter words.

"Why, Mexicans ain't even white folks," he had scoffed. "If'n they ain't white, Babtiss, and from this heah Texas, they ain't worth a damn—yuh hear?"

"She's of pure Spanish stock," Lee had said. "She isn't Anglo, but she's white as you are. Her ancestors were here in Texas long before your daddy and his daddy even thought of coming here. She's no mestizo, no half-breed, no Indian's thrown in somewhere to corrupt her blood. She's no Mexican, Daddy! She's white European like you and me."

"We ain't white European, boy! We's white, Babtiss, Texas-Americans! Thet's what and thet's all and thet's the best goldang stock!"

"No use in talking to you," Lee had said. "You've made up your mind long ago and you won't change it and you won't even meet the girl!"

"Don't hafta!" Ol' Dan'l shouted. "A Mexican's a Mexican!

Yuh can't trust 'em! They'll stab yuh in the back! Yuh mark ma words, boy!

"What she gonna feed yuh? Eh? Ask her thet! What she gonna feed yuh? Frijoles an' chili an' corn tortillas, ah betcha! Ain't fit fer a Texan or any white man! Ah got ta laugh! She gonna be a heapa trouble ta yuh! Sure nuff!"

"You don't understand, Daddy!" Lee had explained. "I'm going to marry her whether I get your blessing or not! I just want to let you know about it and hope you can understand."

"Ah don't unnerstan! Ha! Ah don't unnerstan, he says. Ah unnerstan too good, boy! Ah don't cotton ta any a' ma kiddos being part greaser!"

When Ol' Dan'l said greaser in that gravel-voiced, curled-lip way he used to show his contempt, Lee had burst out the screen door in a fury. He had climbed into the truck and growled, "I could kill that old mulehead!" His face had been raging red with veins showing thick and throbbing on his forehead. She had dared not speak. She had never seen him like that before and it had frightened her.

The next day at dusk Lee had come for her again, but this time they visited his older brother. Toye was married to a local girl, but he had married right for Ol' Dan'l. Again María Dolores had been left to wait in the pickup while Lee talked to Toye in the porch of his home. She remembered exactly how the conversation had gone that evening.

"Toye, you know I'm getting married."

"Ah know," Toye had answered dejectedly. From the truck she could see him with his head cast down, his arm leaning loosely on his leg which was propped up on the porch ledge.

"Is that all you're going to say?" Lee had asked. There was a short pause.

"Well, ah don't know's ah like it much," Toye had finally volunteered.

"You don't think like your daddy, do you? . . . Why, plenty of folks here in Texas have married into Spanish stock, Toye. You know that! Nothing's wrong with it! Some's even bred with Mexican stuff, you know that. Sure, they all hide it like they have T.B. or something. They make out like they're married to French lilies from Louisiana, you know that. Someone asks the maiden name of the bride and the answer is always Chavéss, not Chávez, or Mendés, not Méndez."

"Don't waste your breath none, Lee. Ah don't intend ta

preach ta yuh. Ever'body makes his own bed, ah say. Ain't ma doin' anyways."

And that is the way it had gone with everyone Lee had talked to. It was a long time ago, ten years, but it still hurt to think about it. Why, Lee had not even wanted a baby till Ol' Dan'l's death!

She remembered how it had been at school in Geneva Gap. The tall slim "kickers" would swagger around the school yard in a carefully affected way, lazily, cocksurely, joking at each other and punching playfully at the arms of passersby. Each kicker wore a three-inch wide belt with his name engraved on the back and a huge shiny-faced buckle in the front from which a longhorn or horseshoe image protruded slightly. They all wore tight faded blue Levi's and crumpled grease-smudged Stetsons and high-heeled, thin-toed Tony Lama boots which served well in dogfights with "Meskins" from across the tracks who came over each day to attend classes. The hats and boots were not authentic Stetsons or Tony Lamas, but they liked to call them that whether they wore straw cowboy hats or cheap ready-made boots.

Lee stood out in this crowd. He had been known as a loner and used only the boots of the kickers' uniform. He liked to joke about the kickers to Marie—he had always called her Marie —telling her once that taking the high heels off those drugstore cowboys would steal nearly a foot off their stature, both literally and otherwise. "A head smaller in every way," he would say, and chuckle quietly.

Lee had dared to date Marie consistently. "Playin' 'round with a Meskin gal's awright, jest so yuh never get caught!" the older men would say with a wink of the eye and a nudge in the ribs. Going steady, though, was a horse of a different color. That might lead to something mighty serious and embarrassing. But Robalee was sure a loner, they finally decided.

María Dolores often thought then that they suspected her motives, and she was right. Some Spanish-speaking girls were looking for an opportunity to marry into "Anglo" families, and often when they succeeded they cocked back their heads and spoke derisively of those "Mexicans."

Other girls to the north and west of Texas claimed to be Basques, although most were not, but a Basque was an acceptable person in the minds of many Anglos. And so it was good to be known as a Basque and many young girls looking for an uplifting contact would present themselves as such.

María Dolores felt sorry for those girls. They are always pretending and hiding; they are to be pitied. One must be what one is and not be ashamed or deceitful.

She remembered the girl Lupita who had come across the Rio Bravo to live with the family of María Dolores, the Obregons. Lupita had come to attend American schools in a special program. The girl was of pure Indian blood from the state of Chihuahua and she was not ashamed but quietly proud of her origins.

"In Mexico," she often said, "very few people are concerned with lineage whether of a racial or ethnic kind. There are many different people in Mexico, but we are all simply Mexicans." María Dolores wished so much that here too it would be so; that all could be simply and confidently Americans.

She came back from her daydreaming, for the sun was high overhead and Danny was tugging at her arm and telling her of his deep-growling hunger. She laughed at him and hugged him close and then rose from the ground and took him by the hand into the heavy heat of midday and then into the cool rooms of their home.

María Dolores cooked some huevos rancheros for the boy which he ate with great gulps of delight, for the eggs were well seasoned with freshly-picked green chili that he liked so well. His mother's white tortillas were also delicious, especially when covered with lots of fast-melting butter. And a tall glass of Hippie's cold fresh milk filled out the hungry edges of Danny's stomach to make him feel that he was the foremost beneficiary of good food in the world.

"That was good!" he said. "I was really hungry, Mamá!"

María Dolores brushed back his hair.

In the afternoon she sent the boy to bed for his usual nap. It became very quiet and almost lonely in the big faraway house where she knitted with quick-moving fingers in the old rocking chair by the window facing Sun Mountain. She remembered that deep sickly loneliness she had felt the first year on the ranch and she hoped it would never happen again, although it was a constant threat that she submerged in the recesses of her mind.

That first year the pattern of their lives had been set and she had almost not survived it. Lee had begun his life of many interests and long hours away from home and this life had driven María Dolores to distraction and depression. For days and days she could not speak to anyone for no one was near. In the beginning she had waited up for Lee long into darkness. But often he had come home very late and very tired and their relationship had not gone well. She had become irritable and forgetful and cold. She had felt isolated and alone, trapped by the vast spaces of the Texas plain—and by her man.

María Dolores had been raised in a home where a large family with many visiting relatives had lived and loved and talked freely. She had been used to long conversations over coffee during the day with the many women in the family, and that life had been pleasant and reassuring to the growing insecure girl that she was. But after her marriage to Lee that life had changed abruptly and drastically. Her relatives no longer visited her. They had come to the ranch several times in the first year of her marriage, but such visits were now discontinued. Lee had not been friendly to them. Formally polite, he had never said that they were not welcome, but they had felt his concealed displeasure and so had María Dolores. She knew the reasons Lee didn't welcome her people. Some of her sisters and brothers had married dark-skinned Chicanos, and, anyway, they all liked to speak in Spanish. Lee had no inclination to associate easily with such undesirable elements in Texas society. He would only go so far in breaking the rules of that society, and marrying into a Spanish-speaking family was more than enough. One should not mingle with such people beyond that.

Most of the social life of the Texan, English-speaking people revolved around the churches and so Lee had tried to involve Marie in one of them. But it didn't work. She had insisted on keeping her ties to the Catholic Church in Geneva Gap. Lee had tolerated it for about a month, but after that time he balked at driving her into town on Sunday. He began to deride Catholic services and practices. He was convinced that "those Mexicans" were tied only to the outside forms of the Church. He had said that they liked only the formal, the convenient side of that religion, not the essence of true religion.

María Dolores remembered his exact words now: "They get drunk and spend all their money and don't take care of their families and then they go to confession and tell the priest all their sins and then go out and do the same things all over again because they think they can always wipe the slate of their souls clean by telling some curious preacher their transgressions."

So it was that María Dolores stopped going to church and

lost her last close contact with her friends, her family, and her former life. Her marriage to Lee had gone very badly for a time, but she had finally adjusted to the isolated life of the ranch. And now the bad time was all in the past and she hoped it would never return to plague her again.

María Dolores was now tired of thinking. The rest of the afternoon she worked very hard scrubbing floors of the house so that she would no longer think so much. Danny had awakened too, and with her work and her care for the boy the day went by.

That night María Dolores sat up waiting for her man to come home. Danny talked to her for a time on the front porch steps, but he had become tired and she had tucked him into bed for the night.

Now late into the evening she sat at the kitchen table . . . waiting and thinking.

CHAPTER THREE

That same morning, as Cross drove onto the highway, he glanced back at the ranch and saw Marie waving goodbye, alone at the threshold of their home. *She seems so lonely at this time each day,* he thought, *so frail and helpless and alone. But in a way, it was good she was so isolated. She had no temptations here. In town who knows what might happen. She just had to be set off from the Mexican influence, and the gossipy tongues of Geneva Gap.*

Cross would not admit to any more than that, as he forgot about Marie and had only the familiar highway stretching out like a long black asphalt carpet—only the highway and the onrushing plain—to think about.

The jaunty pickup was free of the hilly country in short order and the flat interminable plain allowed Cross to race the truck easily and comfortably toward Geneva Gap. Cross loved the wide flat country of West Texas. He thought of those insensitive outsiders who drove through this big country and complained of the monotony of the desert. Cross only smiled at such ignorant blindness. Why, they never really looked at the West Texas plain. It did have a variety of colors and moods and vegetation. Really opening the eyes to such wonders was like lifting the old rotting wooden gate holding back the precious water of the irrigation ditch and letting the life-giving fluid flow into the channels and crevices of the fields; opening the jaded, jaundiced eye and allowing the free flow of impressions to inundate the channels and crevices of the brain. "Fertile fields and fertile minds," Cross said to himself.

The old Ford was speeding by the steppe-like region and

leaving it. The face of the countryside was changing rapidly now, the truck rolling on the highway that cut through grassland that was prime grade for the raising of beef cattle. The gramma grass shone pale yellow and grew inches tall and was nourishing for top beef on the hoof. True, the grass did not appear rich and lush; the yellow-tinted blades were still gray-bleached in spots; but it got the job done, so said the cattlemen in these parts. Hundreds of thousands of dollars were still being earned right here in cowpunching. Fact was, providing beef steaks for city folks was the main and practically the only industry in these parts. Of course, some ranchers planted cotton and did fairly well. Everything that grew out of the earth had to be carefully irrigated, but many crops were being cultivated for a profit in this way. "All this country needs is more water, and it would be as green and lush as any. It's still God's country anyway," he uttered in a whisper. The air was clean and a man could breathe and move as he pleased here. No congested, no smelly cities here. You can drive for miles and hours and see hardly one other human being. No folks stomping all over you wherever you go. Elbow room and pure air. God's country!

The cab of the truck was fast becoming kiln-hot. It was the last day of May and high in the eastern horizon the sun radiated glaring rays of heat onto the forehead and eyes of the pensive driver. He began to sweat and cranked down the left-hand window, but the air that gushed in gave no relief. Cross was undisturbed. This was all part of his country and he liked it just fine.

He could see eddying whirlwinds kicking up thin clouds of dust in the distance and he caught sight of a sharp-cutting roadrunner fast-stepping along the barbed wire fence adjoining the highway. Once in a while a thick-wooded, lonely chapparal would appear along the onrushing highway and Cross would see kangeroo rats and prairie squirrels hopping, scurrying, in and out of the thickets.

Now Cross was traveling through an area where cotton fields lined the highway and where, in the close background, rose black-rocked mesas that appeared forbidding to the cultivation below. Cross caught sight of two, three dark Mexicans in Texas-style straw hats moving slowly through the fields and saw for an instant a big house nestled in shade-giving trees at the foot of the black mesas in the distance. These were familiar sights to the intense driver, but they never lost their fascination for him.

The country was wide-out flat again. He could see an occasional windmill in the far horizon with its water tanks and troughs close by. Cross thought of the East African plains which he had seen in the movies in El Paso some time ago. Big country, both. Big country that overwhelmed a man with endless wide-open distance and big high turquoise sky.

To the right Cross saw a tiny speck of black sitting blasphemously alone in the middle of the wide yellow plain. It was a familiar speck. He knew it would grow bigger and bigger to the eye as he sped in its direction. And indeed it began to loom larger as he pushed down harder on the gas pedal that prodded the light pickup to greater speed. Now Cross could distinguish the black silhouette against the pale yellow plain as a big house with impressive upreaching walls and gables and chimneys. It stood tall and proud in the incoming distance of the great yellow plain. Its solitude lent it dignity and strength. It seemed impervious to the wiles and ways of a country daring it to rise there in its heartland, alone. But there it stood, very much aware of itself, it seemed.

The old Ford began to reach the point in the highway where Cross could see the black-looming house more and more directly to his right in the distance. For a few seconds he was even with the house, and his line of vision to it was straight over his right shoulder. Now he could see, as he always saw with a tinge of despair, the thin black line that was the big house—the house that had been so strong and commanding just minutes before. Now he saw as he passed—as he always saw when he passed—the long wooden supports that held up the big house. It was a fraud. The big house was simply a facade. A wooden facade that tricked strangers into thinking that it was indeed a great and magnificent mansion that needed no aid in its lonely struggle against the wide open plain. It was a prop, a Hollywood artifact of make-believe. *It's a phony giant,* thought Cross. *Phony.* Although he had seen it many times, he could never get over it. Just as phony as the film and the novel. Why, Ace Reid says more about Texas in two or three of his cartoons than that female novelist said in 450 pages of pure sham. A giant fraud. Why, she never even considered the little ranchers of Texas. She never even considered the coolie-work, two-dollar day of the ranch hand, the cotton picker, and the cow puncher. *They're real Texas,* thought Cross, *not any dandified, got-rich-quick drifters. Ol' Ace Reid got it all over her.*

Some folks were mighty proud of it all. Why, down in Ft.

Gadsden they still had those autographed pictures hanging on the walls of the dining hall of the hotel. Those movie stars with pearly-white teeth and high-bushy hair smile down at poor, raw-boned, dirt-and-sweat-soaked cowhands who come in occasionally to do the town. Some folks were still mighty impressed with the whole Hollywood rigamarole. It was one of two or three great events in the history of this generation of the Big Bend country. Folks hereabouts were riding a mighty high horse in those days.

Cross drove on. Soon in the distance beyond the highway he could see the massive cathedral-like mountains that surrounded Geneva Gap. Another thirty, forty miles.

Now Cross watched the tall wooden telephone poles whizzing by—poles that he had seen so often in his daily trips to town. They always impressed him. They flashed by his line of vision in a regular row. Every pole stood thirty yards or so from its successor. Some five feet from the top, each pole had a short crossbeam on which electric lines lay and from which they continued to the next. *Each pole like that tree on Calvary. The smooth-shaved, dark brown trunks with life lines connecting one to another symbolized the lives of generations. Memorials to the men who penetrated this country to cut this vital highway through and the Southern Pacific beside it.*

It was late May and the small yucca plants sprouted bulb-shaped blooms at the foot of each live-wire cross. *Life lines of the dead. The ties of Christianity and Western Man*, thought Cross. *All more important than any individual, and yet raising the singular spirit to the unity and dignity and divinity of Humankind and the Godhead. The Good and the Beautiful are never lost in the demise of the particular. All will arise again on that Great Day.*

Cross was now driving into the hills leading to Geneva Gap. He remembered the name the conquistadors had used to describe this place: Puerta de la Paz they had called it. It was quiet and serene and the hills and mountains were showing off their best spring attire. They wore a light gray-green carpet of minute vegetation interspersed with gray-brown rock. And the deep green mesquite stood out vividly from the light-tinted hillsides. Cross marveled at the beauty and peace of this West Texas Eden. Five thousand feet above sea level, cool in summer and mild in winter, it was a catch basin for thunder showers that brought forth life, opening quickly after a storm to absorb the warm sunlight. Cattle grazed on the hillsides, and corrals could be seen intermittently on more level ground, where waterholes lay.

The old Ford dipped long and climbed roaring on the many depressions and upgrades of the hill-country highway. Finally, as the truck crested a high rise, it leveled out onto flatland, and in the distance nestled in low-slung hills stood Geneva Gap. *It's a Pisgah sight all right,* thought Cross. The college dominated the town from its pedestal heights, guardedly surveying Geneva Gap like a medieval fortress. Its buildings rose impressively and massively. Neo-Georgian style. The oblong structures of Cal Davis were mighty forceful all right, and they easily overshadowed the houses lying at the foot of college hill. Framing the college and rising slightly behind it, stood another hill on which the school brand was painted in large whitewashed letters: C Ⓓ C.

The truck followed the long arc of the highway into Geneva Gap. Side roads broke off from the main artery. The buildings came in thicker bunches now as he followed the highway—Main Street—into town. The railroad emerged to the right from between outhouses and rockshops and gas stations and motels. On the other side of the railroad were the ramshackle frame houses and grayish adobe homes of "Mexican Town." Of course the people here knew that Mexican Town was part of Geneva Gap, but they always insisted on a distinction. And Cross adhered to it. He had never thought otherwise.

Driving slowly on Main Street, Cross stopped at the one traffic signal. To his right was the railroad depot where some elderly, tobacco-chewing Mexicans were already lounging and talking as they did every day. To his left the principal commercial buildings of the town showed their wares from behind large plate-glass windows. The store with the biggest displays was Bronstein's on the corner of Main and Center Streets. This store was the Neiman-Marcus of Geneva Gap. Variety and quality were its trademarks. In the show window stood elegantly clothed mannequins, while pressed up flush against the pane was a small oblong sign announcing, "Cambiamos Moneda Mexicana."

Mexican nationals did come over the Rio Bravo early to shop the stores of Geneva Gap. Businessmen welcomed them. They had money to spend. True, they used pesos but such money was hard currency now. Cross saw Mexicans window shopping and browsing along the store fronts. They were Mexican nationals all right; they differed from local Mexicans because they wore suits and had slick-downed hair and smiled politely at the native Texans along the street. They parked their cars along the curb and the license plates identified the owners as being from the state of Chihuahua. They preferred Bronstein's, for the store had styles and colors that were seldom found in the Mexican border towns. Inside Bronstein's they would find not only smartly cut clothes but also book stalls where Texas works written by Tom Lea and J. Frank Dobie and Walter P. Webb sat proudly on the shelves.

The traffic light blinked green and Cross drove past Jake's Barber Shop on the left, past the Frontier Theater, the only movie house in town, and beyond assorted stores and more motels and gas stations and self-service laundries and the big tourist restaurant, which was called the Granada. Now to the left he approached the slightly sloping hill of the college campus. It was enclosed by a fence constructed of medium-sized rocks and boulders. This was rocky country and many homes and fences were made from the sturdy red rock. Cross turned off the highway and the truck rolled under the arch of the gate that identified the institution as Cal Davis College. He steered the old Ford into the big parking lot. There were many cars and trucks parked there, and Cross could see a line of many students already forming in front of the side entrance of the administration building where registration would soon start for the summer session.

The tall man wearing high-heeled boots got out of the truck and pulled out his black valise from the seat. He walked slowly in an easy swaying Texas way on the sidewalk along close-cropped lawns and high-reaching Spanish dagger plants. As he approached the registration queue several people recognized him, smiled, and waved a friendly "Hiyuh Robalee!" Cross acknowledged the greetings with a raise of the arm, a slight nod, and a right friendly "Hiyall." He joined the line at the end and the end happened to be a young couple Cross would call God-fearing, if someone asked him. They said howdy and shook hands with Cross. They were two of his most loyal listeners when he preached on the radio, and he liked them just fine.

Sam Calkin was a rather short stocky Texan who wore Levi's and cowboy boots and a Western-style shirt, but he owned no Stetson and his hair was the color of shining yellow hay, his eyes what Indians called white eyes, his face slightly ruddy with large freckles here and there about the nose. Betty was nearly her husband's height, but she had dark black hair and ebony eyes and unmarked pale skin. They drawled happily to Cross about their first-born baby, and Cross nodded absentmindedly, as he looked far into the distance from the college hill from which he could see most of Geneva Gap and the lowlying mountains around it. Dang pretty sight, he thought.

The line began to move and Cross was glad because he had much to do today. Soon he was hurrying from one desk to another inside the building, securing a library card, paying fees, checking class schedules. The people at the desks were friendly, not very official or self-conscious of their positions. The procedure went quickly.

Cross jumped two steps at a time up the stairway leading to the second floor and the division offices where professors would hand out class cards and sign him up for courses. He went straight to the social science office, and as he walked in he saw both the old and rather young teachers sitting at long desks, smiling and waiting expectantly for their students. Rather old and rather young—very seldom a teacher in between. Hard to keep good teachers here, everyone said. And it was true.

Cross gave them all a big howdy and ambled over to Dr. Sterner to talk small talk, as everyone did with Dr. Sterner, and then ask his advice on schedules and classes and sports, as everyone did with Dr. Sterner.

"Well, hi! Robalee," said Dr. Sterner as he reached out across the desk to shake hands.

"How'reyu?" said Cross and he shook hands, smiling.

"Pretty good, feelin' jest fine. Set yourself down!" he said emphatically.

Dr. Sterner had suffered a heart attack a year or so ago and he was not always well. But he looked good now with his ruddy, well-creased, full-fleshed face and kind blue eyes and thin, white, combed-back hair. His voice was right friendly, too. It seemed as though it always needed clearing. It reminded Cross of the voice of Andy Devine, that lovable side-kick of many a Western movie hero. Lovable and friendly and easygoing. Yep, that was Dr. Sterner, all right. He was a favorite here.

"Whatcha takin' this time 'round?" asked the good doctor.

"Oh, might take your course on Latin American history,"

Cross said. "Also thinking of taking that new professor's course, Sociology 301. Whatcha think?"

"Sounds mighty good," replied Dr. Sterner. "Ah don't know him too good. Ah think he'll be jest fine though. Name's Serveto, yuh know. Probably Eye-talian or somethin' like that."

"Where's he from?" asked Cross.

"California, ah believe."

"Not Berkeley, I hope!"

Dr. Sterner laughed good-naturedly at this comment and said, "Ah don't rightly know. He's not here today, so can't ask him. He seems awright, though. Don't worry none—yuh can always drop the course if yuh don't like it. How's the preachin' comin'?"

"Oh, just fine, Dr. Sterner. Gotta go to the station today and check out my sermon and tape it for tomorrow night. Almost getting to be too much, these three-a-week sermons. But I like it."

"Tuesday, Thursday, and Saturday you're on the air. Ain't that right?" asked Dr. Sterner, smiling because he and everyone knew that he used "ain't" and other such Texanisms deliberately.

"Sure nuff!" said Cross, smiling quickly, going along with the little game. "But those are the Second, Fourth, and Sixth Days," he corrected, seriously now. The preacher refused to use the traditional names for the days of the week because they were derived from pagan sources. So he called Monday the First Day, Tuesday the Second Day, and so on for the rest.

"By the way, I'm going to take the bible course at the Baptist Student Center this summer," said Cross exultantly. "Reckon I better go down the table here and see the Reverend Mr. Jenks about it."

"Be good, preacher. Take it easy—hear?" Dr. Sterner smiled benevolently as he handed Cross a class card for the Latin American history course.

Cross rose from his chair. "Will do! See yuh, Dr. Sterner."

He walked alongside the desk to the opposite end where Mr. Jenks was greeting students. The Reverend Mr. Jenks had been trained in theology at a big Eastern school. He knew where he stood on all questions.

Cross and Mr. Jenks exchanged cursory greetings and the latter set about enrolling the name of Cross in the bible class list. They said no more to each other. Mr. Jenks despised Cross and the feeling was reciprocated. Cross often thought that Jenks hated him because he disliked Robalee's independent preaching, and he did denounce it while he secretly envied it. *He's really quite harmless,* thought Cross. In his official capacity at the college, Mr. Jenks taught philosophy; unofficially he taught bible courses off campus at the Baptist Student Center. All such classes, official and unofficial, were enrolled and assembled in the social science division.

Jenks had finished his hasty scribbling and handed Cross a class card. Cross said, "Thankyee kindly," as Texans in West Texas did, and then stepped alongside the table again to have one of the old women professors sign him up for Dr. Serveto's course.

"Thankyee, ma'am," Cross said, and the shriveled, gray-haired lady with the purplish tint to her hair smiled and handed him another class card.

Cross left the room and walked down the hall for the stairs. He stopped momentarily at the office door of the new professor; there on a 3×5 white card in a slot for such purposes was typed the name Dr. Tomás Serveto. Strange name, wondered Cross, as he continued down the hall.

On the main floor Cross met Jedidiah Sporison, the comptroller of the college. They were good friends. Sporison was corpulent, quite sensitive about this fact, and about another which involved careless people spelling his name Sporozon. Cross never dared look at Jedidiah's belly and kept that name-spelling firmly in mind. They were indeed good friends. Jedidiah, in a rush, invited Cross and Marie to a coffee and cake social that night at 8:00 o'clock sharp. He said hastily, "Y'all come—heah?" Cross answered, "O.K. Jed," and watched Sporison waddle hurriedly down the hall into his office.

Finishing more registration details and chatting some minutes with preoccupied, in-a-hurry acquaintances, Cross left the building and sauntered to his old Ford pickup. He was thinking of his next chore for the day.

*   *   *   *   *   *   *

"Reckon yuh about need your ears lowered again," said Jake Greenfeld as Cross swung open the bell-jingling door of the barber shop where three chairs rested, empty and unswinging.

"Reckon so," Cross said lamely.

Jake rose ponderously from the stiff-backed chair by the

magazine rack and folded the *Geneva Gap Echo* into a neat little pile on the evacuated chair. The barber was a thin slat of a man with long gangling legs and a long slim neck which seemed to stretch and recede like that of a weasel. His hairless head boasted a huge, almond-nostril nose, and hanging from the temples to the neck were large pendulous ears. His skin was like rawhide stretched tight over the bony structure of his skull. No wrinkles sullied the surface. He had large freckled hands—delicate hands—with long fingers and bluish veins channeling under the taut brown skin. His beady hazel eyes peered from behind steel-rimmed glasses, appraising the preacher.

"Where is everybody?" said Cross as he mounted the platform of the chair and sat back into the thick leather-upholstered seat. The chair swung slightly to the right as he settled his big weight and tall frame in it.

"Oh, yuh know Rex Austin! Won't be in till noon prob'ly. Stayin' out late at night with some filly again, ah guess. An' Pepe won't be in till afternoon—damned lazy Mexican!"

He pronounced Pepe like peppy.

"Well, ah guess he won't be gettin' many shoe shines this mornin' anyways," Jake went on. "Thet Pepe's damned lazy— God, he's lazy! Pardon ma talk, Robalee, but ah can't help it. Yuh know what he does when he's here, preacher?"

It was rhetorical and Cross knew it.

"He don't do nothin' but sleep in thet shoe shine chair yonder."

Jake had unfurled the near-white barber's apron around his client's shoulders and pinned it tight around his neck.

"He sits yonder with his head on his propped-up arm and his eyes closed shut. He pretty near falls outa the chair sometimes when his head droops forward slow, but he usually jerks up sudden-like and his eyes are all glazed over but he's awake enough ta keep from fallin' on his punkin head on the cement floor right there in front o' the shoe shine stand. But yuh talk ta him when he jerks hard like thet and he don't hear yuh or nothin'. Ah'll be goldang if he ain't dead ta the world. Pepe prob'ly be jest as well off if he set down in one of them Mexican barber shops acrost the tracks, for all the money he's makin' here. Ain't makin' hardly a dime, all the time sleepin'!"

Snip, snip, snip.

"Well, what can a fella do?" said Jake shrugging his shoulders and looking that helpless look of resignation.

Jake Greenfeld was a descendant of German free-soilers who came to West Texas in the 1850's. The name was Grünfeld originally, but Greenfeld sounded more American. Jake was raised in New Braunfels, but he had been in Geneva Gap now for close to thirty years. There were other barbers in town, but Jake was undoubtedly the best. German precision was what he had in cutting hair, if not in circulating the latest gossip. People liked both.

Jake droned on as he cut hair mechanically. Cross listened with half an ear and scanned the wall opposite his chair. High up the wall near the ceiling hung a stuffed deer's head with large antlers, and next to it and somewhat below, a small showcase displayed Indian flints and arrowheads that Cross knew belonged to Rex Austin. Directly before him on the wall was a large built-in mirror and Cross could study his face in it.

Snip, snip, snip.

The preacher's face was long and thin and rawboned. It was weather-beaten, reddish-tan, with deep lines cutting vertically to his strong slightly protruding jaw. Cross owned a strong, aquiline nose, and his hair was thick and light brown and sandy-colored in spots. His eyes were wide open and deep blue, had a shining, deep-boring quality to them as if they could see right through a man to the quintessence of his being. An almost insane look, it seemed to some. And the brows arched sharply at an angle nearly to the inner edge of the sockets of the eyes that met the nose at the center of the stern, heavy-lined face. Every feature of his face seemed to center about the eyes. And the eyes were what acquaintances most remembered about the man.

Jake was talking about the new members of the faculty now.

Snip, snip, snip.

"Yuh met this Serveto fella yet, Robalee?"

"Can't say that I have, Jake," said Cross. "Heard about him, though."

"Seems lak a right nice fella," volunteered the barber.

"Seems like," agreed Cross. "I expect you've met him, eh?"

"Shore have! Been comin' in for 'bout a month now. 'Pears he jest got off a job for the government down in Peru or somewheres lak thet. One of them missions thet ol' Uncle Sam keeps sendin' ever'wheres ta see ta ever'body's welfare. Giveaways we pay for with our taxes, sure as shootin'!"

"He sounds interesting," said Cross dryly.

"Yep, he's an interesting fella awright," acknowledged the barber. "Worked for government doings in foreign countries many's a time. Speaks dang good spik! Reckon he might jest be one too!"

"What's that?"

"A spik."

"Oh?"

A pause to reflect. Snip, snip, snip.

"I hear tell he's from California," said Cross.

"Yep, says he wanted ta come here so he can be nearer the border."

"What church he belong to?" asked the preacher.

"Don't rightly know, Robalee! Ah don't even know if he goes ta church a-tall!" answered the barber rather gloomily because he was not one to be caught without an answer to such an important question.

Snip, snip, snip, snip.

"Mebbe, yuh can wrangle him the right way, eh preacher?" said Jake, distracting attention from his embarrassment.

"Maybe, Jake," laughing lightly.

Snip, snip, snip.

"Mind turning on the radio, Jake?"

"Shore." The barber walked to the stand by the back door on which sat the old varnished-brown Philco that was shaped like an egg, except that it was like an egg that was cut short and flat down near the three quarters mark in order that it sit in a stable position. It looked like an egg to Jake. Quite an ancient radio really. But it worked.

The livestock market report was on.

"Thet's the Carpenter boy talkin'," said the omniscient barber.

The voice coming from the cloth-covered speaker owned a heavy, hesitating Texas twang. It was telling folks that prices on heifers and feeder cattle was steady. Prices on prize bulls was up three cents, while prices on cows was holding steady.

Then the hesitating Texas twang introduced a Mr. Hankins from Odessa—OH-dessa—to talk about pink eye and the care and cure of the same in beef cattle. A more poised voice like that of an older man drawled out the details of the medication for the infection and advised folks where to write if they needed it all written down on paper.

By now Jake had finished the haircut and Cross had

dropped out of the chair. He was being brushed off with a whisk broom. Cross handed the barber $1.50 and Jake said thankyee kindly.

"Well, see yuh again, Jake."

"See yuh."

As Cross walked out the bell-jingling door, he could hear the voice emanating from the radio asserting in a more confident twang: "This is XYYZ, Geneva Gap, . . . Texas: The Voice of the Last Frontier."

CHAPTER FOUR

Cross had eaten a rib steak and was feeling full to his stomach, picking at his teeth and dillydallying momentarily outside the Granada Restaurant. Across the street the self-service laundry was doing a thriving business. A Mexican family from across the tracks carried bundles and more bundles from an old crestfallen, rattle-doomed Chevie—the Mexican Cadillac people hereabouts called it—and stuffed in loads and more loads of clothes into the new shiny aqua-colored automatic washers. *They sure get their money's worth. If I had a half dozen kids like that, I guess I'd do the same thing.*

Outside the laundry the brown-faced, shoeless children were running about, chasing each other, laughing and jabbering shrilly in "low-down Meskin," as true Texans called that way of speaking. At times Cross felt sorry for those runny-nosed, dirt-splotched children from across the tracks. *They're mighty resilient though, and many of them grow up to be dang good athletes, although they're a mite on the small side for football.*

Cross climbed into the old pickup and drove to the radio station. XYYZ was a small operation. It was located in a building next to Odie Field where the big football games were fought hard in the autumn each year. The antenna tower rose high, sixty feet or so, behind the radio station.

Inside, Cross waited in the narrow hall from which a sound-proof window afforded the visitor a view directly into the small studio and a glimpse at the control room from which an ear-phone-covered head could be seen. The eyes from the partially submerged head directed their gaze at Cross, recognized him, and the head rose up to show much of the rest of "Speedy" Carpenter's long-limbed, slow-moving body.

The heavy metal door of the control room opened at the far end of the hall and Speedy Carpenter dropped down loose-jointedly from the high step.

"Howdy, preacher," he smiled affably.

"Hi," said Cross.

"Reckon yuh wanna tape your sermon," measuring out each word stingily with a heavy twang.

"Uh-huh," nodded Cross.

Speedy led the preacher into the empty studio where the tape recorder was kept on a small wooden table. Cross pulled a chair over, thanked the boy who was already leaving with a shambling gait, and sat down at the table to start.

Cross never preached from a prepared text. He chose a topic and began almost immediately. He had switched on the recorder now and was already speaking into the microphone.

Like a tiny rivulet splashing lightly from a high mountain source, the sermon ran softly, then grew wider and deeper and angrier, as it traveled on its course. It flowed spontaneously. Chapters and verses from the Scriptures, like conjoining springs, added to the increasing power. The preacher quoted from the bible as readily and naturally as an expert canoeist rode the rapids, twisting and turning his weight and working his paddle from side to side, down the big river, down the big river. The preacher was like the canoeist who rode the rapids deep along the sheer Chisos Mountains and finally was carried breathless in one last billowing lunge into the serene waters at the base of Santa Elena Canyon from where he could look up to see a thin strip of bright blue heaven at the crown of the steep dark canyon walls.

Cross had finished, his head bowed over the table, his eyes shut tight. He felt exhausted. The muscles all over his body felt limp and weak and his long limbs shook visibly. He remained at the table in that worked-out posture for a time. The trembling of the legs subsided slowly and his head bobbed slightly and he seemed to be emerging from a deep hypnotic sleep. He stretched his back hard against the upright of the chair and his arms rose stiffly and stretched tightly backward to relieve themselves of the last strains of tension. It was over. And tomorrow he would listen to the sermon virtually for the first time. He never revised his creations.

As Cross walked out of the bare studio into the hall, he saw Speedy talking to two middle-aged, round-middled men. They turned immediately and called to him.

"How's she comin'?" said the one with the curly high pompadour and the turnip-sized nose.

His name was Israel Bronstein and he never failed to amaze Cross. *He didn't have that Semitic aura about him.* Cross couldn't really explain the aura, but he was certain he sensed it. Not in this case, however. *Perhaps it's his blue eyes and dark-reddish hair. Izzie was just fine, though. He was a top business-man and a leading citizen of Geneva Gap and he was reputed to be a real scholar of the Old Testament. All of this appealed to Cross.*

"Mighty fine," the preacher said, smiling in answer to Bronstein's greeting.

Bronstein reached out his big meaty hand and they clasped and shook hands vigorously. Then Old Man Zarler did the same.

Cotton Zarler was said to be the richest man in town. He had money—there was no doubt about that. Behind his back he was called Old Man Zarler or "Cotton-mouth" Zarler. To his face he was called Cotton or Mr. Zarler, depending. No one knew for sure how much money Old Man Zarler stashed away in the bank and what all he was involved in financially, although Jake Greenfeld thought he did. He owned several large cotton spreads within a hundred miles of Geneva Gap, employed and housed Mexican tenants at the cotton fields and profited very well indeed.

"How'reyu," said Old Man Zarler automatically.

Cross nodded and then asked, "How's everything with you two old finaglers?"

Guffaws all around.

"Well," said Old Man Zarler smiling broadly, "yuh got ta ride drag a long ways ta save two old mavericks lak us."

More short bursts of laughter.

"We're paying our dues," said Bronstein, controlling his mirth. "These advertising rates are going up all the time." Now turning to Old Man Zarler: "Can't you do something about that, Cotton? After all, you're part owner of this radio station."

"Don't look at me! Ah got ta pay jest lak you-all!"

More laughter, less boisterous, quicker ending.

"Well yuh both get fair-to-middling results by running commercials on thet program," injected young Speedy Carpenter. His unaccustomed forcefulness surprised the three older men.

"Well, ah reckon we do get dang good customer kickbacks," bawled Old Man Zarler. "Most popular radio broadcast in these parts!"

"I wouldn't put my advertising funds in anything but the Crusading Christians," said Israel Bronstein. "It's a sure winner."

"Why don't yuh let us advertise on your show, preacher?"

"It's not that I don't have a mind to, Cotton—you know that! It's just that Texacut has an exclusive contract for it."

"Oh, these monolithic outfits!" barked Zarler. "They'll run us poor dirt farmers outa business afore yuh know what hitcha. Ain't thet right, Izzie?"

"You're always right, Cotton!"

Everyone laughed again, nodding.

Shuffling of feet and anxious looks. Too long a pause.

"Well, I guess I'd better go peddle some of my wares," said Cross as he moved toward the door. "Can't make money standing around jawing."

"Say, preacher, ah ain't seen thet cutlery you're all the time selling," said Old Man Zarler. "Why don't yuh come over ta ma house right now and show them knives ta me? Ah hear tell ma squaw has money ta squander."

"Be glad to!" said Cross, eyes brightening.

The three older men waved a slight goodbye to young Speedy Carpenter and walked out into the heat of the early afternoon. Cross could feel the burning gravel through the soles of his big boots. His feet felt sweaty and itchy. It was unusually hot for Geneva Gap.

"Ma wagon's right yonder," said Old Man Zarler. "You're comin' too, ain'tcha Izzie?" he bellowed at his Jewish friend.

"No, thanks, Cotton. Gotta run. Somebody's gotta mind the store." He quickened his pace toward his car, looking over his shoulder. "See y'all!"

Old Man Zarler owned a shiny family-style bus. It was a flat-nosed Volkswagen, and at its rear hung a Texas license plate and an extra metal plate above it which boasted large fluorescent block letters spelling ZARLER. The two men climbed in and drove off toward the new housing development where Cotton Zarler had been the first to purchase a new home several years ago.

The Zarler house looked very expensive to Cross. It was a low-slung, ranch-style home constructed of cream-colored brick. It looked unadorned now, because every Christmas season the Zarlers decorated the front lawn very elaborately. Everyone, even strangers, knew the Zarler home at such times.

Last Christmas they had larger-than-life plywood figures of

the three kings, bearing rich gifts, placed on the roof. And the roof was always brightly lighted to afford everyone a good look at any hour. All the shrubbery had been lighted bright with multi-colored Christmas bulbs, and huge five-foot block letters, made of plywood and illuminated glaringly by thousand-watt lamps placed strategically on the lawn, announced the extravaganza's producers: THE ZARLERS. No one could outshine the Zarlers in Geneva Gap. No one even dared.

The snub-nosed Volkswagen stopped before the two-car garage that was linked to the main house. A big shiny Cadillac, comfortable as a house cat, nestled in the carport.

"How do yuh lak the old homestead?" cracked Old Man Zarler.

"Mighty fine-looking house," smiled Cross.

As they walked in, Cotton Zarler let loose a commanding yell: "Hanna! Hanna! Where are yuh? We got company!"

A slight mousy-looking woman in loose-fitting pants and loose-fitting sweater appeared quickly with short nervous steps. To Cross she looked like she was walking on eggs. She had straight shoulder-length blondish hair, a prominent nose, and anxious wide-open eyes. She never impressed people as being the mistress of a wealthy household. She was reticent and plain-looking, and she had a little-lost-girl aura about her. Cross always did like her.

"Yes, dear." She nodded a cursory greeting to Cross.

"Fix us men some coffee," commanded Old Man Zarler.

"Yes, dear," and she was gone.

"Set yourself down, preacher," he ordered in a friendly tone.

Cross sat on the long sumptuous couch and laid his black valise flat on the coffee table and proceeded to open it.

"Now, les take a gander at whatcha got there." Cotton Zarler took up a post next to Cross.

The knives were set in red-felt grooves. The assortment amazed Old Man Zarler. Paring knives, steak knives, butcher knives. Knives, knives, and more knives. Beautiful knives. The blades were gleaming stainless steel and razor sharp and the handles were smooth brownwood plastic and grooved slightly at an angle to fit the fingers and palm for comfort and efficiency.

"Texacut puts out a good product," said the preacher. Cross believed in the soft sell. And he believed in his merchandise.

"They're down right purty," said Old Man Zarler. He was

impressed. He handled them carefully and inspected them closely. "Mighty fine cutlery," he said over and over again between the liftings and turnings and placings. He grunted an amazed "huh!" at times as he brandished the shiny sword-like butcher knife.

Hanna brought the coffee and placed it on the table. Then she disappeared again.

Cross sat back, took the saucer and steaming hot cup of coffee in his hands, and relaxed. He wouldn't have to present his sales pitch here—it was obvious. Nothing to do but pursue his own thoughts. He glanced aimlessly around.

The Early American living room was spacious. On the walls hung several large paintings by Peter Hurd. Cotton Zarler was known in the Southwest and among the more knowledgeable art connoisseurs for his fine collection of Hurds. He was also known for his extensive collection of pre-Columbian Indian art figures from Colima, Nayarit, Monte Albán and elsewhere.

Old Man Zarler spoke fluent Spanish and made frequent trips to Mexico in his private plane. People said he went there to sample deep-sea fishing around Mazatlán or to buy beef cattle at cut rates in Chihuahua or to smuggle valuable artifacts across the border at Laredo. He was never detained by Mexican authorities. He knew all about la mordida. People said he had a pretty brown-skinned mistress, and she was the main reason, so they said, Cotton Zarler flew down there so often. No one was certain of any of his dealings in Mexico, but everyone was sure he benefited right handsomely.

Old Man Zarler was born and raised along the border. He was speaking Mexican before he talked American, people said. His bilingual talents had given him great confidence as a boy. He had astounded Texans with the ease with which he seemed to handle Mexicans on both sides of the Rio Grande and he was always admired by people who could assist him to gain his ambitions. He once had a rich benefactor, people whispered, who sent him to Texas A & M to study business administration, agronomy, and livestock breeding. And it was while at College Station that he met Hanna. She had helped him to pass the required liberal arts courses and he had become forever grateful to her. But she never was quite successful in preventing Cotton from talking Texas. He knew better all right, but he was full-blooded Texan and he was not about to surrender his colorful way of speaking to please anybody.

To the eye Cotton Zarler did not appear a forceful man. He looked retiring, almost ascetic. He wore glasses and was bald at the crown of his head. A kindly, tonsured monk. He was acquiring extra pounds of flesh around the abdomen and his normal gait was slow and sedate.

To the ear Cotton Zarler was often like a West Texas tornado. His deep-toned, booming voice shook people to their neural and skeletal foundations. It was that voice, at times like a jet breaking the sound barrier, that prickled the skin and swung the eyes anxiously.

"Ah take the biggest and best set yuh got," jabbed Old Man Zarler.

"Mighty fine," said Cross, startled back to business. "That's the $120 set."

Cross spent the afternoon and early evening at the Zarlers. Cotton insisted on it and when he did that no one resisted. They closed the deal on the cutlery, they gossiped, they inspected Cotton's gun collection. Cotton insisted Cross handle one of the rifles. The preacher took the weapon reluctantly, blinking at it nervously. "Put it ta your shoulder and get the feel of it," barked Old Man Zarler. "It ain't loaded." So Cross lifted it to his shoulder and grasped it firmly, his left hand forward on the stock, his right hand searching for the trigger. The weapon felt good as the preacher grooved it into his shoulder. Then Cross scanned the room, swinging the weapon in short hesitant arcs seeking an imaginary target. The preacher was surprised at the feel of the weapon. It was sweet. Real sweet. Like an extension of his own body. Slipping into fantasy, he drew a bead on one of Zarler's pre-Columbian pieces set on shelf, the figure of a naked Indian woman squatting open-legged. The preacher peered through the sights moving the weapon down until he could see the circular ridges of baked clay enclosing a slight concavity representing the woman's genitals. The preacher's face reddened as he squeezed the trigger. Click! In his imagination Cross heard the shot fire. But then immediately the preacher snapped out of his fantasy and with an embarrassed feeling of guilt at having relished the weapon and its potential destructiveness, he handed the rifle back to Cotton Zarler who managed a puzzled snicker.

Zarler resumed the conversation. The two men discussed Cotton's brooding Indian idols from Mexico and the breeding of his shepherd dogs from Germany. He told Cross the German police dogs were loyal only to him and vicious enough to scare off any prowlers who came from across the tracks.

The two dogs were named Schatzie and Schnakie. They sure look mean, thought Cross, as he watched from behind sliding glass doors that opened out to the back yard. Old Man Zarler gave commands to sit and heel and pranced the prize dogs around the yard to show off their blue ribbon quality. He took great care to place them in the proper stance for inspection by an imaginary judge and stood back smiling proudly as they froze like statues in their show-dog attitude. They were first rate dogs, all right.

Old Man Zarler boasted good-naturedly. He told Cross about his European tour and his visit to Germany to find the special dogs he wanted. He talked about the great love Germans had for their animals. And, laughing loudly, he joked, "Yuh know preacher, if ol' Adolph had set up concentration camps for dogs and liquidated *them,* there sure woulda been an uproar against him and he woulda been booted outa power sure thing. He knew better 'an ta gas dogs and cremate 'em. That woulda been too much for the Krauts ta swallow all in one gulp!"

He laughed shrilly, tears coursing down his chubby cheeks. Recovering gradually from the fit of laughter, Cotton Zarler noticed the grim-mouthed, sharp-eyed look on the face of his guest.

"Oh, preacher!" he cried. "Don't pay no mind. Ah was jest funnin'."

A short pause. Cotton Zarler gulped down the last gurglings of laughter.

"Yuh stay for supper—heah?" And Cross stayed for supper.

They sat in the large living room after the big meal. Cotton spoke softly now, and Hanna sat in a straight-backed wooden chair off to the side from where the men were seated and nodded occasionally at what her husband was saying. Cross listened attentively, injecting a minor point at times.

*   *   *   *   *   *   *

He left the Zarlers when darkness fell. It was a short walk to the radio station where Cross climbed into the old pickup and drove to Jed Sporison's place out on the old Ft. Gadsden highway north of town.

Sporison's house was on a deeply rutted dirt road off the highway. The truck bumped, rocked, and rattled toward the lights ahead. Several cars and trucks were parked haphazardly in front of the dark-cornered house. Jedidiah greeted him at the door.

"Well, mighty glad yuh could make it, Robalee! Where's Marie?"

Sporison knew very well Cross would not bring her tonight, but he expressed dismay anyway.

"Can't drive back all that distance just to fetch her," said Cross smiling.

"Reckon you're right. Sure sorry she ain't heah, though."

The front room of the Sporison home was sprinkled with people in seated groups of two or three, speaking quietly and sipping politely at cups of fast-cooling coffee. Dr. Sterner and his corpulent wife called Mama were there; so were Mr. Jenks and his small, dark-haired wife; so were Sam and Betty Calkin; and so were Will and Goldie Busbee and many others from the college and the town.

Several people looked up and said howdy to Cross between words of tepid conversations. Will Busbee stopped him for a moment to tell him there was a meeting of all Texacut salesmen tomorrow, and Jed brought him a cup of steaming coffee and some heavily frosted chocolate cake, directing him to a place on the couch next to Dr. Sterner. Sporison knew he and Cross were good friends.

"Did you get through the registration all in one piece?" teased Cross.

"Good ta see yuh here, Robalee," said Dr. Sterner. "Well, registration wasn't too bad—lots of kiddos but no trouble."

The muffled voices of quarreling children could be heard coming from a back bedroom. A tall thin austere woman stood up quickly from a chair across the room and marched down the hall. Cross could hear Linda Sporison shushing her three children.

"They got a television back there," said Dr. Sterner smiling. "Prob'ly fightin' over which show ta see."

"Yep. I can't afford that nuisance," said Cross, "even if I wanted it. First thing, the sets are too expensive, and second the cable hookup costs too much. No wonder there aren't many folks around here that have it."

"Jest an idiot tube anyways," observed Dr. Sterner to be agreeable.

The doorbell buzzed slightly and Sporison waddled over to

answer it. He emitted a yelp of pretended surprise when he opened the door. *Jed's greetings are more expansive than usual,* thought Cross. *He's trying to impress.*

The man entering the room was of moderate height. He had heavy black eyebrows and large dark eyes and a full head of thick black hair that was graying at the temples. He was dressed in a light summer suit.

Dr. Sterner leaned over confidentially to Cross. "That's Dr. Serveto."

Sporison made a big show of introducing Dr. Serveto to each person in the room. The newcomer seemed embarrassed by the fuss.

"An' this heah's Dr. Sterner an' Robalee Cross," introduced Sporison, finally reaching the couch. The usual Texas pleasantries were directed at Dr. Serveto, along with excessively generous handshakes.

"Y'all set down and do some gettin' acquainted," said Sporison, turning away now to tend to his other guests.

"Mighty nice to have you here in Geneva Gap," Cross greeted.

"Thank you. I think I'm going to like it here."

Coffee and cake were brought to the newcomer by Linda Sporison who smiled broadly. He thanked her, nodding slightly and flashing a quick smile.

"You've been here a while, I hear," said Cross.

"Yes, about a month now."

"Have you joined a church yet?" asked the preacher.

"No."

"Yuh might think about joining us," said Dr. Sterner. "We got a right nice Episcopal Church down the hill from the college."

"Oh?"

"Yuh don't wanna go joining one of them evangelical churches," said Dr. Sterner. "They're for lower class folks, yuh know. A better class of people come ta our church."

Serveto nodded in a noncommittal way, staring tight-lipped at the two men.

"Robalee here's a preacher," said Dr. Sterner. "He's independent. He won't be hogtied ta any particular church."

"Oh," said Dr. Serveto. A short pause.

"I understand the man for whom the college is named was once a preacher," observed the newcomer.

"Sure was," said Dr. Sterner proudly. "Ol' Cal Davis was a circuit rider for many a year back there in the nineteenth century. He became chairman of TIP—the Texas Itinerant Preachers Association. And he was a dang sight more 'an thet too!"

"What does Cal stand for?" asked Serveto.

"Calvin. Calvin Davis was his full name," explained Dr. Sterner. "Folks jest shortened it ta Cal Davis—more friendly thataway."

Dr. Serveto listened carefully.

"He was a Texas Ranger during his younger days," continued Dr. Sterner. "Folks said he could shoot the eye out of a chicken hawk at forty paces. During the Civil War he led a Texas cavalry unit here in West Texas and in New Mexico too—Confederate troops invaded that territory, yuh know. Well, anyway, old Cal fought in a battle up near Santa Fe. Glorieta Pass, ah believe. Later was ordered ta defend and hold Ft. Gadsden jest north of here."

"Yuh been ta Ft. Gadsden yet?" asked Dr. Sterner, breaking off the history lesson for a moment.

"No, I haven't."

"Well, you'll like it fine. It's a national historic site. Was built before the Civil War ta protect the trail ta El Paso from the Apache and Comanche. The military even brought in camels ta use in the desert thereabouts. After the war the federal government stationed an all-nigger garrison there—all nigger excepting the officers. Folks hereabouts didn't take ta thet much. Anyway, the old fort was finally abandoned in the 1890's, jest about the time historians were writing thet the frontier was over. No need for the fort anyway. Indians were all whupped and pacified. But jest a few years ago, Ft. Gadsden was resurrected as a national historic site. They're rebuilding it slow but sure, ah reckon."

"That's very interesting," said Dr. Serveto. "It's pretty far from here to Ft. Gadsden, isn't it?"

"Not at all," answered Cross. "A hundred miles or so. Just around the corner in these parts. Driving the highway is a way of life out here. Why, folks think nothing of driving into Odessa or El Paso early in the morning for shopping and coming back the same day. About four hundred and fifty miles round trip. Not far really."

"Amazing," said Dr. Serveto, evenly. "By the way, what does the ring around the *D* on the hill behind the college mean?"

"Oh," said Cross, "that's the school brand. It reads C—circle D—C for Cal Davis College. It's just a brand like most cattle ranches have around here."

"Why should Texas name this college for Calvin Davis? Is it simply because he was a Ranger, a circuit rider, and a Confederate officer? There must be others with the same credentials."

"Not like his," said Dr. Sterner. "Besides, he was governor of this state for nearly four terms in the late nineteenth century. Made a fine record too, like he did in purty near everything."

"Must have been quite a man!" Cross and Dr. Sterner nodded.

Jed Sporison waddled over.

"How'rey'all gettin' along?" he asked, baring gold-filled teeth among yellow-stained, untapped incisors.

"Jest fine," said Dr. Sterner, smiling.

"Did y'all know Dr. Serveto's been down in Mexico many a time?" Sporison inquired, looking at his two fellow Texans. And he began to relate his Mexican tales. He did it at practically every social event.

Serveto eyed Sporison. The comptroller was dressed in a grayish-blue pastel-colored suit. Quite conservative. The first time Dr. Serveto had seen Sporison, however, had been a revelation. Serveto had seen him at the top of the stairway at the college. Sporison was talking animatedly with another man. It was hot that day and Sporison carried his suit jacket over his arm. He wore a short-sleeved shirt which presented a view of his stubby, hairy arms. At his layered neck was a loosened tie which hung listlessly from the open shirt collar that could not contain the coarse chest hair that reached up to his throat. The necktie was wide like a bib and boasted a bright multicolored flower design. Over the shirt and holding up the baggy, high-water pants stretched an unbelievably wide pair of tense suspenders. And on his leaden, high-arched feet, rose a pair of magnificent two-toned shoes. The hayseed motif was then perfectly complemented and topped by a heavy porcine head, the face red, the cheeks chubby, the hair a swirl of loose strands on reflecting baldness.

"Yuh were in Mexico in 19 and 51, weren't yuh? . . . Weren't yuh?" Sporison's brows curled toward his nose in irritation. Serveto was oblivious to the question, his eyes unresponding and gazing aside blankly.

"Oh, yes! Yes, of course!" replied Dr. Serveto, finally tuning in.

"Yes," he said again. "I was there that time from 1949 to 1952. I was attached to a joint U.S.-Mexican commission trying to stamp out foot and mouth disease in Mexican cattle. I lived near Guadalajara most of the time. We camped out on the range. I was one of several Spanish-speaking Americans working there on the project. It was a very good experience, although I did pick up some pesky amoebas that still bother my stomach occasionally. But I wouldn't trade those years for anything!"

The three Texans looked dubious.

"I'm a social anthropologist and Latin America is my special field."

"Oh," said Cross. And the three Texans nodded soberly.

"I understand this town was once called Puerta de la Paz," observed Serveto, sensing the need for a change of topic.

"It was for a while," added Dr. Sterner, "before the real Texans come here in the 1830's. They couldn't pronounce the name right. They called it Purta Pass or Purty Pass or something like thet. So they decided ta call it Geneva Gap instead, named partly for that great center of the Protestant Reformation in the Alps. The name stuck!"

It was Serveto's turn to appear skeptical.

"Well, it's a right purty pass, all right," volunteered Sporison. Everyone laughed.

"Y'all come now ta fill the cup," said the rotund host. And Sporison led them to the table where a large coffee percolator stood among cups and saucers and spoons and pans of frosted cake.

"How do you like our socials?" asked Cross, as he and Serveto waited their turn at the coffee spigot.

"Very nice."

"I suppose this is different from what you're used to."

"Well, yes, in a way. In California people usually have cocktail parties when they get together."

"I thought so," said the preacher evenly. "We don't do that here."

Sporison heard their remarks and turned to them from slicing a generous hunk of chocolate cake. "Jest 'furriners' drink hard liquor hereabouts." He chuckled as he said it.

"Some folks on the faculty from the Midwest have cocktail parties. But they keep ta themselves," Dr. Sterner chimed in.

"Did ah ever tell yuh about the time ah was stationed in Oklahoma City?" asked Sporison. No reaction.

"Well, them days Oklahoma was dry—legally thet is! Huh! Ah never seen sich a wet state in ma life! Hard liquor ever' wheres. Folks kept a glassa 3.2 beer on the table and under the table they smuggled in some 100-proof Kentucky whiskey. Ever'body did it!"

"You too, Jed?" asked Cross, smiling.

"Well, gosh darn, preacher! Yuh know dog-goned well and good ah wouldn't do sich a thing!" replied Sporison laughing.

Patting his water-logged belly, he continued his tale, "Them was the days ah was slim and trim. Ah looked mighty sharp in them Air Force togs, ah guar-an-TEE! An' ever' time we hitch-hiked into town them taxi drivers would pull over ta the curb and ask us if we wanted this or thet commodity—all supposed ta be illegal of course. But dang if thet wasn't the most wide open town ah ever been in!"

The four men gathered in a circle now.

"Shame on yuh!" said Dr. Sterner in mock astonishment.

Everyone laughed lightly and then focused again on Jed Sporison.

"Most of this is second-hand, mind yuh," said Jed laughing. "Well, anyways, one evening me and ma buddies was walkin' 'round town lookin' fer mischief, when here come this taxi bar-reling up the street sixty-odd mile an hour. He spots us sudden-like and slams on the brakes an' thet ol' car pretty near jack-knifed. Scared the tar outa us! Well, anyways, he tole us about this place we could get some liquor. So we say fine and climb in the cab. Well, he took us ta this real nice neighborhood—real middle class. Lawns cut real nice and picket fences whitewashed and flowers ever'wheres. Real respectable. Well, we stop in front of this nice, neat little house and go in the gate and ring the doorbell. Can yuh figger who answered the door? Well, this lit-tle ol' lady in tennis shoes . . ."—Everyone laughed—"No, not really. Jest a little ol' lady. She shows us in, and goldang if we didn't see a sight! Right there on the couch was bottles and bottles and more bottles! Ever'thing from tequila ta vodka ta rye whiskey. Anything yuh want!"

Everyone laughed again, lightly.

"Not really very funny, though," continued Jed, assuming a serious demeanor. "She was crippled. She was in a wheel chair. And this is the way she made a livin'. Pitiful. Real pitiful."

Everyone nodded.

"Ah feel like whiskey's a real damnation. Don't yuh believe so?" said Dr. Sterner gazing at Serveto.

"I think it can be."

"Ah feel like it ruins ever'body thet drinks it. Don't yuh believe so?" challenged Dr. Sterner.

"I don't know that it does," replied Serveto.

"Ah feel like these folks thet don't have hardly nuthin' must be alcoholics. Don't yuh believe so?"

"I think perhaps it's true sometimes."

"Ah feel like those niggers thet have kids one-after-another and don't know even who the daddy is are probably real barflies. Don't know what they're doin'! Don't yuh believe so?"

"I don't know."

"Ah feel like the federal government's too easy on the niggers. Welfare checks ever' month and they don't work a lick! Drink the whole check down! And their little pickaninnies go 'round half naked and fulla lice and barefooted. Don't yuh believe so, Dr. Serveto?"

"I don't know."

"Ah feel like thet's social irresponsibility. And the government pays for thet out of our pockets! Best thing thet woulda happened was the American Colonization Society back there in the early nineteenth century woulda shipped them all back ta Africa where they come from! Don't yuh believe so?"

"I don't think so," said Dr. Serveto dryly.

"Well, ah feel like it woulda saved us much grief," added Sterner, looking annoyed. "Anyway, their own nigger organizations want their own country. Yuh ever listen ta the Black Muslims? . . . Well, they want it. Ah believe the government should do something about them. Ah feel like they should sterilize them or somethin'. Get these pickaninny-producing machines and perform hysterectomies or somethin'. Don't yuh believe so?"

"I don't think so," repeated Dr. Serveto.

"Ah feel like no amount of education will help them much either. They're jest low class. Don't yuh believe so?"

"I don't think so."

"Ah believe it. Ah feel like it's so," concluded Sterner firmly, vigorously nodding his head. Thet's the gospel truth! Ah believe it!"

"Now, Dr. Sterner," said Sporison amiably, "don't go riling up ma guests!"

Everyone laughed self-consciously. Sporison broke up the circle by taking Dr. Serveto aside to meet some other newcomers. The four men began to move among the other talking guests. Cross was embarrassed for himself and the others. *Dr. Sterner should not have been so frank about his beliefs.*

Later in the evening Cross made a special effort to talk to Serveto alone. He told the newcomer about Big Bend National Park and about the dedication some years earlier. Dr. Serveto was interested and he listened carefully.

He seems to like this country all right, thought the preacher. Still, he was wary.

CHAPTER FIVE

Cross was feeling guilty. Yesterday Marie had begged him to come home early and instead he had gone to Jed Sporison's party and stayed out very late. By the time he arrived home it was two o'clock in the morning. He glanced anxiously at her.

Marie looked sad. The few words that passed between them on this late Saturday morning concerned items of no importance uttered in dry flat tones. Marie sighed deeply and the edges of her sensual mouth were turned down in little lines that showed her unhappiness. She cried softly at the smallest things that went amiss in the kitchen. Her eyes were cast down and their gaze withdrawn.

Cross was uneasy. He was sitting at the kitchen table eating a late breakfast. The food was tasteless, for his mind was preoccupied. He spoke now as if nothing were wrong, his voice betraying a pleading quality, hoping to elicit some response from the distracted woman.

"The party was right nice last night," he told her. "Jed was awful sorry you couldn't be there. So was I . . . I wish he would've told me earlier about it."

Marie stood at the stove, her back to her husband, stirring pots of cooking food that needed no stirring.

"Dr. Serveto was there," Cross went on, attempting to arouse interest. "You know who he is, don't you honey? You know! He's the new man on the faculty. I hear he speaks Spanish. He should! Why, he's been in Mexico and other parts of Latin America many times. He's a nice feller, seems like."

Cross hoped his saying that would please Marie. There was

no response. She stirred, the arm moving in nervous circles, the rest of her body immobile and cold.

"He reminded me a little of that Mexican politician from San Antonio. What's his name? Oh, yeah, Sánchez—Celso Sánchez! You remember him, don't you honey?"

There was no response.

"Remember the San Jacinto ceremonies last month?" Cross forgot today was the first day of June. "My God! what a ruckus he started with that speech about Texans overcoming their history. He's got guts—I give him credit for that! But to tell folks they should scrap a patriotic slogan is pushing too far. Can you imagine true Texans shouting, 'Obliterate the Alamo'? 'Olvidamos el Alamo!' he said. Remember? No wonder Dr. Sterner and the others were fighting mad! That young upstart Sánchez was asking for trouble! I feel like Dr. Serveto may be that kind too. But I like him okay to this point."

A door slammed hard and the rat-a-tat-tat of light running feet could be heard approaching, growing louder, louder quickly. Danny burst open the swinging door and nearly fell headlong into the kitchen.

"Whoa there, cowboy!" said Cross laughing, catching the sinewy bronco up into his arms and onto his lap. "Whatcha up to, Son?"

"Papa!" said Danny, gasping for breath. "The bruja is here! She's going to get me! La bruja!" He snuggled trembling to his father's breast.

"La bruja!" said Cross, eyes narrowing. "What's he talking about, Marie? A witch? What's he talking about?"

"Oh, it's just Brigitta. You know the old lady who goes around selling tamales." She walked hurriedly out of the kitchen, wiping her hands on her apron as she left.

Cross took Danny by the hand and followed. The boy carried his rattle in the other hand, jiggling it nervously.

The old lady standing on the threshold outside the screen door was dressed totally in black. A black mantilla framed a bony, sharp-featured face that owned all the mystery of ancient witchery. She was old, very old. Wrinkled and grizzled.

"Quiero una docena," said Marie.

With jerky, trembling motions, the old woman grabbed at the wet, warm-smelling rags that covered the tamales in the old dented bucket that she carried on her arm but now dropped to the stone step to dig into more easily with sharp-nailed hands.

She laid the steaming, husk-covered corn rolls in an old newspaper.

"You're not fixing to buy any food from her, are you?" Cross asked in an irritated tone.

"Yes, I am," answered Marie, still watching the old woman. Danny clung to his father's leg.

"First she scares hell outa the boy and then she sells you rotten, evil-smelling tamales! You must be plumb loco to insist on buying food from her!"

"Danny and I have had them before, Lee. They're all right."

"You've bought them before? Ahhhhh," he moaned, shaking his head.

"How do you know what she puts in them? Probably stuffs cat meat in that corn meal. You know what folks say about these tamale peddlers, Marie! Honest, I just can't figure you out! How you can play with your own health and Danny's too!"

The old woman wrapped the hot dripping tamales in a tight bundle and waited momentarily as Marie opened the screen door, and she handed the warm package to Marie and took the dollar anxiously with a toothless grin.

"Gracias. Muchísimas gracias, señora," she almost whispered in a low gravelly voice, head bowing.

"You git! You git, now!" growled Cross. "And don't let me see hide nor hair of you around here again!"

The old woman looked sharply into the eyes of Robby Lee Cross and their steel gazes clashed. She turned and shuffled off, humpbacked, bucket dangling, up the dusty yard toward the arroyo bridge and the dirt road that led to the highway.

In a hot temper Cross wheeled sharply, his gaze like a laser on Marie's back as she marched into the house with her bundle. She had cast a barbed look at Lee before entering and her eyelids had moved automatically shut and open again as if in disgust at the sight of him. Cross was glad. They would have it out now. He launched after her. Danny remained at the screen door, eyes fixed on the black shuffling figure working her way toward the highway. His hand was shaking the rattle nervously.

"What in hell are you buying Mexican slop from the likes of her," shouted Cross angrily, "And then feeding it to Danny! I never heard of such idiocy!"

They glared at each other in the kitchen. Marie was unwrapping the tamales.

"Who is that old witch anyway?"

"Brigitta," said Marie, sighing with impatience. "Brigitta Obispo. She's that old lady who lives the other side of Sun Mountain."

"She does? Well, who is she? What is she? Why does she frighten Danny?"

"She doesn't do it on purpose. She scares children and superstitious old ladies because she looks so withered and old. That's all. She means no harm. And her tamales are probably the most sanitary you can buy."

"I'll bet!" Cross said cuttingly.

"You don't have to yell at me, Lee!" snapped Marie angrily.

"Who's yelling?" Cross exploded. "When you don't have more sense 'an to give the boy that Mexican garbage, don't you think a person has cause to get all riled up? You aren't very considerate of your own kin, I reckon."

Marie could contain her tears no longer. Her voice broke as she complained bitterly. "Lee! Don't shout at me! You've hurt me terribly! You stayed out late last night even though I asked you special to come home early! I don't like to stay home alone with the boy late at night. I'm afraid, Lee. I'm afraid. . . ." The woman broke down and began to sob.

"Oh! honey." He felt ashamed now, what with all the quarreling and shouting. "There's nothing to be afraid of. There's nobody gonna hurt you. We're safe here. We're perfectly safe here." He came up behind her and put his hands on her shoulders. "Don't worry none, honey. This is the safest place on earth. Our home is secure."

Marie went to the table, away from her husband, and dabbed at her eyes with the apron tied around her waist. She sighed deeply and choked off the crying spasm. Cross shifted nervously near the stove. He wanted to prevent any more tears. He waited for Marie to compose herself, and then in a soft voice he asked, "Why does the old witch dress all in black like that? Is she in mourning?"

"In a way, yes," answered his wife, wiping her nose with a handkerchief to stop her sniffling.

"What way? How is she in mourning?"

Marie sat down at the table. Her anger had subsided and she was thoughtful. Lee sat down across from her.

"Most of her life is wrapped in old maids' tales. It's hard to tell myth and truth apart." Lee was interested and Marie knew it. She told how, years before, Brigitta Obispo fell madly in love with a Mexican boy who had come across the river. He had come to work and he found a job as a blacksmith in old Santo Domingo, now a ghost town. Marie said that Brigitta had never been pretty and that the boy seduced her and then took her for a convenient affair once he saw she loved him. They got along all right for a while, till the boy began to court another girl who was very beautiful. This made Brigitta insanely jealous, and the old maiden aunts said she put a hex on the boy and his new love. Then, one night in a terrible thunderstorm, as the boy and his beauty were going home from a dance in a borrowed buckboard, they were caught in a flash flood that spilled over the banks of an arroyo and the rushing water washed them away and they were never seen again. The old maiden aunts charged that it was Brigitta who conjured up that thunder shower. Marie told how Brigitta dressed all in black after the accident and how she had never dressed in any other color since. She told how Brigitta became uglier and more eccentric and how she became a scapegoat for anyone who had troubles. She was tormented constantly by the people of Santo Domingo, so she went to live alone in an old shack on the other side of Sun Mountain. The old maids connived and conspired even more against Brigitta when Santo Domingo itself became a ghost town. "They're sure it was Brigitta who put a hex on the old town. Poor thing. I feel so sorry for the old lady. Her life is very sad and the old comadres don't give her peace."

"I don't like her one bit," muttered Cross mildly. "How does she get around anyway?"

"I don't know. Nobody knows. People see her walking along the highway and then she shows up in faraway towns in a very short time. The old maiden aunts say she can change herself into a lobo or a cougar or anything else she wants."

"A lobo?" Cross exclaimed.

"A black lobo," said Marie.

"Hmmm," mused Cross. Then he said: "There's no connection of course, but did you know I saw a black lobo by the corral the other night? I didn't tell you about it, not to frighten you."

Cross regarded Marie with a steady gaze and she looked back into his eyes, thoughtfully.

"Oh, this is ridiculous," he went on, "There's no connection."

Cross got up from the chair and in one sweeping motion lifted Marie to her feet and embraced her hard against his body and kissed her. She responded warmly. He could feel her body, its warm soft contours pressed against him.

"I'm awful sorry I was so late last night, honey," he apologized. And he kissed her again. "You feel better now?"

The woman nodded.

"Lee, I got something to tell you." Marie hesitated, searching for the right words.

"What is it, honey?" Lee took her chin on the ledge of his curled forefinger and lifted her face to his, still holding her close.

"I'm going to have a baby, Lee."

"What?"

"I'm going to have a baby!"

"Sure enough?" A questioning smile was on his lips. "Really?"

"Yes, Lee. It's true."

"The doctor say so?"

"Yes, he did."

"Well, gosh darn!" he gurgled happily. "Sure is good news, honey."

Marie smiled broadly as Lee held her tightly. He couldn't get over the idea—another son maybe. "Gosh darn," he repeated over and over again. "Sure is good news." Cross laughed happily. Then he took Marie's face in his hands and looked seriously into her eyes. "I'll be more careful here on out," he told her as he kissed her lightly.

Danny swung open the kitchen door.

"How'reyu now, Son?" asked his father with a smile.

"I'm okay," said the boy.

Cross lifted his son into his arms. "No need to be afraid, Son. She's just an old lady. And you're a man now and you're not scared of any old hag, now are you?"

"No sir," replied the boy. "I'm not a-scared."

"Good."

The boy wrapped himself around his father's body with his arms and legs, and father and son felt close and warm. The father kissed the boy's cheek and brushed back his unruly hair and told him of the new baby. Danny wasn't sure what it all meant, but he liked the happiness he saw on their faces.

"Now you two homebodies put your mind to your chores! I

gotta spend the day trying to sell some cutlery. I got a meeting this afternoon too."

The boy was unclasped by his father's strong hands and put on his feet, and the boy ran out the back door yelling, "S'long, Papa!"

Cross moved purposefully about the house now, preparing for his trip into town. He took the black valise last, and as he moved towards the front door, he told Marie about the big sale he had made at the Zarler's the day before. They sure could use the money now with the baby. He kissed her more carefully than usual and he climbed into the old pickup and drove over the rough bridge, past the woods, up the dusty road. As he turned onto the highway, he looked back to the house and waved to Marie—and to the boy now as he ran, arms waving, from behind the house.

Cross made two stops along the way, both at isolated ranches where people might have a need for good new kitchen knives. He sold a small set; then he drove on.

In the glaring sunlight, he saw the vultures circling above the onrushing highway. Desert animals were often struck and mutilated by indifferent men and machines speeding on to nowhere. Slowing the old pickup, he watched a flock of black bald vultures gorging in the distance. Then, bloated with carrion, they performed what seemed a ritual dance, hopping and bouncing while flapping their anxious wings. Try as they would, their wings were no longer strong enough to carry them up into the wind where all would be well. So they hopped and flapped and squawked in a bizarre dance of death.

Then, with a kick of its talons against a fence post, a flap of the wings, and straight graceful glide, another black vulture landed hopping on the highway by a carrion feast and began pecking greedily at the choice parts. Cross braked the pickup slightly, but the eyes of the vulture were keen and its instincts true, and it flew away as the pickup loomed menacingly. Cross now accelerated the old Ford to get away quickly from the grisly scene.

Soon he saw the mountains surrounding Geneva Gap and he geared down to take the foothill upgrades. The air cooled off nicely and Cross was glad the heat wave had rolled by.

Cross drove directly to the old emasculated gas station on Center Street. For some time now the garage had been stripped of its fuel pumps, its car lift, its repairing devices, and all else that identified it as a gas station. The previous owner had gone bankrupt trying to compete independently against the big American chain stations. He had tried to compete with cheap gas bought from Mexican sources, so people said. Then, when he sold out to the big companies, the local Texacut agency had acquired a twenty-five year lease on the property. The building was located on a corner and had good parking. Texacut was pleased, and its meetings were held in the large back hall that once served as a garage for repairing broken-down cars.

Cross parked the pickup in the driveway of the converted gas station. There were other cars standing there. It was clear the meeting would soon start.

Inside a small crowd was gathering in the garage behind the front office. The hall was humming with voices and the air was choking with cigar smoke. Cross caught sight of Rex Austin and Will Busbee talking in a corner of the hall. They saw him too and motioned him over.

"Howdy, preacher," said Rex Austin.

"Howdy right back," he shot back to the two men.

Rex is always mighty friendly, thought Cross. He was about twenty-eight years old, open-faced and extroverted, and tending toward a certain obesity. He had a nondescript face that was pockmarked and bulged a bit at the jaw line, and his eyes were friendly but showed a certain shallowness. His favorite topic was "female wimmin."

"Rex was just telling me about his new girl friend and another one he's got an eye on," commented Will Busbee, laughing.

"I figured he'd be talking shop," joked Cross. The three men laughed.

"How's business?" asked Busbee.

"Picking up, I reckon. It's about time too! Man can't live on faith alone," philosophized the preacher. "How're you doing in spreading the Word?"

"Oh, fine! I've got two prospects here today who seem to have that old drive and determination to spread the Texacut Word. I'm optimistic!"

Will Busbee was chief coordinator for sales and personnel in the Big Bend country. He was also an instructor of business administration at Cal Davis. He was involved. People liked that. Originally from Michigan, he became involved in the community. People liked that. People liked Will Busbee. He was a most agreeable chap. He belonged. He belonged to the Rotary Club, the Lion's Club, the Junior Chamber of Commerce, the college International Club, and he was an honorary member of the American Legion post of Geneva Gap. If the NAACP and Ku Klux Klan had established chapters in Geneva Gap, Will Busbee would have belonged—he would have been the first to join. He was a most agreeable fellow.

Will Busbee called out, "I guess we ought to get this show on the road." He cleared his throat and raised his voice: "Take your seats, gentlemen!"

Will Busbee stepped up onto the platform at the front of the hall, stood at the desk with his famous smile, and waited patiently for the meeting to come to order. Behind his head on the wall hung a large banner proclaiming:

TEXACUT CUTLERY
MADE IN TEXAS, BY TEXANS, FOR TEXANS
Texas Cutlery Company of Dallas

The flag of the Lone Star State was unfurled to the right and pinned to the wall.

Will Busbee stared out at the audience with a fortunate smile on his face, nodding occasionally, mumbling "Hiyuh Ed" and "Hiyuh Tom" to friends looking for empty seats among the unfolded metal chairs.

Busbee's face was nondescript, much like Rex Austin's. The difference lay in the fact that Busbee's face afforded discriminating people the impression of a chalk drawing on a blackboard that had been partially blurred by a careless flick of an eraser. People invariably forgot the face but remembered the pleasant manner about Will Busbee.

The chief coordinator now turned his head to check the clock on the wall behind. He unwittingly exhibited the bald spot at the back incline of his head.

Will Busbee was young. Only twenty-four. But he had to pamper his rapidly thinning hair. This misfortune embarrassed him constantly. He was molting terribly and every morning he had the difficult choice of combing his remaining black feathers forward to hide the shiny flatness of an imperialistic forehead or of combing them in reverse to cover the platter-shaped expanse of skin at the back. It was humiliating to make such a choice, but usually Will Busbee decided on a forward thrust of

the comb. And so today, as on many a day, the bare disk at the
back of the head shone brightly.

"Will this congregation please come to order," he intoned.
"Let's all stand now and sing a hymn to our master product,
Texacut Cutlery."

The metallic scrapings and groanings of displaced chairs
were heard along with muffled shufflings and utterings of rising
men. Cross had found a hymn sheet on the chair beforehand
and now raised it to eye level.

"Let's start with number two. It's a rousing song and it'll
put us in the mood." Will Busbee hummed a note, waved his
arm like a baton, and led the serious men in song.

> "C-C-C Cutlery, beautiful cutlery,
> It's just got to be fine Texacut.
> When the s-sun shines over the mountain,
> We'll all be selling Texacut cutlery.
>
> "C-C-C Cutlery, beautiful cutlery,
> Everybody takes a cut with Texacut.
> When the siz-iz-ling steaks are a-frying,
> We'll be standing round around with Texacut.
>
> "C-C-C Cutlery, beautiful cutlery,
> Trim your beef and slice your bread with Texacut.
> When G-G-G Gabriel blows on that trumpet,
> We will all go marching in with Texacut."

The salesmen snickered and looked at each other and applauded
vigorously on their own behalf. The chief coordinator motioned
everyone to take his seat. "Now, for the benefit of our newcomers, we'll give our little spiel on the Texacut creed. You-all
help me out now!"

Everyone applauded again and nodded smiling.

"Texacut," continued Will Busbee, "Texacut doesn't believe
in subjecting itself to common, ordinary sales methods. It
doesn't sell retail in any store or shop. You will never find Texacut in your local department store. Nosiree!

"Texacut believes in going directly to the people with dedi-
cated believers carrying the word of our master product. It is a
master product. We don't cringe in conscience at our sales pitch.
Why? Because we have a master product. We believe in our
product. We don't have to deceive like other companies. We

have the master product. Carry on there, Robalee," concluded Busbee, pointing to Cross. "Carry on!"

"Sure will," said the preacher, standing. "We all must show the benefits of Texacut to all the people. When you make a contact, tell them to pass the Word. Give them your name card with the Texacut slogan on it: 'Made in Texas, by Texans, for Texans.' We want folks not only to think Texacut, we want 'em to believe Texacut! Have faith and keep the faith! Think Texacut! Believe Texacut! Texacut is the only cutlery product which has an iron-clad guarantee that no other company can approach. We got the master product!"

"Great, Robalee, great!" said Will Busbee. "Rex! you tell them about the rewards."

Rex Austin stood up, and with a silly grin on his face he said, "The rewards is real great! Texacut appreciates successful service in this here business. Prizes are given ever' year ta the salesmen who top the list of total sales. In 1963 Will Busbee won a trip to Grand Canyon for a week, all expenses paid, for hisself and his purty wife Goldie. This year a vacation to that entertainment Mecca in the desert, Las Vegas, is promised to the top salesman in the region—all expenses paid by Texacut! So the trail to better sales is mighty invitin' and the rewards is right shiny and brassy! And this all is jest icing on the cake, 'cause y'all 'ill be makin' money—good money—all along!"

Rex Austin sat down very pleased at his performance. Everyone applauded.

"That's great—real great!" approved Will Busbee. "You newcomers can see me after the meeting about your samples, about your contracts, and whatever else you feel you need. Now let's talk about the annual outing we're planning for next week."

The meeting continued. Arrangements were made for the picnic of all Texacut salesmen and their families at Big Bend National Park. Cross listened impassively.

When the planning session ended, Will Busbee took up his hymn sheet again and called out, "Let's close this sales meeting with my favorite song. Number one on your hymn sheet, please!"

Again Will Busbee hummed a note, waved his arm like a conductor, and brayed out the militant hymn.

Onward Texacut Salesmen,
Marching as to war,

With the Texacut banner,
Going on before.

Texacut the master product,
Leads against the foe.
Forward into kitchens,
See the sales flow.

Onward Texacut Salesmen,
Marching as to war,
With the Texacut banner,
Going on before.

All you butchers take note,
All you housewives too.
Cut right through that gristle,
See how Texacut's true.

Onward Texacut Salesmen,
Marching as to war,
With the Texacut banner,
Going on before.

Soon all Texans will respond,
And all Americans too.
Cast that dulling knife aside,
Texacut's the knife for you!

Onward Texacut Salesmen,
Marching as to war,
With the Texacut banner,
Going on before.

The salesmen laughed, looked self-consciously around the room, while applauding vigorously. Then they began picking up their belongings and uttering small talk to neighbors and leaving the converted repair station.

Cross waited in the hall to talk to Will Busbee who was busy indoctrinating the two new salesmen. He wanted to congratulate Busbee for the job he had done in adapting the Texacut gospel to the music of traditional songs. Cross was not really so impressed. The adaptations were crude, but Cross was a courteous person, especially with the right people. Yet he was certain he could have done a better job.

Cross waited patiently. He could hear Rex Austin in the

small outer office relating kiss-and-tell tales to some prurient bystanders.

"Lord, yuh ain't about ta know the things ah seen," he was saying. "That's why ah like this job real good. Yuh never know what's goin' ta happen! One time, ah walks up ta this house in El Paso ta sell ma knives—and Lord! what opened the door near batted ma eyes out! This gorgeous filly come out bare-ass naked! Lord, she was built! Real blonde too! Thet's the God-honest truth! Ah tore off like a bat outa hell—Lord knows what she had up her sleeve—oh! pardon me! ah mean up her poon-tang!"

Raucous laughter emanated from the front office.

"Ah found out later thet she was asleep after her bath when ah come up there, and the doorbell jest woke her up enough ta lead her ta the door. She didn't realize she had nary a stitch on!"

"How'd yuh find out about the bath?" asked a voice unknown to Cross. More laughter.

"Well, yuh studs don't think ah'd leave well enough alone, do yuh? Ah went right back the next day and she was real embarrassed but real nice too. She bought ma biggest seta knives and explained the whole thing. She was real nice! Ah thought ta maself then—Lord, ah'd lak ta tickle her innards! Sure nuff, hardly a week and ah was in lak Flynn! Ah shot her old man clean outa the saddle! And Lord! did she have a bellyful o' bed-springs! A millionaire's mattress, ah tell yuh! Bucked hell outa me!"

More raucous laughter from the front office, and Cross shook his head in disgust. He decided to leave without speaking to Will Busbee. As he walked through the front office, he heard Rex Austin shout, "See yuh, preacher!" Cross did not look back.

Cross visited five homes in the Geneva Gap area trying to sell his merchandise. The people were friendly but Cross sold nothing the long afternoon. He became discouraged and felt tired. He decided it would be good to surprise Marie by coming home early. He stopped to fill the tank and he was off, wheels spinning, dust flying, onto the smooth asphalt highway.

Cross felt good now, driving on the highway. The day had not gone well and he looked forward to a relaxing evening at home. He would forget the bad day and build a small fire in the fireplace and they would make a good evening together and talk of the baby. He could already feel the comfort of the fireplace and the soft warmth of her body. His penis began to throb and he tried hard to suppress the sensual longings in his loins. He pressed down hard on the accelerator.

The sun was dropping toward the western horizon and its glaring rays struck his eyes, burning and causing them to water. He would be glad when it reached the dark clouds on the horizon. In minutes the glare had abated. The earth's atmosphere now allowed Cross to stare for seconds into the sun. It was a huge yellowish-red ball on the horizon and the clouds around it reflected vivid reds and yellows and pinks. *Nobody has really seen a sunset till they view one here in West Texas,* thought Cross. *This was God's country, all right. Nothing can match nature in West Texas.*

The sun had disappeared, darkness rose swiftly, and in the near distance before the highway loomed black-purple clouds in one vast apron threatening to unload heavy rains. It grew darker, blacker in minutes. Soon big rain drops splattered down but far between as if they were an advance guard surveying the lay of the land. Then in an instant came the showers, heavy, like thick gray curtains on the windshield of the old Ford pickup. The wipers on the window before the eyes of the lonely driver were swamped in the rushing downpour. *Sisyphus labor,* thought Cross about the windshield wipers. He gazed intently on the highway before him, fearing the blinding rain might cause an approaching car to swerve in his direction. He slowed down and pressed his foot down on the switch that snapped the headlights to brightest intensity.

It was well into night when the old truck turned off the highway onto the muddy road leading to the ranch. The rain was falling less heavily.

Marie and the boy glowed with joy when Cross entered the house. Marie's face was bright and smiling, her eyes happily attentive, as she administered to him with great care.

Cross had a springy kick to his heels as he walked about the house now.

"Do you have any of those tamales left, honey?" He rummaged through the refrigerator.

"No. I didn't think you cared for them, so Danny and I ate them up. I'm sorry."

"Oh, that's all right. Ol' Brigitta probably put a hex on 'em, anyway."

They laughed happily and he kissed her lightly on the cheek as he passed to take a chair at the table.

After supper Cross kindled a fire in the big brick fireplace. The large living room smelled of smoke at first, but soon the fire was burning brightly, warming the large room. Danny lay on his stomach before the crackling fire, while Cross and Marie sat on the couch whispering about the baby and listening quietly to the radio. The Grand Old Opry was coming straight from Nashville. Twanging hill-country music with screeching fiddles circled and promenaded and danced about the large room. Then it was over.

"My program's on next," said Cross.

Speedy Carpenter's nasal, jerky stutter announced this was the voice of the last frontier. Then a pause.

Organ music beat the eardrums now as a recording of "That Old Rugged Cross" was played on the air. It was the theme hymn of the program. Now Speedy Carpenter informed listeners that the program was sponsored by Texacut products of Dallas, Texas. "And now the Reverend Robby Lee Cross," said the announcer with a heavy twang.

The next voice sounded strange to Robby Lee Cross as it always did when he assumed his radio personality.

"I am the seeker," said Cross's voice gravely. "I seek the truth on the highways and byways of this great country. And I find it in the valleys and in the backwoods, in the cities and in the villages. I am the seeker. I am the seeker after truth and salvation. I seek the absolute."

Cross never altered the introduction. Now he presented the subject for the day's sermon.

The Cola Generation. We are living in the Cola generation. . . .

Some people say that God is dead. And they are right. They are right! A new god has been created by the Cola generation. A hedonic Odin has been raised to the new cathedral spire—the roof-top apartment—the playboy pad—that is the sanctuary of the hedonic Odin! A sanctuary where female beings transformed to crouching animals sink to their short-skirted knees and adore the new pagan god. A sanctuary where sex throbs set to strings and drums and brass arouse the vestal sex ducts to jerking spellbound movements. They rise from all fours and commence to rush and jump and stomp out vibrating crotch frenzies. Then male beings in skin-tight garments, exhibiting sex bulges, jump into the spine-tingling orgy. Throbs, stomps, shakes! Where the action is!

Eyeball to eyeball, nostril to nostril, taste bud to taste bud, hand fall to hand fall, hand feel to hand feel, sex bulge to sex bulge! Pneumatic dollies! Huxley's hedonism! Where the action is! The hedonic Odin rules over all from his sex pad in the sky! Sodom and Gomorrah!

Do not listen to fake prophets who sell visceral pleasures wrapped in cerebral falsies! Heed St. Paul's epistle: "Be not deceived: neither fornicators, nor idolaters, nor adulterers, nor effeminates, nor abusers of themselves with mankind, nor thieves, nor covetous, nor drunkards, nor revilers, nor extortioners, shall inherit the kingdom of God."

My hair falls out and a cancer corrodes my bowels. My fingers refuse to halt their insane tapping. My face is twisted by pressure and pain. I sell my smile, I sell my arms, I sell my soul. I smile mechanically at the vegetating, walking Jack-O'-lanterns about me, because I must sell my soul. I have placed it on the auction block to be presented to the highest bidder. I feel myself a dog, an animal, an organism without semblance of divinity. I am the frothing dog chasing the steaming bitch. I am sold to the order of numbing machines and numbing anaesthetics. The lever is my brain and the sexpot is my soul. I am the Cola generation!

And to whom and to what do we owe our plight? In centuries past mankind had fallen to moral degeneracy. But never before, except perhaps in Sodom and Gomorrah, has a society raised to a virtue, an ideal, the sinkhole of immorality, amorality, and sexual perversion. Virtuous immorality is now being established on a national scale, as a national ideal. Beware the false prophets! Beware the moral relativists and the relative moralists and the absolute amoralists! Beware the Freudian pickers of the brain! The bible warns: "They became vain in their imaginations, and their foolish heart was darkened. Professing themselves to be wise, they became fools, . . . and changed the truth of God into a lie!"

And what do the Freudian devils tell us? They use science to warp the truth of God. They tell us that Man was always an animal of crass necessity and they cite scientific revelation to support their assertions.

In ancient times, they say, Man was like a minor god believing himself to be the center of the universe. His senses indicated so. His eyes described a circle about him of 360 degrees with everything converging on himself as the center. The earth, his abode, was the absolute center of the universe. Suns and planets and hither worlds revolved about his domain. But then a revealing shock occurred. Copernicus and Galileo and Newton destroyed his visions of grandeur, making the earth but a minute speck in a universe possessing a thousand upon a thousand centers. . . . But the trauma passed.

Next, Man considered himself at least supreme on his own planet. Here he was king. Here he occupied the upper strata of a Great Chain of Being reaching to the Godhead. But another shock wave swept his egotism to the point of nearly collapsing it. Along came Darwin and Haeckel and Huxley and they relegated Man to an evolutionary phase in the development of the animal. The nuclear bomb could not create more havoc. Man was an animal with the actions and reactions of an animal. . . . But this trauma also passed.

Man could always be supreme in his own inner being, in his brain, in his soul. Rude shock! Along came Freud and Jung and Pavlov to show that Man was in greater disintegration within himself. Man could be conditioned, even determined, by impulses and machines and conditioning factors. Rude trauma set in once and for all!

Why struggle, why battle to perfect and improve oneself? Such questions Man asked of himself. Better to forget, to anaesthetize, to succumb to animal pleasures. And there arose the Cola generation! A generation defeated! No need to fight the good fight. No need to struggle to improve and perfect one's character and morality and one's very own soul. No need to think. Such things are obsolete! Hedonism is the new god. The hedonic Odin watches carefully over all. A sensual Utopia is upon us! Heaven on earth is upon us in the form of an uninhibited hedonism. The little speck to which we cling in the universe is whirling on to infinity—an infinity of fearsome unknowability. Better to take our pleasure today! Who knows what lurks in the misty expanses of infinity! Take that drug and dance the sex frenzy and take the sex outlet wherever it may be!

Oh, Jerusalem, Jerusalem! The new Jerusalem! The new Utopia! The new frontier! The great society! Jerusalem, Jerusalem! Where art thou going? Think! Stop to think! Have faith! Stop to have faith! The great Jehovah has not abandoned you!

His immortal Son has not forsaken you! Dispel false prophecies —expel false prophets! Renew the faith of your fathers! Faith can move mountains! Faith can drive the very atom to nothingness! Faith can move oceans and orbits and the very heavens! Reform and revive! Revive and reform! Heed the Word: "Put on the new man, which is renewed in knowledge after the image of him that created him."

Read the Bible! It will revive you and transform you to righteousness. Reject the false prophets! Agitate yourself away from being a mere accident, a mere mechanism, a mere hungry animal.

Organ music now blasted forth and a choir could be heard singing "The Old Rugged Cross." The program was over.

Marie switched off the radio and leaned back on the couch. "It was a very good sermon," she said in a whisper.

Cross sat still, his hand covering his eyes. He did not speak.

Marie watched him sadly for several minutes. Then she turned to the fireplace. The fire was out and the room was becoming chilly. Marie looked at Danny, asleep on the floor. She shivered as she rose from the couch and lifted the boy gently to carry him to the back bedroom.

Cross remained in the darkened room, his head bowed, his eyes covered with his hand. It was a long time before he moved at all. Finally he rose from the couch and walked to the back bedroom, slowly, almost painfully.

In the dark he undressed without thinking. He rolled into bed beside her warm naked body. He placed his hand on the soft roundness of her hip, the smoothness of her thigh. Then he removed the hand and turned his back and closed his eyes, quickly sinking into a dead sleep.

Marie lay still, her eyes wide open. She lay awake the entire night.

CHAPTER SIX

On Sunday Cross arose early. It was his habit to awaken before the sun appeared on the Seventh Day and to walk around his land in a form of adoration to his deity.

He got up carefully, quietly, anxious not to disturb his woman whose eyes had finally closed and for whom a profound sleep had finally come. He dressed quickly and then tiptoed out the bedroom into the kitchen where he lit a burner on the butane gas stove to heat some leftover coffee. In the dim light of early morn he sat at the table, thinking. The chill of the dissipating night caused goose flesh to break out on his arms, and Cross rubbed them vigorously, hoping the friction would warm up his body. It helped a little. He poured a big cupful of coffee and took great gulps of the hot steaming liquid. That helped even more. He grew warmer.

He grabbed a blue Levi jacket off a hook in the kitchen and armed his way into it. Then he walked out the back door into the half light of the cool early morning.

The air was fresh and moist. Dew clung in beads to the sprouting greens of the garden. The birds in the woods were warbling, the throaty singing losing itself in the expansive quietness of the early morn. Cross inhaled deeply. The cool moist air seemed to wash out clean the cavities of his head and the lungs of his broad chest. This was God's country, all right.

He walked over the rough-hewn bridge spanning the arroyo and watched the highway in the near distance. It was undisturbed, no car or truck speeding on it on this early Seventh Day. It appeared gloomy and lonely.

Cross skirted the edges of the tiny forest, because among the trees darkness still ruled and he would only stumble and wrench his ankles and scratch his legs and arms on underbrush and protruding branches as he walked along the pathway. The difficulties of penetrating the dark woods would simply distract him from his meditation. So he walked along the edges of the woods, away from the ranch, with head bowed and gaze cast to the ground before him, concentrating on the wonders of the Godhead.

After trudging some three miles, Cross turned on his heel and took the forest path back to the ranch, for now the sun was casting flashing rays over the rim of Sun Mountain and the light entered the dark woods in long ethereal fingers. The human intruder caught glimpses of forest creatures from time to time as he walked alone among the trees. Rabbits and squirrels scurried everywhere and curious deer watched him warily from a safe distance. The birds now seemed to be singing more happily in the sunlight. Cross felt warm and reassured and strong. He felt he had spoken well with his Creator.

Back at the ranch, he attended to the old goat in the barn and the two mares in the corral. Then he went into the house and began preparing breakfast for his family. Marie usually rose early, but today she remained in bed, sleeping, because of some reason that escaped Robby Lee Cross.

It was not long, however, before Marie rushed into the kitchen, still buttoning her gingham housedress and looking at her husband with swollen eyes and saying, "I'll do that, Lee." Cross allowed her to take over, because when she insisted so, it was wise to acquiesce. He helped her by unwrapping some pork sausage and setting three places at the table. Danny was up early too.

The day went by quietly. Cross read the bible. It was his way of keeping the Sabbath holy. When he came upon a particularly interesting and significant passage in the Scriptures, he would read it aloud to Marie who was knitting busily, and the boy who was paging lazily through picture books. Otherwise Cross read quietly and the day passed quickly.

That night, as Cross sat on the bed removing his boots, Marie walked out of the bathroom, naked. She carried a towel which she had been using to dry her body, and now she flung it on a chair and climbed into bed. The sudden emergence of the woman in all her nudity had aroused Cross uncomfortably.

Eyes averted, he said, "You shouldn't traipse around like that with Danny in the room. He has to learn modesty."

Unbelieving, Marie riveted her eyes on her husband. Danny was fast asleep in the large crib. Before she could answer, Cross switched off the light and rolled into bed. The man and the woman lay on their backs, eyes wide open, tension between them like a neural coiled spring.

"Marie, I don't want to indulge in sex for a while," said Cross bluntly. The woman did not answer.

"A person should learn to discipline himself in matters of the flesh. There's too much sensuality in the world . . . too much self-indulgence . . . too much sex just for the sake of sex. People no longer discipline themselves. One should learn abstinence. The Penitentes of northern New Mexico are on the right track, though they go to extremes. But there are extremes on the other side too—sex frenzies and giving way to self-indulgence. There must be a happy medium."

There was a pause, as if the preacher wanted the message to sink in good. Then he continued.

"I think folks need to discipline their animal hungers once in a while. It will make them better people, better Christians. Jesus disciplined himself. He fasted for forty days and forty nights. He should be our model, our guide. . . ."

Another pause ensued. Then: "Let's discipline ourselves. . . . Is that all right, honey? Besides, you're pregnant now, and we can't be too careful about the baby you're carrying. All right?"

"If that's what you want, Lee."

"Put on a night gown from now on," he admonished.

Marie rose from bed in the dark and fumbled at a chest of drawers, searching for a night gown, and then she found one. She slipped it on over her head and returned to bed.

He leaned over and kissed her lightly on the cheek. The man and the woman lay far apart on the large bed.

* * * * * * *

The first week of classes at Cal Davis went well for Cross. The Reverend Mr. Jenks was somber, introducing him to different interpretations of the bible. Dr. Serveto was relaxed but precise and very interesting despite his "typical Berkeley" attitudes. And Dr. Sterner was his usual stimulating, wise-cracking self. All in all it seemed that it would be a good summer session.

His selling was going slowly, as usual. But his sermons were developing more power and people complimented him on their distinctiveness and effectiveness. His topic continued to be modern immorality and the need for spiritual rejuvenation. Folks are taking to the theme just fine, he thought happily. But his selling worried him at times. Yet he was looking forward to the annual picnic Texacut had planned for the weekend.

As the Sixth Day approached, Cross thought more and more about the outing. He decided to camp out the evening of the picnic, although no one else would. The others were simply going for the day, but Cross thought it would be good to sleep along the Rio Grande and worship there on the morning of the Seventh Day. He suggested the plan to Marie, half expecting and half hoping she would reject it for herself and the boy. And she did. Marie recognized her husband's unexpressed wishes and determined to stay home with the boy on Saturday. It would be better that way. Then Lee could sleep under the heavens by himself and really meditate. Cross kissed her lightly on the cheek for her decision. He was happy.

The Sixth Day rose hot and blinding bright. The salesmen and their families gathered at the converted gas station in Geneva Gap. Trucks and cars and station wagons were crammed full with blankets and baskets and beach chairs. Yelling children and chattering wives filled in the nooks and crannies of the over-stuffed vehicles. A happy, carefree mood pervaded the caravan as it snaked its way out of Geneva Gap southward toward the Big Bend of the Rio Grande.

Cross led the way on the highway in his old Ford pickup, followed closely by Will and Goldie Busbee in a foreign sports-car, the others trailing behind in various vehicles imported from Detroit.

The highway became exceedingly narrow, twisting and turning up and down knolls and small-rising hills. It grew hotter and hotter as the caravan moved farther southward.

At this time of year the Big Bend would be hitting near a hundred degrees or more. "We better find a good cool spot right quick," Cross whispered to himself.

He began to sing loudly to take his mind off the increasing heat.

> "You'll take the high road
> And I'll take the low road
> And I'll be in Scotland afore yuh.

But me and my true love
We'll never meet again
On the bonnie, bonnie banks
Of Loch Lomond."

The farther south they drove, the more forbidding became the countryside. Glaring reflections of sun on gray-bleached rock stung the eyes of the travelers. The predominant color was a whitish, glaring, sun-reflecting gray. Few shrubs graced the landscape. It was barren land, hot and shimmering bright. At times a lonely lizard slithered along the roadside on white-dazzling chips of rock, then it would disappear into sun-burnt, deathlike vegetation. And it was hot, stifling hot. The rays of the sun blazed down unmercifully on the cheeks and foreheads and arms of the travelers and they sweated freely and felt uncomfortably sticky all over their bodies. A fine dust permeated the air. It was stifling.

The caravan was moving closer to Big Bend. Cross was now driving hard up the first mountains that introduced the traveler to the vicinity of the park. The mountains here seemed to be covered with alkali, no vegetation, with slides and banks of black and dirty-looking gray. Cross switched to low gear because the mountain climb was steep and winding and the old Ford was whining, almost hesitating, struggling mightily. In the rear-view mirror Cross could see the Busbees in the low-slung sportscar. They were having no difficulty. Then Cross spotted a motorcycle with two people riding on it roaring past the long caravan. *Dang fools, passing on a narrow winding mountain road like this.* But the young man driving and the girl with long blonde hair flying and arms clinging hard to the body of the confident driver gained their objective without incident as they sped up the mountain and curved out of sight. Before they rounded the bend, Cross had caught sight of the block letters on the girl's leather jacket. "Happiness is coming," they proclaimed blatantly. The preacher grunted in disgust. "Longhair beat-niks!" he growled.

The old pickup was heating up badly. Cross watched the gauge on the dashboard, anxiously. Through the rear-view mirror again, he could see the cars inching up the steep highway behind him. The old truck roared and snorted slowly up the steep incline. Finally, it topped the mountain and now it was easy going down. The engine of the old pickup no longer heated up to the danger point; the indicator dropped quickly. Cross had to brake the old truck lightly as it sped down with increasing force. He steered around one curve on the highway but was carried over the median line by the high speed of the vehicle, and so now he shifted to low gear to increase the braking action.

To his right, bordering the highway, rose high cliffs; to his left off the lane of oncoming traffic was a sheer drop, down, far down. There was very little room to maneuver if any car coming up or going down crossed the median line. A yellow, black-bordered sign warned extreme caution.

Cross braked harder. Another curve lay ahead with the highway disappearing behind the rock shelf on the right. Suddenly, driving slowly around the corner, he saw it. An accident. A man stood in the middle of the highway frantically waving his arms for the oncoming traffic to stop. Quickly, Cross brought the truck to a dead halt by stepping on the pedal and pulling the hand brake at the same time. The cars behind stopped. "It's a dang good thing I was going so slow," Cross whispered to himself as he jumped out of the cab of the truck. Then, with a worried frown, he walked on to the scene of the accident.

A huge van had crashed into the steep mountainside. The front of the heavy truck indicated it had been coming up the highway and had swerved towards the mountain shelf in an attempt to avoid hitting someone who had crossed the median coming down. And it was so. A motorcycle was pinned tight against the rock cliff by the nose of the massive van. On the pavement several yards farther down lay two mutilated bodies, arms and legs broken, twisted in all directions like puppets whose strings had been cut in mid-act and had fallen in a pile of bizarre-lying limbs. Cross moved closer. Glazed, wide-open eyes greeted his gaze—dead eyes of surprise—eyes that had seen for a terrible instant their own fate. Blood painted the highway in fragmented smears, for the bodies had been dragged some distance. From wet-matted heads, two streams of human life flowed down the highway—one deep red, one a mawkish yellow-white. Cross turned his head away, suddenly sick to his stomach. He felt weak and faint, his knees buckling beneath him. "Happiness is coming," flashed through his mind. He walked rubber-legged to a large boulder by the side of the highway and sat down, his head between his hands. "Happiness is coming."

Will and Goldie Busbee marched over. They were un-affected. Wrecks were everyday occurrences here. Many people stood around the bodies, watching. The blonde girl, lying broken on the ground, her long hair matted deep crimson in spots, moaned faintly once and then there was nothing. No sound. No wisp of life. And the dazzling sun beat down upon them, the living and the dead.

It was a long, hot hour before the caravan could move out again toward the Big Bend of the Rio Grande. Meanwhile, am-bulance attendants from Geneva Gap had gathered up the frac-tured corpses. Only the wayward tire markings, the evaporating human liquid, and the hard dried blood remained on the high-way. Footprints made by curious bystanders, like fossil im-prints, had burned into the asphalt pavement, for the highway was squashy soft on the surface from the unbearable heat.

Will and Goldie Busbee led the way now. Their sportscar could make up the lost time. Cross brought up the rear.

The caravan finally arrived at the main basin of Big Bend National Park. It presented a beautiful panorama with tall pines reaching skyward on the rocky slopes of the Chisos Mountains. The basin was a tourist center with cabins, cafés, and other con-cessions. It was too crowded. So the salesmen and their families moved out again, heading toward the Presidio—Ojinaga road leading away from the park and trailing along the Rio Grande. They hoped to discover a secluded spot along the river to spend the rest of the day.

It was well past noontime when they found a shady grove of trees along the banks of the big river. It was like an oasis. The weary travelers climbed out of their cars and walked in the heat-filled, powdery dirt to the grove near the river. People now for-got the accident and the long hot trip and settled down for an enjoyable afternoon. Blankets were spread, beach chairs un-folded, baskets emptied, and food was traded and tasted and consumed with great relish, and the afternoon went well.

Cross sat under an old weeping willow with Will and Goldie Busbee. With them was another salesman—a watchful husband—with his wife and teenage daughter, and the ubiquitous and iniquitous, Rex Austin. Austin was drinking beer, and he and Goldie Busbee were jabbering, laughing, and joking with jagged fervor.

"You looked like a ghost out there at the accident," said Goldie Busbee, directing her mischievous gaze at Robby Lee

Cross. "You were deathly pale—a big man like you! Shame on you!" she and Rex Austin laughed uncontrollably. The others only smiled uncomfortably.

"I reckon this just isn't my day," he said sadly, now forcing a wry smile. The preacher was thinking of the taunting woman sitting before him.

Sadie Wethercock Busbee: Wethercock her maiden name, Sadie her given name. She had exchanged the latter for Goldie because she thought it fit her personality much better. She was from Michigan like her husband.

Goldie Busbee was sweet, people said. She was very sweet indeed, like honey that edged into tooth decay. Yet she liked to add a dash of tabasco to her personality on occasion—whenever appropriate or charming. Whenever a weak or defenseless or sensitive person happened to appear, she assumed her tabasco-tinged personality—hot and searing, digging, digging, to jab at a root. Goldie Busbee took great pleasure in playing and manipulating. Tattered nerves and tattered souls were all fair game.

And she was picture-pretty. She had cold pale blue eyes and peroxide-blonde hair. Goldie Wethercock Busbee altered the color of her hair as she changed the color of her personality—arbitrarily, whimsically, it seemed.

"Oh, the preacher's awright," said Rex Austin. "Ah feel lak he was a-prayin' for them folks back yonder on the highway. Thet semi tore hell out of 'em! You was prayin'! Ain't thet right, preacher?"

"It might do us all some good to do some praying once in a while," Cross snapped, "instead of running off at the mouth."

Everyone laughed, except Rex Austin and the preacher.

"I guess he told you a thing or two," chided Will Busbee.

"Oh, fer Chrisakes!" exclaimed Rex Austin, red-faced. "The preacher don't like ma waya livin', thet's all!"

Goldie Busbee wrung the beer can from Rex Austin's grasp and took a long drink of the yellow foaming liquid.

"Chug-a-lug!" coaxed Rex Austin, smirking. He was eminently flattered at the close attention paid him by Goldie Busbee, while her husband stared vacantly at them.

A short distance away some of the teenagers and smaller children were preparing to go into the river for a swim. Cross could see them bob up and down in the back seats of cars and station wagons as they undressed and slipped into bathing suits. Then they emerged, showing whole bodies of pale white skin—a paleness that reached down their arms just below the shoulder and up near their necks. Their faces and necks and arms were deeply suntanned or sun-reddened and freckled. They ran down the sandy bank of the river, while the women walked down the steep embankment to watch closely.

From their vantage point a little above the river, Cross and the other men in his party could see the youngsters splashing and diving in the muddy-brown waters. Little whirlpools could be seen in the steady flow of the big river. Mothers cautioned smaller children to stay near the bank in shallow water. Cross stood up and leaned against the gnarled tree and watched the frantic action below and listened to the happy yelps and shouts of the young people. A smile played on his lips.

Still seated, Will Busbee, Rex Austin, and the watchful husband talked on. Rex Austin began to dominate the conversation, casting challenging glances at the preacher from time to time.

Nearby, under a sapling that afforded a tenuous shade from the blinding sun, a fat, thick-legged, red-faced woman with her hair pinned back in a bun, snapped on a portable radio and the screeching strains of country and western music blared forth—coming direct from Clint, Texas! A heavy twang reported on the latest sales going on at Clint—patent medicine, corn plasters, hernia remedies, and Tex Ritter records. You want it, Clint had it! Just mail your request to Clint, Texas, and the bargain would sure come C.O.D. Now a love song, Texas-style, with a moaning electric guitar and a sad bass voice crawled lazily on the air waves. A song of unrequited love.

Rex Austin was saying, "Ah'd dip ma wick in a tar baby!"

Cross squinted across the dazzling sunlit space toward the river and across to Mexico. He was thinking. *That desolate, scrub-brush land over yonder shows the hunger and desperation of those people. They're miserably poor, ragged, downtrodden poor. No wonder they come over here illegally. Nothing to lose. Once they came in legally as braceros; this year they're wetbacks. No wonder the American border patrol is recruiting men more than ever to stop illegals.* Sometimes, the preacher felt real sorry for those Mexicans.

Rex Austin was still talking. "Thet's good eatin' stuff, yuh betcher boots!"

"Oh, you're talking about some of these brownies?" asked Will Busbee mischievously.

"Well, now thet yuh mention it—dang right! Looks mighty good!"

"It'll make you fat," joked Will Busbee, handing him a slice of the flat-pan chocolate cake.

"A good rooster never grows fat!" retorted Rex Austin.

Will Busbee laughed. "Well, I see where you're putting on some extra pounds here and there."

"Well, yuh-all's incitin' some long teeth ta grow in ma jaw with all them goodies!"

The three men laughed. They munched absent-mindedly on the frosted brownies.

Then Will Busbee questioned, "Did you see Dr. Serveto this week at school?"

The two men nodded, then looked expectantly at Busbee.

"Some people think he looks like one of those Mafia gangsters or a Tammany Hall ward heeler."

"Oh, yuh mean 'cause he's kinda dark and wears them dark glasses round campus," said Rex Austin.

"Yes."

"Well, maybe he's got the right idea," interjected Cross. "After all, it is mighty bright in these parts with that sun and all!"

No reply from the three seated men. They sat impassively, squinting into the bright sunshine.

"It's hot! Ah'm glad ah'm jest takin' one course at the college this summer. Too danged hot!" said Rex Austin. "Even in Geneva Gap it's been mighty sticky here of lates."

"You're right there," agreed Will Busbee.

A pause ensued. The men gazed absent-mindedly at the river and the splashing children.

Then Rex Austin thought of something. "They got too many old maids at the college. Goldang! if they's goin' ta hire wimmin-folk, how come they don't get some's as got some shape ta 'em! Ah swear ta God, them wimmin professors are old and scrawny or old and pudgy! 'Ceptin' one—Corazon Dankhaus—she's got the darn nicest rump roast ah seen on any filly! She's half Mexican, yuh know! . . . No chance with her, though. She all the time follows them three old maids round school and off campus. And they watch her like a hawk! . . . Ah lak ta call 'em the 'Three Mouthketeers'! All the time jawin' and gossipin' and leadin' little Miss Dankhaus down the trail ta an old maids' home. Gossipin', connivin' administrators—all three! Ain't one person in a whole school—the whole town—they ain't talked about and tore ta pieces!"

Suddenly a fearful scream sliced the air. Cross started, and for a heart-stopping instant, he froze. Then he saw people running down the banks of the river to the figure of a woman who was tramping wildly back and forth at the water's edge and screaming hysterically. Cross found himself scrambling down the sandy banks and elbowing his way through the crowd to console the weeping woman. He put his arm around her shoulders and in a shout, above the din of the crowd and the woman's shrieking, he asked her what was the matter. The distracted, sobbing woman, heavy veins throbbing on her forehead, babbled incoherently about her daughter being pulled under by the current, a whirlpool maybe, and disappearing down the river. Cross now recognized her as the wife of the watchful husband. A picture flashed through the preacher's mind, the picture of the mother and daughter and the watchful husband all happy and carefree an hour earlier under the weeping willow. Now the husband came rushing up to them, tears welling up in his watchful eyes.

Meanwhile, two men had jumped into the river, diving deep to find the lost girl. Cross snatched off his boots and dove head-long into the reddish-brown waters. He could hardly see deep under. His eyes burned. But he swam deeper, turning his head from side to side hoping to glimpse the lost daughter. Then he let himself be carried up to the surface by the pressure of the water and he emerged with one gulping gasp for air. He bobbed on the surface for a second, panting, plunging again like a knife down into the murky waters.

It was all in vain. No one saw the girl. The mood was dark as Cross splashed out of the river and stood soaking in pasted-down clothes, his eyes staring blankly at the grim crowd around the watchful husband and the sobbing, mumbling woman. The preacher felt a numbing helplessness.

Someone had driven to the ranger station in the park to telephone for help, and later the rescue squad from Geneva Gap arrived in a small van, sirens screaming. The rescuers immediately donned scuba gear. The search would be for a body. There was no hope for the girl's survival.

They plunged into the reddish-brown waters time and time again. They followed the current of the big river, searching every sinkhole, every cranny along underbrush on the banks. The rescue operation went on for hours.

Meanwhile, the holiday swimmers had dressed and they and their parents watched sad-eyed and grim-mouthed. Hardly a word was spoken.

Soon the salesmen and their families began to leave the picnic grounds. It was getting late. The drive back would be long. But the heat had moderated a bit and the dusk drive would be tolerably warm, almost cool in comparison to earlier hours. It would be a bitter return to Geneva Gap. The lost daughter had not been found.

The rescue squad stopped diving at dusk. They would make camp for the night and begin again in the morning. Cross would have grim company the long night. Bedrolls were laid out and a campfire struck. The preacher and the rescuers sipped coffee and talked in low, mournful tones through the early evening. Soon they all crawled into their bedrolls and the exertions of the day drugged them rapidly to sleep.

The next day, the Seventh Day, would not be one of rest and reflection for the preacher. Cross was content to aid the rescue mission—to find a lost sheep was the work of the Lord. There were three scuba suits with air tanks and four men—three trained rescuers and Robby Lee Cross. The latter was an excellent swimmer and the squad knew it and so the four men alternated in using the diving gear. One man always remained on the river bank to rest and to watch closely for any signs of discovery and any need for assistance in bringing the body to shore.

The search began at dawn and continued for hours. Rubber rafts were now being used to comb the water farther downstream. The operation was gruelling, exhausting work. The sun was hurling blazing hot, blinding rays on the struggling rescue party.

Cross was inspecting a sinkhole under a ledge of the river bank when he surfaced and heard the cries of a rescuer. The body had been found. Cross swam to the spot of the discovery and helped pull the purplish-pale, helplessly weaving body out of the deep water. The fourth man scrambled along the shore to help, as the lost daughter was dragged to a narrow beach and the men sank exhausted to their knees and snatched off the leaden equipment and sat back on their haunches and breathed heavily.

Later the body was bundled in a black plastic bag and stored in the van for the trip into town. The three rescuers thanked the preacher for his help and then drove away.

Cross dressed slowly beside his truck and then sat on the river bank under the weeping willow and stared into the reddish-brown waters. He sat very still, bone-tired, his mind a blank. Finally after some time had elapsed, he got up and walked down to the river's edge. He took off his boots, unbuckled his belt, and stepped out of his tight Levi's and waded into the shallow water along the bank. Resurrection plants waved calmly in the knee-deep water and the preacher picked up three. He bundled the loose leaves and stems together in a ball and went back to shore. He laid the resurrection plants on the ground to dry in the cruel sunshine.

CHAPTER SEVEN

For Marie the days and weeks slipped by in a pattern that was undeviating and joyless. Lee was becoming more and more preoccupied with his selling and his religious meditations. Ever since the violent deaths of the three young people on the journey to Big Bend, he had become even more withdrawn, quiet, and cold.

He had come home late that Sunday evening and placed the three resurrection plants in wide glass bowls of water on the ledge above the fireplace, lighting two candles there as if they were a guard to protect the mementoes. He had spoken few words to her since. When he forced himself to speak, his voice was low and weak and far away.

Marie longed for the warmth and strength of his embrace. If only he would show some little affection. Even a smile, like a tidbit thrown to a pet from the dinner table, would have caused her heart to leap. She hungered for him. Her body ached for him.

Cross was experiencing a profound spiritual crisis. He saw the portents of great evil. God was warning him, he was sure. The Almighty must be displeased. Else why the horrible deaths on a journey which he had envisioned as a kind of pilgrimage to the big river to adore Him. The wrath of God was clear to him. "I must think this out alone. It must have some dreadful meaning." For the downcast preacher the days and weeks went by in fearful contemplation.

With that sad withdrawn expression on his face, one day Cross drove into town. All the way into Geneva Gap he was so engrossed in his thoughts that he hardly noticed the wide flat

country he loved so well. Nothing distracted him from his meditations. But as he drove into the mountains before Geneva Gap,
he began to revive from his reverie and recognize the familiar
sights in the Puerta de la Paz.

Suddenly, deep in the mountains, Cross caught sight of a
prostrate calf on a ledge off the highway to the right. On one
side of the sick heifer stood the cow that had suckled it and on
the other, crouching grotesquely and patiently, was a huge
black vulture. Cross braked the pickup quickly, its tires burning
rubber, screeching in apparent anguish. He shifted to reverse
and drove slowly and cautiously back to the spot of the quiet
struggle. As he stopped he could see and hear the cow, head
upturned, lowing pitifully to its young. The black vulture
squatted at a safe distance, undisturbed by the mournful calls.

Out of the truck, Cross snatched a rock off the bald side of
the ledge and hurled it at the obscene bird. The vulture
squawked and hopped two bouncing steps as the missile kicked
up dust near its talons, but it did not leave. "Damned devil." He
grabbed another rock and this time he was true with it. The vulture squawked again and flew into the sky, circled overhead and
then swooped down onto a perch high up the hill. "Damn that
bird," Cross snarled. But there was nothing more he could do
and he climbed back into the truck and drove on to Geneva
Gap.

It was not long before he turned the truck off the highway,
under the arch of the college gate, and stopped near the main
building. He took his black case of cutlery samples with him.

Inside, he stopped at the men's room to urinate. As he
stood above the toilet bowl, his eyes fixed on some pencil
scratchings on the wall before him. "NIGGER DICKS ARE
BIGGER," proclaimed the erratically printed letters stretching
over a crude drawing of a long thick phallus. Colored black.
Cross turned away in disgust as he zipped up the fly of his
pants.

He walked down the hall toward Dr. Serveto's class. The
hall was jammed with students moving, reluctantly it seemed,
from one classroom to another. Most of the young men wore
big wide-brimmed Stetsons, which they wore on their heads
everywhere, even to class. Professors had difficulty in persuad-
ing them to remove their cowboy hats in the college buildings.
The young men seemed to consider the hats rising from their
heads as essential to their appearance as the noses extending

from their faces. Cross often wondered if they dared remove those sacred Stetsons on going to bed. He doubted it.

Cross dropped into a desk chair near the rear of the classroom. Students strolled into the room in a steady flow. Big gangling cowboys, their long legs stretching out before them as if challenging someone to hop over them, slouched down in the small desk chairs. One casual student was chewing intently on a big wad of tobacco that puffed out his cheek in a ball. From time to time he would pick up a paper cup with the words Coca-Cola emblazoned on it and spit a big splash of tobacco juice in it.

Cross was fidgety. On the small wooden desk before him were written and carved all kinds of disturbing daydreams. Mostly obscenities: "Doris screws Mexicans" and "Billy Joe sucks" and "John David is a queer." Cross knew that most of the wooden desks on the college campus were like that. It was nothing new, though it was still disturbing to him. Administrators tried desperately but unsuccessfully to curb it. Janitors from across the tracks scrubbed the desks hard and even sandpapered them to obliterate the obscenities. Deans lectured the young men on preserving public property and controlling lascivious urges. But nothing helped much. The obscenities always reappeared.

On the wall next to Cross, a would-be poet had scrawled a verse about youthful frustration.

SHOVE LOVE

I crawled between the sheets that night,
Between those legs so fair:
Crawl, crawl, crawl,
Ball, ball, ball.

I lay upon the body mat
Tresses wet and blonde:
Foul, foul, foul,
Bawl, bawl, bawl.

She lies between the sheets again,
Her legs so high outstretched:
Foal, foal, foal,
Soul, soul, soul.

So now I crawl to bed each night,

Too tight, too long those legs do hold:
Shove—shove—shove
Love, love, love.

Cross stood up and went down the hall to the men's room again, this time to moisten a paper towel. He came back to the classroom and wiped the disturbing poem off the wall. Two girls, sitting nearby, giggled and exchanged knowing glances.

Dr. Serveto walked in the classroom just as the bell clanged loudly.

Today the lecture concerned minority groups in a democracy. *Dr. Serveto's feeding us those Yankee attitudes again*, thought Cross. The preacher grunted in disgust. Other students also showed alienation in their faces.

Cross finally spoke out, his words shooting forth with intense feeling, the first outward sign of emotion in several weeks.

"I'm sick and tired of all this propaganda that's been thrown at us about the nigrah and the other colored minorities! It's like the myth of the noble savage that was applied to the Indian at one time. Why, right here in Geneva Gap recently that movie 'A Patch of Blue' was shown—not too long—thank God, and fired-up lots of citizens! That nigrah Sidney Poitier is the epitome of the new myth of the noble savage in our culture! The white girl in the story was blind, but you better believe the bible isn't color blind!"

Serveto listened impassively. He enjoyed a response from students, although the question of race often brought an uncomfortable feeling to a class. But he disliked a class in which the students tried to impress the professor simply to gain favorable grades. In such cases, discussions developed into a game of verbal ping-pong with the unspoken rule being that there be no hard smash to the professor's backhand.

"I'm against giving too many rights to nigrahs," Cross continued. "There's always got to be some people on the bottom of things. It's just natural. Some folks are predestined to assume certain lower positions in society and be the menials. Besides, you give them too many rights and they'll be wanting to marry your daughter!"

"I'm afraid that's a bogus argument," replied Dr. Serveto. "That's what reactionaries say to scare people away from affording full democracy in America. The human rights movement has nothing to do with Blacks or Chicanos or Indians mixing sexually with Whites. It does have a great deal to do, however, with providing them with full political rights and equal opportunity in the economy and in the community. Miscegenation is a bugaboo created by racists. And after all, if you look at history, when did the most miscegenation occur? Well, it occurred during the era of slavery in America. Many a female slave gave birth to the offspring of the master. Of course, very seldom if ever did the master acknowledge such mulatto children as his own. Today many near-white Negroes are really mulattoes whose ancestry includes the blood of white masters of the ante-bellum period or white bosses of the period after the Civil War.

"There's fear today in America," he continued. "There's a cancerous fear eating at the hearts of some Americans. The fear of the 'black stud' or the 'Latin lover.' A fear that the Black or someone else just may be more of a man than they. That is what's behind the concern for the inviolability of white womanhood. Some white men fear the sexual prowess of the Black man, as if he were more virile and even superior physically to the White man. This is the other side of the feeling of white superiority. And both are false! But racists play on such fears and feed them constantly. Why do you think some people sketch on the walls of public toilets and scribble graffiti indicating the potency of the 'black stud'? Fear! It's fear! It's simply fear! And some people swallow it all too willingly."

The students looked sullenly at Dr. Serveto. He wondered if they were really listening, and yet he recognized the intense interest of at least one student. Robby Lee Cross was listening.

Dr. Serveto went on, "It seems to me that there are superior individuals in every racial grouping. Some are superior physically, others intellectually, others morally, if you will. But no group has a monopoly on excellence, either physical or intellectual. Here on earth there is a kind of natural aristocracy very much like that which Thomas Jefferson wrote about years ago. It's an aristocracy of virtue and talents. But it's not based on race or money, or religion. And every ethnic group has representatives in it."

Cross blurted out, "Would you let some nigrah marry your daughter?"

Dr. Serveto smiled. "That's really irrelevant since I'm not married. I don't know how much I would have to say about it anyway. Young ladies are very willful today. And in any case this is a free country. We boast that it is. No, I wouldn't willingly allow some Negro—if that means any Negro—to marry my fictitious daughter. Just as I wouldn't willingly allow some Caucasian—if that means any Caucasian—to marry her. I think I would apply the same standards to every suitor. Is he aesthetically pleasing? Is he morally good? Is he intellectually capable? These would be the questions needing answers. And when I speak of aesthetic criteria, I'm referring not only to physical qualities but also to qualities of character and personality. A person may be rather homely and even ugly physically, but his character may be so fine and appealing that he's really quite beautiful. In other words, the standard of aesthetics includes attributes of morality and intellect and physique. Stripped to the nakedness of mind and body, is this man a human being of aesthetically pleasing refinement and goodness? That is the question."

Cross was seething with emotion. "I don't believe white liberals! They accept nigrahs fully only in the abstract but not in the particular and in the flesh."

"Well, it doesn't really matter if they do or not. Some people of color and some Whites will cohabitate and marry as they wish. Nothing can stop them in most places. This is still a free country. And as democracy progresses it will be more accepted as a particular phenomenon in our society. It's really unavoidable. But just as in nature, like will breed with like. Generally, people will marry and have children with those who look most like themselves. That seems to be human nature and the rule of nature generally. It is more comfortable for people that way; and the few who deviate will eventually not be looked at askance. At least I hope so. A free society can't forceably and feasibly prevent such personal contracts between people of different races. When several races live together in one country there is bound to be a man or woman who is attracted to the slant of the eye or the cut of the mouth or the curve of the body or the intonations of the voice or the goodness of the heart of another human being, black or white or brown. And they will live together. And I wish them happiness in their choice."

The students looked at Serveto and were silent. He knew he had lost them. The rapport he had built up so carefully over the weeks had now virtually disappeared in the throes of the racial question. For the rest of the class period Dr. Serveto avoided the more controversial aspects of the topic.

* * * * * * *

Several days later, Robby Lee Cross went to Cotton Zarler's annual Mexican supper. Everybody who was anybody was there that night. Cross brought Marie along. He thought it would be good for her to get away from the ranch; she seemed so despondent lately. At first she was reluctant to go because of Danny, but when Cross said she could leave the boy at the home of her parents, she agreed. She decided it would make the boy happy to see "Gramma and Grampa." It had been so long since she and Danny had visited them. And Marie was glad to talk to them if only for a few minutes as she and Lee dropped Danny off at the old Obregon home in Mexican Town.

Cross grumbled about the rugged, potholed road as he drove through Mexican Town. He didn't like this side of Geneva Gap one bit. He complained of the gray adobe houses with their windows tilting awry and the broken-down appearance of the walls which seemed to be washing away with every thunder shower. Cross pointed disgustedly at the back yards of the Chicano homes where old tires and old rotting outhouses and rocking chairs and battered old hulks of cars without wheels lay around in careless disarray. "Why don't they take more pride in their homes?" he complained. Marie did not answer. As they passed the Spanish mission-style church which was named Nuestra Señora de la Paz, Marie made the sign of the cross. The preacher grunted sourly.

At the party Lee introduced her to Dr. Serveto. Marie sensed a certain uneasiness between the two men. They exchanged a few words, then Lee left her alone to talk to Serveto while he went off to meet other people at the party.

At first she felt a little afraid of the confident young man before her. But soon she discovered she could talk to Serveto easily and comfortably. She knew she could not do so with most of the other guests and that included the host himself.

Cotton Zarler was all mouth and thunder that night. He spoke boomingly to a circle of friends that included Izzie Bronstein. Cotton was having a good time. He was saying he believed Adolph Hitler and George Lincoln Rockwell did have some good ideas. He thought Germany in the 1930's was the best time for women. They knew their place and were happy with it.

"Ol' Adolph knew right well what pleases a real woman and brings her ta blossom. The three K's: Küche, Kirche, und Kinder! Cooking, church-going, and raising children—thet's

what puts the color in a woman's cheek and raises a healthy
bosom ta heaven! Ha ha ha! Yuh ladies don't believe thet! Ha
ha ha!"

Cotton sure was having a good time. Everyone said so. Some
people began to suspect Old Man Zarler was putting more than
cream in his cup of coffee. He was the life of the party, all right.

He played the attentive host now, rounding up his guests for
a taste of "some real cooking." He spotted Marie and Dr.
Serveto and came over.

"Qué tal, hombre," as he put his arm around Serveto's
shoulders. "Vamos a comer algo. We got lots ta eat over yonder.
Come on yuh two. Vamonos!"

He stepped between them and locked his arms in theirs and
maneuvered them over to the long, food-laden table.

Hanna Zarler had laid out a rich feast. The tastefully ar-
ranged foods stimulated the eye and the spicy aromas made
mouths water. Almost every kind of Mexican dish was represented on the long, spotless table. Tortillas, tacos, tamales, tostadas, enchiladas, chili con queso, guacamole, and posole.

With big serving spoons of fine sterling silver, people were
digging in, piling a conglomeration of food on paper plates, dip-
ping with tostadas into the bowls of hot-tasting appetizers. Cotton Zarler handed plates and forks to his guests and made a
motion for them to dig in.

Will Busbee stood nearby eating from a heavy plate of food.

"This stuff's real good, Cotton!" he said, still chewing a
mouthful.

"Glad yuh lak it," rejoined the smiling host.

"Old Cotton's a real liberal to serve Mexican food around
here."

Dr. Serveto glanced aside at Will Busbee. The host was
laughing half-heartedly at Will's comment.

"Yuh-all's liberals ta eat thet hot stuff too!" jabbed Old
Man Zarler.

Dr. Serveto was spooning into a tamale dish. "Do you have
to be a liberal to serve Mexican food in Geneva Gap?"

"Almost," said Will Busbee, smirking.

"Don't mention the name o' Cotton Zarler in the same
breath with liberals. They ain't ma kinda folks. Ah jest like
Mexican food and ah don't give a hoot who don't lak ma eatin'
it! Anyways, most folks hereabouts really do lak this stuff.
They's jest too goldanged afraid of what other folks 'ill say. But

when they come ta ma house, they know it's awright. They gobble it up! Of course, ah know right well tomorrow some 'ill say ah pretty near forced 'em ta eat this stuff! Ha ha ha!''

Will Busbee laughed too.

Marie and Dr. Serveto finished serving themselves and stood in a circle with the jolly host and the coordinator of Texacut sales. Cotton Zarler was the only one not eating, so he continued his monologue.

"Of course, some of these dishes are jest foods from good ol' Dixie thet has been Mexicanized with hot sauce. Thet posole yonder is nuthin' but hominy grits and sow belly made up with hot red chili. Yuh can't tell me thet ain't nuthin' but a adaptation! Ah reckon thet guacamole is too! These Mexicans hereabouts jest took some of our foods and peppered 'em, thet's all!''

The expression on Serveto's face told the host the professor was dubious. So Cotton looked at him as if inviting him to speak. He did.

"Why do you call the people from across the tracks 'Mexicans'? They're not Mexican nationals. I don't see them carrying passports. People around here talk as if they were aliens or something. They're Americans! It's just that they're of Mexican heritage. That's all. But they're American citizens. They aren't aliens! The accurate term is 'Chicano,' really.''

Cotton Zarler chuckled. "Well, of course you're right. But you're jest being technical. We know right well thet they're born American citizens. But they ain't lak us. When we say a fella's a Mexican, ever'body knows right off what we're talkin' about. It's easier thetaway.''

"Maybe it is easier," countered Serveto. "But it seems to me that it does create disaffection when one group of citizens is so studiously segregated in one way or another.''

"Well, they go ta our high school on this side of the tracks," said Cotton Zarler somewhat defensively. "Don't get me wrong! Ah lak Mexicans jest fine! Why, ah handled Mexicans since ah was knee high ta a grasshopper. Ah know them folks but good. They's good folks, if yuh know how ta handle 'em right.''

Across the room Rex Austin and Goldie Busbee were engaged in a confidential conversation. They stood close to each other, talking half in a whisper. Cross was seated nearby, absentmindedly picking with a fork at a plate of food. The preacher caught snatches of the intimate conversation.

"Husband of mine . . . in bed . . . like instant tea . . . no control . . . wet dish rag . . . sometimes . . . I . . . caged animal . . . feel as if . . . chastity belt. . . ."

Cross saw Rex Austin move his hand carefully over the fine hair of Goldie Busbee's forearm. Her face flushed hot as if in a fever. For a moment they gazed at each other in fixed-eyed silence, the passion that gripped them almost sparkling in the space between.

The man and the woman seemed to awaken suddenly to where they were and they peered nervously around the room as if checking to assure themselves no one had been watching. Then Goldie Busbee whispered something, turned, and marched across the room to the group of pattering people. Cross watched her closely. Her face assumed a mask of pain, as she pleaded with her husband, raising her hand to her forehead. She motioned towards Rex Austin, indicating he would give her a ride home. Will Busbee nodded. He seemed only mildly interested but he said something about her feeling better before he turned back to the conversation being conducted by Cotton Zarler. Cross noticed Marie watching the Busbees with interest as they spoke, and then she glanced after Rex Austin and Goldie Busbee as they left the party. Cross could have sworn he saw Austin caress Mrs. Busbee's round, well-shaped buttocks as the two scurried nervously out the front door. Cross was visibly agitated and a look of disgust descended over the features of his long ascetic face.

The preacher put his plate aside and stood up now and ambled over to where Marie was standing and began listening to the conversation. Dr. Serveto was answering someone's question.

"Well, I find the students here are fairly good. An intellectual atmosphere is definitely lacking, though. Sometimes I almost feel the anti-intellectualism. It seems to me most of the students come to Cal Davis just to get a degree, not to learn. There's no biting urge to question and open up the mind and consider new ideas. And I'm often startled by some things that happen. For example, not too long ago, a student criticized a book for having too many facts in it, and then another time one of my students couldn't tell me who Winston Churchill was. I was dumbfounded. The boy did tell me about the great Sam Houston and the evil Santa Anna but practically nothing about Churchill and Hitler. Oh, of course, he knew vaguely that Hitler was some kind of dictator somewhere. But that's all."

"Well," countered Cotton Zarler as if insulted, "yuh got ta realize this here area's pretty near all rural. Most kiddos live out on a ranch somewheres and sometimes hafta travel miles by county bus ta get some schooling. Anyways, folks hereabouts ain't rich. School taxes hurt! And, anyways, ah feel lak Texans should learn about Texas first, foremost, and always!"

"What do you think of the Mexican students here?" asked Cross, looking at Dr. Serveto.

"Oh, don't call 'em Mexicans!" interrupted Zarler, laughing wryly.

Dr. Serveto smiled. "Chicanos are a little below the other students, generally speaking. This is because they don't get a solid start in elementary school. They're bilingual. Some hash up both languages. They really speak something like the language some call pachuco talk in California. Or Tex-Mex here."

"Coyote Jameson does a lot of that," said Will Busbee.

"Yes, a little," agreed Dr. Serveto.

"Who in hell's Coyote Jameson?" inquired Cotton Zarler brusquely.

Cross answered: "He's that fella from Lareda that's going to Cal Davis. He's pretty much a protege of yours, isn't he?" Cross was addressing Dr. Serveto.

"Yes, sort of."

Cotton Zarler was still mystified. "What they call him Coyote for?"

"That's always been his name, I guess," answered Serveto. "He's part Chicano and part Anglo. He's always in trouble, it seems. He likes to brag that he's well named. He insists a coyote is half wolf and half fox and he says the fox part is his Mexican heritage and the wolf part the American."

Cotton Zarler whirled around and walked away, mumbling something, a look of sarcasm playing on his face. Will Busbee laughed haltingly. He didn't know whether to laugh or keep silent. Serveto didn't hear Zarler's words, but he knew they were not friendly.

Lee was tired. Marie could see the fatigue in his face. He shook hands with those around him and excused himself and his wife for having to leave early. And as they left, Marie noticed again the rising antagonism between her husband and Dr. Serveto. The frigidity in Lee's eyes and the coldness of his manner in dealing with the professor told her enough.

They stopped in Mexican Town to pick up Danny. He was sound asleep and they carried him into the truck where he lay on Marie's lap. They bid a hasty farewell to Marie's parents and drove off.

On the highway going home, Lee drove the little pickup hard, almost recklessly. Marie was frightened by the excessive speed and careless manner of her husband. Now she was sure that he was angry.

Once a jack rabbit jumped into the path of the charging vehicle and was crunched underneath the wheels with a dull thud, and Lee nearly lost control of the truck as it jerked hard to the right on the ridge of the dirt embankment off the highway. But it was all right. He swerved the truck back onto the highway. Marie had gasped for a nerve-tingling second.

"Please slow down, Lee."

He did not answer. He would not look at her. He sat straight and stiff as a statue, only his arms moving slightly on the steering wheel.

Marie couldn't stand the silence.

"Please, Lee, tell me what's the matter!"

At first he did not answer. Then slowly, coldly, he said, "You were really fascinated by Dr. Serveto, weren't you? Real enchanted!"

For a minute Marie was speechless. Then, holding back tears, she asked, "What do you mean, Lee? What are you getting at?"

Cross did not answer. He looked straight ahead, eyes narrowed, mouth grim. The preacher was thinking of the words of distrust Ol' Dan'l had once uttered about Mexicans.

"What do you mean, Lee? What are you getting at?"

There was no answer.

"What are you accusing me of, Lee?"

CHAPTER EIGHT

Cross slept spasmodically. He dozed briefly and then woke up with a start, his heart pounding, his legs aching. He guessed extreme exhaustion caused his restlessness, but it was only partially so. Incoherent thinking plagued his brain. His mind constantly returned to the party of the previous evening, and a confused plethora of jabbering voices and disconnected words and sensual conversations saturated his brain. Then he drifted into a nervous sleep again, a sleep that was thin and tenuous, a sleep that could not switch off the confused consciousness that squirmed tenaciously in his head. His mind was working, harassing, gnawing, torturing, and under the thin sheet of sleep Cross was ever aware of himself on the bed as if his mind had left its bony shell and was observing his reclining body from afar.

He began to dream: *A faceless preacher floating in a cold gray mist reading from a book of prayer in a staccato, foghorn voice: "Heil Hitler! full of clap . . . the Jews are with thee . . . . Blessed art thou among semen . . . and cursed are the pangs of thy womb, bastard!" Faceless preacher in white flowing robes . . . a hood with a high peak rising from his head. Voices! Hard, echoing voices singing off key with notes trailing off in distorted hard-metallic swirls . . . singing the "Old Rugged Cross" . . . . . Big fat nigger woman on black velvet swing—rocking, swinging back and forth, back and forth . . . . Big black lips moving—fits and starts—over sharp pearly teeth: "Come own, big daddy . . . . Come own, preacher man . . . . Come own, wizard man! Oh! Oh! Oh! Ah'm comin', ah'm comin', ah'm comin' —Oh! Oh! Oh! . . . Big black thighs writhing open on black vel-*

97

vet swing—deep black bottomless pit . . . . Preacher trembling hard . . . . "Look down!" Enormous white ulcerous phallus . . . dripping . . . thick, long, hard, erect . . . . dripping . . . . "Oh! Oh! Oh! . . . Deep scarlet blood shooting forth . . . deep harlot . . . ." Oh! Oh! Oh! . . . Faceless preacher . . . exploding rage . . . swinging arm with cutting edge of a machete . . .-black woman's head lopped off . . . rolling, rolling, rolling like a bowling ball down a slick black highway . . . .

In his sleep Cross was struggling mightily to awaken. Every muscle tensed. He felt he was going under . . . down . . . down . . . under something terrible he could not understand. Panic-stricken, he worked harder to stir his body from its lethargy. The part of his mind he still controlled struggled to force its way through. It pushed, it pressed, it groaned. It broke through, and Cross awoke with a loud shocking scream. He found himself sitting up in a cold sweat with Marie tugging at his arm, whispering in a hoarse tremulous voice, "It's all right, Lee! You just had a nightmare! It's all right!"

Cross moaned. He was shaking all over. Marie caressed his cheek and spoke comforting words. Cross moaned again and cried softly. He could feel the bed wet with sweat. He lay his head on his arms that were held flat on his propped-up legs, and he trembled with a chill. Calming down now. It was only a dream.

Cross lay back on the pillow. Marie moved her soft hand under his nightshirt and began massaging his aching body. The softness of her touch soothed him and he began dropping off to sleep.

But suddenly he was wide awake again. Clumsily, he lifted Marie's long nightgown. He began feeling her body, his big hand roughly fondling her breasts and squeezing hard so that it hurt. His big hand moved down to the secret, mystical grooves and fissures between her legs and again his hand movements were rough and crude. His fingers jabbed and stroked and the woman was frightened by the aggressive sallies.

Like a wild man trembling in anticipation, he climbed upon her body and beat savagely down and up, up and down, down and around—hard strokes into the marrow of her being. Sharp pains cut into her abdomen and the woman could not hold back the tears that streamed down her cheeks onto the pillow. She moaned and gasped at the sharp impact of his body. Then she cried out in anguish at the fullness of a final thumping stroke that cut at her so that she thought she would die of its terrible slashing.

It was over. Lee rolled off her body and lay exhausted. It was as if Lee had wanted to hurt her, to feel her body suffer. She turned away from him and covered her naked body in shame.

Cross awoke the next day with a stinging headache and a growling temper. Marie tried to please him by attending closely to his needs, but he would turn on her in a furious rage. She could do nothing right for him. So she avoided him, keeping out of his way. He slammed doors and marched about the house shouting and snarling in choleric fits whenever a drawer would not open or a button would not hold.

Danny was awakened by the turmoil and got up and tiptoed into the kitchen, his eyes wide with fear. Marie brushed back his hair with the full palm of her hand and the boy began to feel better.

The gray mood in the faraway house matched the gray light and the gray skies outside. It had rained hard during the night, and now in early morning there was a fine mist of rain pervading the valley.

Cross burst into the kitchen causing the door to swing wildly back and forth. He grabbed his black valise, and standing near the sink he gulped down some hot black coffee. Marie and the boy sat at the table, stolid and mute. When Cross swung out the door, Marie called after him to take his poncho along because of the rain. He ignored her.

Driving on the highway, Cross heard great rumbles of thunder and saw great streaks of lightning break jaggedly across the huge purple clouds that formed a giant waterfall above. The steady rain was soothing and the air was fresh and pure. The sweet pungent smell of wet sagebrush tinged the air. Beyond the barbed wire fences cattle grazing on the open range were cooled by the rain. Once in a while a bolt of lightning would carom with a booming jolt across the land and onto the highway and Cross would feel his heart jump in his breast and he would breathe hard for a minute and his heart would pound anxiously. But most of the time the rain shower was soothing to the jittery nerves of Robby Lee Cross.

In Geneva Gap, Cross drove directly to the college. He attended classes faithfully, but nothing seemed to make much of an impression on his befuddled brain.

*   *   *   *   *   *   *

Cross was glad to go to Jake Greenfeld's barber shop. He needed some diversion and he looked forward to Jake's skilled fingers massaging his sore, nerve-wracked scalp.

"Hiyuh, Robalee!" Jake grinned, as the preacher entered. He was trimming the scarce hair on Jed Sporison's shiny head. Jed was mighty happy.

"How yuh lak this rain?"

"Just fine, Jed. Just fine," said Cross.

"Reckon the ranchers 'ill lak it."

"Yep, sure will," said Cross as he sat down and picked up the *Geneva Gap Echo* from a neighboring chair.

"You all alone today, Jake?" asked Cross.

"Reckon so. Rex tole me he wouldn't be in today 'cause he's goin' ta mix sellin' with pleasure. Goin' ta hustle some cutlery and hunt up some more arrowheads. Prob'ly goin' ta dig up more 'an jest flints, ah'd say!"

Jed Sporison laughed loudly. "Gosh darn! Nobody with a skirt on is safe around thet lecher. Joke's around town thet when he was at the Astrodome last summer on vacation he pretty near raped one o' the men on the Scottish bagpipe corps thet was there. Ha ha ha! Damn fool skirt chaser! Ha ha ha!"

"Hold still, Jed! Yuh don't want one o' your ears clipped off, do yuh?" Jake was disgruntled. He was the joke teller around here.

Cross glanced at the newspaper. There had been another accident.

"Yuh readin' about them kids got killed last night?" asked the barber.

"Yes."

"Ah don't know about them kids," Jake confessed, shaking his head. "Here they go up ta Carlsbad ta see the caverns and try ta make it all in one day! Must be five, six hundred mile round trip! All four was killed instantly. Man! ah don't know about these kids!"

"Did you know any of them?" the preacher asked.

"Ah knew 'em all," added Jed Sporison quickly. "The two girls was from San Angelo and the boys—they was brothers, yuh know—was from 'Little Texas.' Ah reckon they was from Carlsbad, somewheres in southeastern New Mexico anyways. Ah feel lak they was from Carlsbad. No! Roswell! Thet's right! Ah remember now. They was from Roswell. Transferred here from the military institute. Their folks was from Odessa originally and they wanted the boys ta be educated in West Texas. Thet's right."

"Did yuh read how they got killed yet?" The barber gave Cross no time to answer. "Can yuh imagine thet? They tried ta beat a train ta a railroad crossing! And at night and raining ta top it all off! The boy driving was one of the best rodeo performers Cal Davis had. Helped put Cal Davis on the map for its rodeo team. It's jest sorry! Jest a sorry mess. Goldang! if some of them kids don't run around lak chickens with their heads cut off! Ah swear!"

Snip, snip, snip.

"One of the girls was national rodeo queen last year," continued Jed Sporison. "She sure laked ta ride. Her folks own one of the best horse stables in West Texas. She'll never ride one o' them palominos again—poor little ol' gal!"

The barber had finished cutting Jed Sporison's hair and he took off the wide near-white apron from Jed's neck and swung it aside to shake it off and he snapped it down hard so that it cracked like a whip. Jed Sporison belched loudly and made a wheezing noise as he struggled out of the barber chair. His damp pants were glued tightly to his massive buttocks and he jigged ponderously to relieve the pressure and then hitched up his tentlike trousers over his ballooning paunch. He handed the barber some money and waited for his change.

"Thankyee, Jed," said the barber.

Sporison adjusted his necktie in front of the long mirror; then he said "See yuh, preacher" and "See yuh, Jake" and waddled out the bell-tingling door. Through the large plate-glass window, Cross watched the corpulent comptroller plod across Main Street to his car.

"Jed's getting awful fat," said Cross. He was already seated in the barber chair.

"Yeah, sure is. Ain't no wonder with all he eats. Puts away plenty. Ah hear tell he can gorge down two, three T-bones at one sittin'."

The barber unfurled the apron around the preacher's shoulders and secured it firmly behind his neck. He began to use the electric clippers deftly around the ears and neck of his customer.

"Did yuh know some folks is callin' Dr. Serveto a Commie?" Jake asked casually.

"No. Who is?"

"Hear tell Old Cotton and Dr. Sterner think so. So do other folks. A student called him a danged red socialist in heah the other day."

Cross did not reply. He looked down at his fingernails that were bitten down to small wedges, over which bulged the fleshy edges of the fingers like red berries where once long, normal-sized nails had grown. Cross was surprised at the grubby, chewed-down appearance. He hadn't realized how much he had been nibbling nervously at his nails.

The barber droned on. "Thet Serveto's goin' ta get into hot water mighty fast. Yuh know what he's a-doin', Roba-lee? . . . Folks say he's organizin' the Mexicans from acrost the tracks ta hire a lawyer so's they can bring suit ta get back the land they lost in the past. Somethin' about land grants made by the King of Spain way back there in colonial times and some-thin' about the personal land they lost after the Mexican War ta us Texans! Can yuh imagine thet? Man! what they're goin' ta think of next! Thet Serveto's a troublemaker, seems lak!"

"Who's been telling you all this, Jake?"

"Ol' Pepe fer one. Afore ah had ta let him go the other day, he tole me all about Serveto nosing around about land grants and what all."

"You fired Pepe?"

"Yep. Couldn't hardly do otherwise. He ain't worth a good goldang!"

Cross nodded but said nothing.

"Say, Robalee, ah found out what church thet Serveto be-longs to," said the barber proudly. "Ah hear tell he's a Uni-tarian, or somethin' like thet. He won't accept the worda God in the Holy Bible 'ceptin' if it agrees with science. He was in heah the other day an' he tole me he don't believe Jesus Christ was divine. He figgered Jesus Christ was a reformer, but not a redeemer. He says he figgers he was no messiah, jest a great per-son in history. Can yuh imagine thet, preacher?"

Cross shook his head and grunted in disbelief.

"Thet's not all he done said either," continued Jake confi-dentially. "He denied the virgin birth o' Jesus Christ and kinda ridiculed the doctrine of the Trinity! He said he wouldn't swal-low no article of faith thet don't agree with scientific principles! Ain't thet the limit, preacher?"

Cross shook his head disgustedly. And for the rest of the

time he spent in the barber shop, the preacher listened impassively and only occasionally to Jake's toneless monologue. The preacher was developing a theme for a sermon scheduled today.

*   *   *   *   *   *   *

At the radio station Cross talked to Speedy Carpenter a moment before he went into the studio to record his sermon. Speedy was very polite as usual and brought the preacher a cup of coffee which he placed next to the tape recorder on the small wooden table.

In a short time Cross began the sermon. "I am the seeker. I seek the truth on the highways and byways of this great country. And I find it in the valleys and in the backwoods, in the cities and in the villages. I am the seeker. I am the seeker after truth and salvation. I seek the absolute. . . ."

A City upon a Hill. . . .

The almighty scientists of our day supply us with so many answers. Oh! how proud they are of their almighty achievements! They have unlocked the secrets of the atom—the secrets of almost infinite energy! They are delving into the possibility of suspended animation and prolonged life and they are solving the mysteries of the human brain in its various workings for good or evil. They have even found a replacement for the most important organ of our existence—the heart. The heart itself is being replaced by a synthetic pumping mechanism. And who knows what other wonders will arise to amaze us poor mortals—what almighty wonders will come from the almighty men of science.

So many wonders! So many wonders! It takes your breath away!

But I ask you one and all. Have the almighty scientists asked the most crucial of questions? And have they answered the ultimate questions? No. The answer is no. They are afraid of the ultimate, the crucial questions. They avoid them. They only ask the "what" and "how" of controlling the environment and men's diseases. They avoid the whys and wherefores of existence. And consequently they have not given answers to how man should live in peace with his fellow man. How man should live morally in this world of gadgets and easy money and easy pleasures. No. They have no such answers. They are struck dumb!

Remember! Oh, remember! God does not play dice! He has given us answers to the crucial, the ultimate questions. He does not gamble viciously and mischievously with our lives like chips in a game of roulette. He has given us the answers. And they are absolute. And they are irrevocable and immutable.

Whence do I come? Why am I here? Where am I going? In essence: What am I? These are the ultimate, the crucial questions! And the critical answers lie in the bible as given by the Lord God of Israel!

Whence do I come? Man came from the dust of the earth and was formed like clay into a pale image of the Godhead through the divine breath of a soul. "And God said, Let us make man in our image, after our likeness: and let them have dominion over the fish of the sea, and over the fowl of the air, and over the cattle, and over all the earth. . . . So God created man in his own image, in the image of God created he him; male and female created he them." Thus it was. And in the particular instance, we come from the divine creation acting through the instrumentality of two human beings joining together in a divine act of procreation. Sex was instilled in man's body to aid in the creation of new souls. And it is a divine function to be used for divine purposes. As St. Paul wrote so well: ". . . Now the body is not for fornication, but for the Lord; and the Lord for the body. . . . Know ye not that your bodies are the members of Christ? shall I then take the members of Christ, and make them the members of a harlot? God forbid. . . . Flee fornication. Every sin that a man doeth is without the body; but he that committeth fornication sinneth against his own body. What? know ye not that your body is the temple of the Holy Ghost which is in you, which ye have of God. . . ."

The scientists tell us we are following an evolutionary process in the incubation of the foetus. No. It is not so! Rather we are recapitulating for the Lord God in our clumsy way the scene of that first creation of Adam and Eve by the Absolute Being. In coitus we poor mortals come closest to divinity. We create a new soul. A new life! We are therefore the mere instruments of the Godhead. It is a divine function to be used for divine purposes.

Why am I here? This life is a testing ground of our possibilities for eternal life. It is very much a Vale of Tears to prove our worth. We have been cast out of the Garden of Eden into this Vale of Tears for the great test of our election! We are being put to trial for election into an eternity of bliss. We must not fail, for it would mean an eternity of sorrow. You may ask, why am

*I as an individual here? What is my function? What is my place?
Yes, to find the place, the niche, the job that God has predestined for you in this great task of earthly life is jarring to
your conscience.*

*And we here in Geneva Gap, we here in Texas, have a spe-
cial calling. I firmly believe that our isolation is divine Providence working for us. We are more detached from the temptations and tribulations and corruptions of modern life. We have
been placed here for a special purpose, a divine mission. We are
like a city upon a hill! We who live close to the land, who live in
the quiet solitude of the frontier, we above all can think and
meditate more clearly on our duties to the Godhead. We are
very much God's chosen people! Like the God of Israel, Jesus
Christ dwells among His people—advising, counseling, directing,
inspiring. Because we are so favored our mission is manifest: To
be pure and upright in mind and body and to show the sinful
world the glories of Christian righteousness. We are like a city
upon a hill. All eyes are directed to Texas, to Geneva Gap.
From small beginnings we here can bring a great reformation of
spirit and religion to the unregenerate people of the world. We
are like a new Eden opening to all the joys and tranquilities of
Paradise. The land of milk and honey is right here in our own
back yard. We are like the secure buckle on the bible belt that
upholds the righteousness of revealed Christianity to unregenerate humanity.*

*Beware those who say God is dead—who say that the last
Christian died on the cross! We here in Geneva Gap, we here in
Texas, must raise high the banner of Jesus Christ—to show our
true colors—to bring wayward humanity to the teachings and
examples of Jesus Christ our Lord and Savior.*

*Where are we going? The answer lies deep in our souls. We
are like the thieves on Calvary crucified with Jesus Christ on
that terrible day. On the one hand, there was the unrepentant,
cynical robber who cursed our Lord God. His destiny was surely
eternal damnation in the fires of hell! On the other hand, was
the good thief who was sorry for his sins and only pleaded
mercy. To this good thief, the Lord God said: "Verily I say unto thee, To-day shalt thou be with me in paradise." So it is with
each and every one of us. The choice is there: to be like the
good thief or like the cynical criminal. The last Christian did
not die upon the cross of Calvary! We are Christians like the
good thief to whom all eyes are directed and for whom a*

mission of leadership to bring righteousness and eternal happiness is provided by the Lord God.

And finally we ask the basic question: What am I? God is not dead and God has not been created by man in his image. Man has not created God. Man is a combination of the mortal and divine. His soul is immortal, divine; his flesh is mortal, destructible. Man through his personal soul—his personal divinity—is a minute fraction of the all-encompassing Soul, the Ultimate Being, the Godhead. And since the raw stuff of personal divinity, the personal soul, comes from the Absolute Source of All, so man becomes one with the Lord God in his struggle to attain the Absolute. Man will be joined to the Lord God in Paradise. The Absolute Being will have called His own to His nest like a mother hen encompassing its chicks in its feathery bosom.

The eyes of Texas are upon you! The eyes of the sinful world are upon you! Do not disappoint the Lord God of the new Israel, the new Promised Land!

The sermon was over. The preacher bowed his head low over the table, praying.

When Cross walked out of the studio, his face was drawn and his eyes bloodshot. He was in no mood for idle talk, so he hurried out of the radio station before Speedy Carpenter could leave the control room.

It was still raining. Cross ran to the truck. He decided to drive to Ft. Gadsden to try to sell some cutlery.

Driving through the mountains toward Ft. Gadsden, Cross was caught in a blinding downpour of rain and hail. He had to slow the little Ford to a creep. The crackling thunder and lightning caused goose flesh to break out on the preacher's arms and legs, and he said a prayer whenever a bolt of lightning skipped threateningly across the highway.

In Ft. Gadsden Cross didn't sell his cutlery. There had been a severe electrical storm and tornado, striking homes and buildings, causing damage and some fires and many jangled nerves. Cross drove around town viewing the damage, and at times he would stop the truck and climb out to talk to bystanders about the storm and console the victims of the disaster. His mood was dark. The preacher pondered the awful meaning of these heavenly portents.

Before he drove out of Ft. Gadsden, Cross drank a cup of coffee at a small cafe on the highway leading out of town. It was nearly all the nourishment the preacher had taken that day. He was tired and despondent and he longed to be home.

On the highway, the rain suddenly ceased. Soon a big yellow moon like the eye of the Godhead peered down from between huge purple clouds.

It was dark when the little truck bumped over the cattle guard, brushed by the trees of the woods, rolled over the crude bridge, and came to a stop at the side of the house. Cross saw Marie squinting out the lighted window to investigate.

She met him at the door and led him to the couch, and while she helped him take off his boots she told him of the two visitors to the ranch that day. She told him Brigitta Obispo had come by to sell her tamales and how, when she handed her the money, the old woman had taken her hand, her face drawn with fear, and had wailed like a sick coyote at the sight of the lines in Marie's palm. She had asked the old woman the reason for her mournful cries, but she hadn't answered and had shuffled off with repeated glances back. Sitting on the couch, Cross growled angrily at the presumptuousness of the old witch.

"It was nothing, Lee. She's going insane, I'm sure. She has a look as if the devil himself is in her soul. I won't allow her around here any more. So don't worry, Lee. It's nothing to worry about."

Cross was not convinced but he was anxious to know who else had been at the ranch that day.

"A man selling cutlery like yours," she said. "He told me he had been out to look for Indian flints but that it was too wet, so he asked to come in and show his knives."

"Did he give his name?" asked Cross with wide fearful eyes.

"Rex Austin. I think I saw him at the party the other night."

"Yes, he was there." Cross was angry. "Why did you let him come in? Did he do anything?"

"No, honey." Marie was taken aback. "Don't be mad. It was nothing. I let him in because it was raining so hard and I told him you sold cutlery too and he said he knew you. I gave him some coffee to warm him up and he was very nice."

"That son-of-a-bitch!" snarled the preacher. "What did you say to him? Where was Danny?"

"Danny was right here, Lee! There's no need to be mad. He just stayed for a few minutes and he said nice things about you."

"That God-damned lecher! And I suppose you led him on! Don't you know better 'an to let that bastard in here! He's the one's been running around with Will Busbee's wife!"

"I thought after he left that it was him, Lee. But honest! I didn't recognize him before that! You know I don't get around much. I don't know those people."

Marie began to cry and she covered her face with her hands; then she swung around and left the room in a rush.

Cross was burning with rage. He would get that s.o.b. sure! He believed in swift retribution. Swift and sure.

That night Cross lay on the couch. It was a long time before he fell asleep and then he slept only fitfully.

*   *   *   *   *   *   *

The next day was the last day of summer school classes. But Cross did not care. He had other things on his mind. He arose early and drank a cup of cold coffee and was on the highway even before Marie had awakened.

The drive into Geneva Gap made no impression on the preacher's mind. He was driving as if in a daze, and it was only when he reached the outskirts of town that his mind seemed to snap into focus to recognize the location. He drove straight to Jake Greenfeld's barber shop.

The old barber was already cranking out the awning over the large window of his shop. The sun was out and casting blistering rays down on the early risers of Geneva Gap as if it had to compensate for yesterday's rainy sunless gloom. Cross parked at the curb in front of the barber shop and shouted at Jake Greenfeld.

"Where's Rex? Is he coming in today?"

"Well, hiyuh Robalee!" The barber stepped over to the truck. "Yep. He's supposed ta. Reckon he won't be in till later as usual. Has a class this morning, ah believe. What's a-cooking?"

Cross did not reply. He revved up the engine of his little pickup and was off in a cloud of dust. The barber looked in amazement as the truck sped away.

"Well I'll be damned!" he muttered.

Cross was sweating heavily when he walked into the main building on the college campus. He asked in the registrar's office for Rex Austin's class schedule and he learned what he wanted. Then he went up to the second floor, taking the stairs two and three at a time. He was sweating profusely, beads of perspiration hanging on his forehead and rolling down his cheeks. He took a position near the door of a classroom and waited.

He watched the hall very closely, scrutinizing every group of students coming up the stairs. His savage eyes darted back and forth and gazed intently up and down the hall. But no Rex Austin.

Just when Cross thought he had missed his quarry, he caught sight of Rex Austin swinging the door into the men's room and marching in. Cross sprang after him.

Rex Austin was combing his hair in front of a mirror, turning his head this way and that, inspecting pimples and wrinkles, generally admiring the reflection before him. Through the mirror he saw Cross barge in.

"Howdy, preacher!"

"Don't howdy me, you jackassed bastard!" hissed Cross. As Austin turned towards him in astonishment, the preacher slammed his fist hard against the nose so that Cross felt bone and cartilage crunch under the force of bare knuckles. Blood spurted out of Rex Austin's nose and he cringed against the wash basin, raising his arms over his head for protection against the stunning blows of Robby Lee Cross.

"Don't preacher! Ah ain't done nothin'."

Cross grabbed him by the collar and lifted him from his crouch.

"Look me in the eye, you yellow-belly!" yelled Cross, gasping for breath. "What were you doing with my wife? What were you doing out at the ranch? Huh? What did you have in mind? Answer me, you son-of-a-bitch!"

Cross cracked Rex Austin on the head again with his rock-hard fist. Austin cowered, bowing his head away from the blow. Blood flowed over the preacher's shirt.

"Ah jest stopped by mistake! Ah ain't done nothin'! Honest, Robalee! Ah swear ta God ah done no wrong!"

Rex Austin was sobbing uncontrollably now and the blood from his nose left a gory mess on his clothes.

Cross sneered at the hulking figure before him. "You aren't worth teaching a lesson to! But you better hear good! You come near my wife again and I'll kill you—hear?"

Cross let go of Rex Austin's collar, and the sobbing figure sank to the floor. Cross tore off a paper towel from a rack and wiped off some of the blood from his clothes. When he walked into the hall, he was relieved that classes were already in session. Only two people saw him leave the building and they looked after him in bewilderment.

That night at home Cross slept on the couch again. A strong acrid smell of whiskey permeated the air of the living room. The preacher's sleep was erratic and restless and he dreamed of the cold hard steel of a gun barrel pressed tightly to his brain.

CHAPTER NINE

Summer classes over, Cross spent most of his time going through the motions of selling his cutlery. He had lost his moorings. His comings and goings were now irregular and confused. He would start out some time in the morning, drive the pickup on the highway in the direction of Geneva Gap, but often he would leave the main highway and strike out for some distant point on the horizon that attracted his shifting eye and disoriented mind. The roads were mostly unpaved and mined with potholes, but the preacher hardly noticed as he drove for hours through rough country, savoring the effects of the fatigue which created a dulling, numbing, anaesthetic feeling throughout his body and his mind.

It was on such a day, while driving recklessly along a dirt road with hot dust trailing behind, that Cross came upon a spot in the dry desert called Beer. Population: 13, so said the sign. There was not much to the town. An old clapboard house that served simultaneously as a general store, saloon, motel, and gas station. One reddish gas pump stood alone and discolored in front of this local shopping center. One type of gas—regular; one type of price—high. Cross saw it as he pulled up alongside the pump—53¢ per gallon. Cross blinked once but told the hard-eyed, bleach-blonde woman in coveralls who slumped out the door to fill 'er up anyway.

The preacher climbed out of the pickup and stretched his legs as he surveyed the town of Beer. A row of rundown cottages slouched forlornly to the rear of the store. Two pickups stood nearby, one a dull gray but apparently in running order, the other a dull gray which hovered over a pit in the ground where Cross could catch a glimpse of grease-smeared hands straining at bolts and screws.

Across the dusty road stood a shaded home with a sway-backed horse hitched to one of the trees. But that was it. That was Beer. Beyond this cluster of ramshackle buildings lay miles and miles of flat, empty, desert. Cross gazed into the distance, shading his squinting eyes from the blistering sun with upraised hand. The heat shimmered along the bald thirsty earth.

"Reckon it's mighty hot ta yuh, eh honey?"

Cross turned to the hard-eyed, whining woman pumping gas.

"Nah, ain't too bad," said Cross, lying a bit.

"Well, mebbe so." The woman filled the tank of the preacher's pickup, smeared the windshield with a dirty rag, and took the preacher's money. She dug into her coveralls for some change and handed him some coins, saying "Thankyee kindly."

"Got something to drink in there?"

"Shore thing," answered the woman. "High octane fuel for the wagon and high octane fuel for the soul. We got 'em both. Y'all come on in and set a spell."

Cross followed the woman into the clapboard building which looked like any other small general store. An electric fan whirred busily from a ledge above the counter, stirring the languid air this way and that, providing no relief from the stifling heat.

"Jest go in inta the back room yonder," admonished the woman. "Ah'll serve yuh some real good cactus juice ina minute, oncet ah get inta sumpin more ladylike."

The preacher sauntered into the small dark bar room in the rear of the building and was surprised at the coolness. This part of the store was made of adobe and that accounted for the more comfortable air. Two small wooden tables with several chairs stood nearby. The bar itself was about as long as an office desk and sported a shiny brass rail, but no stools. Cross leaned on the aged, worn-down bar, put his foot on the rail, and peered sharply at the rows of bottled liquor along the wall.

Must pay someone off to show that booze like that, thought Cross. *Maybe they get away with it because this is a store, though everyone knows only package liquor can be sold, and only beer can be served in a bar. Or maybe this place is so far from anything or anyone, it doesn't make any difference.*

Then Cross saw the painting. It was hung above the shelves

of liquor and barely visible at first to the preacher's unadjusted eyes. It startled him and made his heart skip a beat. As his eyes adjusted to the darkness of the room, he saw more and it bothered him. It was a painting of a nude woman sitting in the midst of vivid scarlet and black striations. The painting fairly burned with passion. The preacher gaped at the woman. Her hair was long and jetblack, the skin was light pink and almost alive, and the delicate fingers played with the flowing strands of cascading hair. The eyes were black devilish eyes with the brazen slant of a strumpet. And the breasts and curves of *Eve Eternal* were voluptuous and seemed to hypnotize the preacher with their vivid sensuality. Fiery abandon marked the portrait. The preacher stared at the woman. She bore a striking resemblance to María Dolores.

The cheek of Robby Lee Cross twitched convulsively as he riveted his eyes on the picture.

The nasal-voiced woman swung into the room, noticing the fixed stare of the preacher. "Yuh lak her? Mighty good-looking ass, eh cowboy!"

She smiled knowingly and winked at the preacher, who quickly took his eyes off the painting.

"Ah could get yuh some pussy jest lak thet, if yuh wanna. Jest twenty dollahs, honey."

Cross blushed visibly and turned away.

"Ah ain't funnin'," said the woman. "Ah jest could get yuh a little ol' Mexican gal lives ina motel heah. She jest lu-uvs big white Texans. Whyn't yuh try 'er, come own, honey. Nobody ain't gonna know no different."

"I'm not interested," said Cross evenly.

"Well, okay," she sighed. "Don't say ah ain't tried ta hep yuh out."

"Gimme some of that rotgut yuh got there."

"Shore," answered the woman as she reached for the bottle. "How much yuh want?"

"Double shot and a beer chaser."

The woman poured the whiskey and opened a Lone Star beer. Cross paid her and watched as she turned to place the money in the cash register. She wore a print dress now and showed a little plumpness around the waist and hips. Cross thought she probably made some money on the side in the motel too.

The preacher drank at a measured pace all afternoon. The

woman chattered incessantly and kept busy pouring drinks for
Cross and keeping an eye on the store. No one came into the
bar the long afternoon, except for the mechanic whose hands
Cross had seen earlier in the pit outside. He had marched into
the bar covered with oily grime, demanded a tall beer, and
drank it all down in one long tip of the glass. He told the
woman he called Jael that he couldn't get the danged pickup
fixed anyway and then he stormed out the back door toward
one of the motel rooms, or so thought the preacher.

Toward dusk one and then another old grizzled prospector
shuffled into the bar, plopped down in the chairs along the wall
away from the bar, and ordered whiskey and beer chasers. The
two boney, unshaven prospectors drank quietly, staring vacantly straight ahead. A little later two and three more customers
walked in and soon after, as the lights were switched on, the bar
room was fairly packed with dusty, thirsty cowboys rolling
cigarettes, drinking beer, mumbling incoherencies, and staring
frothingly at *Eve Eternal.* Beechnut chewing tobacco was offered and passed from one mouth to another, the juice trickling
down the edges of scrubby looking chins. The heavy step of
drunken men in boots clumped against the wooden, tobacco-
stained floor, and occasionally a cowboy would take hesitant,
staggering steps to the juke box to play a whining, plunking
record by Tex Ritter or Hank Williams. The preacher was leaning heavily on the bar now, his eyes half shut, his head swaying
slowly from side to side. He felt glued to the bar. He wanted to
move but he just couldn't seem to shake the sodden lethargy
from his body. It seemed so comfortable just hanging heavily on
the bar and peering through half-lidded eyes at the shadowy,
unfocused figures skirting by his line of vision. He heard voices
and laughter that seemed to vibrate loudly and sharply for a
second and then muffled and droning the next. He felt sharp
elbows and sweaty arms poke or lean on him pressingly. He inhaled the smoke of sweet-smelling tobacco and at times an acrid
odor of what seemed like burning weeds. Once in a while a
drunken cowboy, Stetson askew on his head, would yell over to
Jael and demand to know if Magda was ready for a "real stud."
Getting the word he wanted and fortified with liquor, he would
struggle out the door.

Cross took a deep breath, squared his shoulders, and
marched bravely toward the back door, swaying slightly as he
moved. Jael reached the door first.

"Ah thought yuh didn't want no humpin', honey. Magda is busy jest now."

"I wasn't looking for that," the preacher mumbled.

"Oh, yuh wanna take a piss? Whyn't yuh say so. Jest out back there—don't trip over your own feet down them steps—hear?"

Cross staggered carelessly out the bar and swayed resolutely toward the gray outhouse. He wrenched his ankle twice on knots of crab grass that rose in little mounds from the bare loose sand. He reached the outhouse, unlatched the wooden door, and stepped up into the cubicle, catching the fumes in his nostrils and feeling a sudden urge to retch. He reached down, unbuttoned his fly, adjusted his penis and then leaned forward, his right arm stretched out before him acting as a brace against the back of the splintery wooden outhouse, while his left hand served as a gas mask, the forefinger and thumb pinching the nose to shut off the sickening odors. His aim was poor, and he wet the wooden seat, but it didn't seem to matter since it was already well urinated. The preacher cursed and spat into the dark, stinking pit.

Outside he stumbled to the wooden walkway bordering the motel cottages and sat down clumsily on the rough planks. He breathed deeply. The cooling night air bathed his nostrils and lungs clean, and he unthinkingly thanked the Lord for such pleasure. He closed his eyes and savored the emerging nocturnal coolness, a careless smile playing on his lips. He sat there for a long time, enjoying the darkness, the coolness, the quietness, the self-sufficiency of the moment. Only muffled sounds emanated from the saloon, and that added to the enchantment of the moment.

"Whatcha doin', honey?" a voice in the dark inquired gently.

Cross opened his eyes and gazed at the shadow of the woman called Jael.

"Yuh feelin' okay? Huh? Yuh okay?"

"Sure," mumbled the preacher.

Jael honkered momentarily and then sat down next to the preacher and snuggled close.

"Ah got offa work. About time Josh took over. Ah'm real tuckered out, honey."

She yawned widely. Then she lapsed into momentary silence. Cross regarded her in the darkness, liking the aroma of

toilet water on her neck and the soft warmth of her breasts
brushing his arm. He liked her nasal Texas voice with its down-
country accents. It had been many years since he had been this
close to a real Texas woman. Something stirred deep in the pit
of his stomach and surged into his throat, the feeling clutching
the muscles at his neck. His heart pounded and the palms of his
hands broke out in sweat. He trembled as if in the presence of
something fearful and sacrosanct. The strong surge of excitement made him dizzy and nauseous. He put his hand to his
head.

"Gosh darn! I guess I drunk too much."

"Whatsa matter, honey?" cooed Jael. "Not feelin' too good,
huh! Wanna come in an' lay ona bed a minute?"

"Guess I should. Just a minute and I'll be all right."

Cross struggled to his feet, Jael helping him with her strong
arm around his waist. He leaned on her heavily as they stumbled
on the boardwalk. Unlocking a door, she led him into the musty
motel room and leaned him gently onto the squeaky bed, Cross
falling like dead weight from her neck. He lay on the bed, his
forehead beaded with sweat, his breathing heavy and wheezing
as he dozed off into a tenuous sleep.

When he awoke he saw Jael above him applying cool com-
presses to his head. She smiled.

"What time is it?"

"Not late, honey. Jest been sleepin' a while. Yuh jest rest a
spell. When yuh feel better, ah got sumpin' ta eat ta fix yuh up.
Now yuh jest take 'er easy—hear?"

Cross would have none of it. He insisted on sitting up in the
brass bed and having a shot or two of whiskey.

"Shore, honey, if that's whatcha want!" agreed Jael. "Be
right back. Don'tcha go away!"

The preacher swung his legs off the bed and sat hunched
over the edge. He reached over to where Jael had placed coffee,
goat cheese, beef jerky, and thick slices of home-made bread.
Jael returned with a bottle and Cross poured some of the bitter
liquor into his coffee.

Soon Cross was in a whirling little world of careless laughter
and rabid hunger. He devoured the cheese, tore at the jerky
with his teeth, and stuffed his mouth with huge chunks of
bread. Jael hugged and bussed him as he ate, and he laughed
loudly at her gossipy humor.

"Wanna try some Mary Jane?"

"Sure," slurred the preacher absent-mindedly, not understanding the offer.

Jael lit a roll-your-own and inhaled deeply, then put it to the preacher's lips.

Cross tasted the bitter smoke as it filled his lungs and knew what he had smelled in the bar earlier. The smoke took his breath away and he suddenly coughed in a choking spasm, shooting the smoke from his nostrils.

"Ain't yuh ever smoked before?" snickered Jael. "Yuh wastin' the stuff, yuh punkinhead! Gimme that reefer!"

She snatched the joint from the preacher and sucked greedily. Her eyes bugged out, as she straightened her back and puffed out her chest. She held her breath for a minute, closing her eyes in the ritual. Then she let it all out in a long sudden burst.

"Now yuh do thet," she ordered. "This here's the best goldanged Mary Jane yuh kin get. Real special, honey, so don't waste none. Now yuh do it lak ah sez. Here—take it!"

The preacher fingered the joint nervously and imitated the woman's ritual. He puffed mightily at the joint, Jael enjoining him to take it all in, and sitting close, she directed the long joint time and again into the preacher's mouth. Cross complained of the bitter taste and harsh dryness in his throat. Jael reached for the bottle and the preacher washed down the side effects with great gulps of the stinging liquor. Tears filled his eyes from the strong potion, but Cross laughed carelessly.

"That stuff is the best germ-killing mouth wash, I reckon," gasping to catch his breath. "Mary Jane tastes so bad, but feels soooo good!"

And Cross laughed uproariously. An uncontrollable giddiness overwhelmed him. He giggled constantly. He felt his whole being sink into a comfortable warm nesting place where all was prickly warm burrowing sensation. He felt himself a yolklike mass of warm, disjointed, undifferentiated, dormant protoplasm. He felt no urge to move. No desire, no passion, no hunger, no conflict, no thought. Life was simply throbbing. Simple and throbbing. Warm. Complete.

When he awoke the woman was gone. The light from the bed lamp glared in his eyes. Cross covered them with his arm and felt the piercing pains in his head. Sharp, piercing reverberating pains. He groaned and felt a nausea well up in his stomach and rush to his throat. He struggled moaning out of bed and staggered to the door, sank to his knees outside on the boardwalk, and vomited painfully onto the sterile sand. His heart pounded and his temples ached with piercing pain.

When the preacher returned to the room, he felt a hollow emptiness and a limp bloodless weakness in his loins. He felt he had lost his soul. Sick, aching remorse enveloped his brain. He cried softly in his misery, as he sat, head bowed, on the edge of the big brass bed.

Cross stirred slightly, reached over to the bedside clock, and tipped its face toward him. It was 3:30. Maybe he could catch one of those all-night stations from across the border and listen to some preaching. That would help him overcome his feeling of sinfulness. He stumbled to the door and looked out. No use. A horrible still blackness suffused the outside beyond the pale light emanating from the room. He could find no radio now. Nothing could be seen, not even a starry heaven. Pitch black everywhere.

Cross closed the door in despair. He sat on the bed again and took some cold coffee from the night stand and drank it slowly, his face twisted in agony. His head throbbed viciously, pains shooting through the temples. He was wide awake and nothing seemed at hand to drive out the devils of pain and conscience. Tears streamed down his cheeks, and Cross took his head in his hands and lamented his wickedness.

Now he recalled that most motels had bibles placed in each room by the Gideon Society. He rose anxiously from the bed and pulled out the drawer of the nightstand in search of deliverance. No luck. He found nothing but two finger-stained, dog-eared paperbacks; one was *God's Little Acre* by Erskine Caldwell and the other *I, the Jury* by Mickey Spillane. He saw the provocative covers and knew these books held no answers. Or, on second thought, maybe they did. Obviously some people thought so. Anyway, he was a fervent reader. He reopened the drawer, pulled out the paperbacks, and sat down to scan their message. In a short time, the preacher grunted in disgust and threw the offending books into a waste basket.

Now he resumed his search for a bible. He rummaged through bureau drawers that stored nothing but cockroaches and black widow spiders. There was no other furniture in the musty room. There must be a bible somewhere, thought Cross. But where?

Cross returned to the bed and lay down. He tried to sleep

but the headache and his thoughts allowed no such luxury. Then, as he opened his eyes he caught sight of a book serving as a window stopper to let in the night air. He rose quickly and snatched away the book, causing the window to fall banging on the ledge. Yes, it was a bible. The preacher sighed in relief.

Cross sat on the edge of the bed, paged through the bible under the light of the bed lamp, fixing his eyes on chapter and verse, and went on to another. He whispered the biblical words and that seemed to have a sedative effect on his troubled spirit. His entire manner calmed down now and he read the sacred words with great reverence and concentration. He turned the pages again and came upon a book mark in Leviticus. It was a foreign postcard with a picture of Madonna and Child by some artist named Sandro Boticelli. Cross was enchanted by the fine lines and soft colors and heavenly expressions on the Madonna and Child. Their features were delicate and sensitive. Exquisite perfection. Pure white skin, sandy hair, and eyes that shone like perfect blue jewels. Calmness and coolness and dignity and reverent beauty pervaded the painting. The preacher could scarcely take his eyes off the portrait of the ideal woman. He stared at the picture as if transfixed. And the piercing headache was soon gone.

He finally lay the picture on the bed and began reading the bible again, glancing aside occasionally to enjoy the Madonna.

Reading aloud, he came upon a passage that made his eyes widen with excitement. Mosaic law had the answers. He read faster now, his face growing brighter. *Here were the answers! All the answers! Of course, why had he not referred to the sacred book before!* And the preacher pored over Leviticus and Deuteronomy and Numbers. His mind was transported far off into the wisdom of ancient times. He read and reread passages that held particular interest for him. He repeated the words slowly, savoring the sounds as they rolled from his tongue. Here was the test!

Cross finally lay the book down on the nightstand. He looked at the clock and made a decision. He picked up the picture of the Madonna and Child and regarded it closely. He was thinking of *Eve Eternal.*

* * * * * * *

A faint light graced the eastern horizon as Cross braked the pickup alongside his home. He peered at the window as he clambered out of the cab of the truck. There was still a light on in the house.

He marched energetically to the house, stepped through the porch, and into the living room. He shivered slightly from the morning coolness as he closed the door. Marie was lying on the couch, fast asleep in her clothes. Her mouth was slightly agape, her eyelids red as if from weeping, her hair and clothes disheveled. She looked a sight.

The preacher knelt beside her, closed his eyes, and whispered a prayer. Then he put his hand to her shoulder and shook her gently.

"Marie!" he whispered firmly. "Wake up, Marie."

The woman opened her eyes and looked at her husband, at first unconsciously, then fearfully.

"Get up, Marie!" the preacher commanded. "We have to bathe right away and then pray to the Lord before the day breaks. Come on, now; get up and do as I say."

The woman sat up and faced Lee in bewilderment.

"I don't understand," she muttered.

"Don't worry. Just do as I say. Go in and take a shower. Cleanse yourself thoroughly, comb out your hair, and then put on your long white gown that you used at our wedding."

Marie looked in wonderment.

"Now, get going! Do as I say!"

Marie rose painfully from the couch and did the preacher's bidding.

Cross watched her go into the bathroom and then went outdoors to the barn. He kicked at the goat obstructing the doorway, and Hippie bleated in protest as it got to its feet and scurried away from the door. Cross pushed the goat by its hindquarters into a corral, lit a coal oil lamp, and then began raking a spot of ground clean of its straw and alfalfa. Finishing that chore, he searched in a feed bin and finally emerged with some barley. He placed the grain on the stool used to milk the goat, then stood back and thought over the preparations carefully.

I must do this right, he thought. Good thing I'm a preacher.

Cross returned to the house and searched the kitchen for an earthenware jug he had bought in Mexico long ago. He found it in a cupboard below the sink, hidden behind dusty glass jars and old milk bottles. He blew off the dust and washed it out in the sink. It was made of reddish clay, globular, with a long horn-like spout.

The preacher took the jug and marched out the back door toward the arroyo. The morning was growing lighter as he passed the barn and began climbing the gradual rise leading to Sun Mountain, from which the cloudburst rainwater of the arroyo traveled. He ducked under mesquite bordering the arroyo and finally reached the slope of the mountain where among the mesquite and Spanish swords he found a rivulet trickling from under a large boulder. It was clear, pure water. Holy water. The preacher filled the earthen vessel.

Later at the house Cross showered and shaved, dressed in his best Sunday suit, a Western tie, and well-polished boots. Then he took his own bible from a shelf in the living room, clutched it in his left hand against his heart, and walked reverently to the couch where Marie was seated, waiting patiently. He offered his right arm and she rose and took it, and they walked arm-in-arm out through the kitchen to the barn. The sun would rise soon, but it was now clear and cool and quiet, only the woodland birds breaking the sacred silence with a choirlike warbling.

The preacher and his wife entered the barn and faced a makeshift altar composed of a large wooden crate on which two lighted candles stood, glued to the top with dried wax drippings. Between the candles sat a bowl of barley grain and beside it the earthen vessel. Marie looked wearily at the setting but said nothing.

The preacher brought her before the altar and bade her kneel. She obeyed, bowing her head. Cross stepped before her, placed his hands on her hooded head and prayed silently, his lips moving, his eyes shut. Then the preacher uncovered Marie's head, reached back for some grains of barley, and placed them in her cupped hands. Taking the earthen vessel in his left hand by the spout and kneeling on the ground, he picked up some dust in his fingers and dropped it into the water.

He stood before the woman again and whispered gravely: "Marie, you must take this oath that I will read to you from the bible. Do not question me! Just do as I say. Listen to it and when I finish, say Amen."

The woman, head bowed, did not move or utter a word.

The preacher placed the jug on the altar and took the bible in his hands and commenced to read.

"If no man have lain with thee, and if thou hast not gone aside to uncleanness with another instead of thy husband, be thou free from this bitter water that causeth the curse: But if thou hast gone aside to another instead of thy husband, and if thou be defiled, and some man have lain with thee beside thine husband: The Lord make thee a curse and an oath among thy people, when the Lord doth make thy thigh to rot, and thy belly to swell; and this water that causeth the curse shall go into thy bowels, to make thy belly to swell, and thy thigh to rot!"

The preacher stopped and awaited the appropriate response. There was a moment of silence. Marie looked up to her man, tears on her cheeks, and gazed at the tight-lipped, stone-wall figure above her.

"Amen," she cried.

The preacher turned to lift the jug of water, and he lowered it to the woman's lips.

"Drink," he commanded.

Marie opened her mouth slightly and Lee tipped the vessel, and the woman drank. Some of the water spilled from her mouth onto the ground.

Then the preacher withdrew the vessel, took the barley from her hands, placed it back in the bowl, and tipped the fire of the candle to the grain. The barley smoked, and when the preacher thought the grain sufficiently burned, he held the candle upright and ordered Marie to drink from the water jug again and then leave.

When Cross finally emerged from the barn, the sun was shining brightly, heating the little valley much earlier than usual. Cross surveyed the landscape, squinting. He felt terribly sick and exhausted. His eyes burned and his head ached viciously. He dragged his weary body into the house and collapsed on the couch.

The preacher slept all the day long and into the night.

CHAPTER TEN

The August sun beat down without mercy upon the snug valley. Marie sweated long hours in the garden, and soon she would harvest the fruits and vegetables for the family table.

Lee remained aloof and preoccupied. His meditations, his sermons, his selling continued to steal the days away from Marie whose desire was to be one with him again. His indifference hurt. Sometimes in the evening she would enter the living room where Lee insisted on sleeping and she would find it reeking of whiskey. Alone in bed at night she pondered for long hours the meaning of all these fearful changes.

Cross was restless. He submerged his consciousness deep inside himself, seldom noticing either his appearance, his environment, or his fellow man. His contacts with others through his preaching and his selling were mere interludes between his deepening thoughts on life and death, the devil and the deity. Doubt tormented his mind. Piercing headaches left him trembling and enervated. And the long hot days seemed to make his head swim with ugly thoughts, depressing thoughts, thoughts projecting little faith in the Lord God. Cross felt terribly alone and dispossessed and disheartened. He felt sick with fear, despairing. He felt like giving up, doubting his life, wishing for death. Something fearful clutched tightly at his throat so that he thought he could not breathe and the same fearful something made his heart race uncontrollably until he believed it would burst from his breast.

One blazing hot Saturday as Cross rose late from bed, he saw Marie from the window laboring in the heat of the garden and he saw Danny playing on the cool earth underneath the trees of the little forest. He hesitated at the window, then turned and went into the bathroom. He washed quickly. Then he tiptoed back into the living room and began dressing slowly, thinking intently. He pulled a sock onto his foot and then sat with his hands folded across his lap. Minutes went by and the preacher did not move. He gazed straight ahead into nothingness. Then he stirred and pulled on the other sock. Immediately he relapsed into reverie. Finally he stood up, climbed into his Levi's and dug his feet into his boots. He was ready now.

The heavy heat hit him like a slap in the face as he walked out into the sunshine, squinting. Marie saw him climb into the pickup and she wondered why he was not carrying his black valise.

She called to him, "You forgot your samples, Lee!"

Cross took no notice of her. He started the old Ford, made a U-turn in the yard, and drove over the rough bridge and past the boy waving to him from the shade of the woods. Stopping at the junction of the highway, he wheeled left in the opposite direction from Geneva Gap, and the woman left behind gazed in wonderment.

On the highway Cross felt free and lighthearted. He determined not to think. He would make a holiday of the trip to El Paso. He needed it. He had been working too hard lately. He deserved a holiday, he was sure. Maybe the headaches would disappear too.

The country through which he drove was wide and flat, sandy and desolate. Prickly cactus and gray sagebrush and stick-like ocotillo dotted the quivering landscape, and occasionally in the background rose bare and gray and gullied mountains that appeared leathery like the wrinkled hide of a bull elephant. From such perches black bald vultures glided gracefully high up in the sky in ever-widening circles. Far in the bleak sun-glaring distance Cross could see high-rising whirlwinds dancing in great billows of dust.

He sped through the main streets of adobe villages, barely able to catch the signs that told him these were not merely other natural phenomena. He entered one end of a scanty town and in seconds it was left in the hot dust behind. It was a "ghost" town of the desert kind where people hibernated in cool dark adobe catacombs in the high heat of the long afternoon.

Cross felt suddenly weak then giddy and dizzy and faint. He slowed the pace of the pickup. He felt an urge to stop at that godforsaken adobe mound there in the middle of nowhere and order some of those tall cool drinks pictured on that sign hanging dejectedly on that fence post yonder. But instead he pushed down hard on the foot pedal to prod the old Ford pickup past the forbidding land more quickly.

The hot wind began to blow. It arrived first as a gentle heat-filled breeze, but soon it was kicking up great clouds of desert dust, slapping hard against the side of the truck, making a hissing sound as the fine particles of sand ricocheted off the speeding metal frame of the old Ford pickup. A fine dust settled on the dashboard of the truck and the sifted sand blew into the mouth and nose of the lonely driver. Cross could feel the minute particles grate on his teeth as he shifted his tongue in his mouth. His eyes were becoming red with the fine dust and glaring sunshine.

The wind roared madly across the desert stretches, carrying a cargo of brownish-red sand. Tumbleweeds charged wildly across the highway. It became more and more difficult to control the little pickup as the aggressive wind slammed against it. The giant dust storm shoved and stung and blinded frail vehicles and their drivers crawling anxiously on the highway. At times it seemed to the preacher that the monstrous wind, flexing its gritty muscles, would hurl the helpless truck off the highway and out over the long stretches of the desert nowhere. He clung tightly to the steering wheel.

Several hours of tense-muscled driving went by before Cross saw the El Paso skyline in the hazy distance. He breathed a sigh of relief, for he was tired and stiff from the concentrated handling of the truck in the forceful dust storm. He was glad his objective lay just minutes ahead. Soon Cross caught the heavy odor of the oil refineries encircling the city. At least the wind had blown away some of the smoke and fumes which usually hung over the place.

As the preacher drove through the outskirts, he glimpsed the huge oil tanks of Shell and Texaco and Standard Oil. In the background innumerable metal smoke stacks, like shiny brass steeples, belched out fumes in the process of refining crude oil among the maze of curves and bends of silvery steel pipe. Slick motels and modern low-slung company buildings and housing developments whizzed by the preacher's line of vision as he drove toward the center of the city.

Cross took Santa Fe Street toward the toll bridge leading to Mexico. He parked the pickup on the El Paso side in one of the many lots that boasted large signs informing tourists of their nominal fifty-cent charge for parking under protective canopies of corrugated tin.

The dust storm was still whistling madly as Cross, his face averted from the blast, leaned his body into the wind and jogged towards the bridge. He asked for change at the toll window and then dropped two pennies in the coin depository. Now barefoot Mexican boys trotted around him with skinny arms stretching in the ageless pose of alms begging. Cross ignored them at first, but when they became too insistent he made a sweeping motion with his arm and barked out a conclusive, "No!" That turned most of the beggars away and they swiftly scanned the passageway across the bridge for another prospect. But one persistent beggar, no more than eight years old Cross guessed, hung onto the preacher asking for pennies. Cross disliked giving charity to the children. He thought it would ruin them for life.

When Cross reached Juarez Avenue, the boy wheeled around and scampered back across the bridge to join his friends who were already working on another American in a big Stetson who was walking through the passageway.

The preacher walked confidently down the street. He felt the eyes of the dark-visaged street hawkers follow him and he heard taxi drivers call to him, suggesting a visit to the girls. Cross pretended not to hear them. He stopped a moment to throw some coins in the old crumpled hat of a blind man whose pupils were cockeyed and half-lidded and bleached almost white.

Cross entered the Reno Steak House where he knew a quiet American-style bar with soft lighting was located in the rear. He walked resolutely through the busy dining room, and sat at the bar. It was pleasingly cool and dark. No one but the bartender was there.

"¿Mande?"

"A double shot of American whiskey and a bottle of Carta Blanca," said Cross.

"Yes, sir."

The Mexican placed the shot glass on the bar and filled it

and then opened the beer. Cross handed him a dollar and got back some change that the bartender slapped down on the counter. The preacher gulped down the whiskey in one big swig, the glass upturned high, his head thrown back, his eyes cast upward as if searching for heaven. Then he grabbed the beer bottle quickly and took great gulps of the cold chaser. He never used a glass for beer on this side of the border.

The hard liquor worked its magic well. In no time at all the preacher was feeling no pain. Since he had started drinking a few weeks back he had experienced some qualms of conscience. After all, hardly anyone drank hard liquor where he came from. Ol' Dan'l had been an unswerving prohibitionist. But the preacher rationalized his drinking with the explanation that he had to take alcohol for its medicinal qualities. It calmed his nerves and soothed the pains in his head and caused him to forget his morbid thoughts. It was a necessity but only a temporary necessity. He was sure he could discard it whenever it had served its purpose.

Cross ordered another double shot. This time he sipped cautiously at the head-dizzying liquid. He ordered no more whiskey the rest of the afternoon and he nursed the few bottles of Carta Blanca that he bought in order to stay in the quiet dark bar and avoid the dusty winds outside.

About dusk the wind diminished and died. Cross was glad because he was tired of watching the tiny bugs that crawled along the bar and he wanted nothing more to drink and besides he was developing a ravenous appetite. He dropped off the stool and went out a side door into the dingy street. The sidewalks were more crowded now as darkness approached and the neon signs of the strip joints were lighted and loud brassy music emanated from dark hallways. Cross walked down Juarez Avenue, and again he was approached by taxi drivers and pimps and little boys selling flesh. He ignored them all, but sometimes he had to jerk away from the grasp of an overanxious salesman.

Cross was waiting at a corner for a traffic light to change when he saw Sam and Betty Calkin at the door of the Florida Restaurant waving at him to come over. Cross smiled happily and waved back. He wanted to eat at the Florida anyway and it would be good to dine with friends.

"Howdy, preacher," said Sam Calkin, reaching to shake hands.

"Good to see you," rejoined Cross.

Betty Calkin said, "We're waiting for a table in here and if you haven't eaten yet we'd like for you to join us."

"Sure would. I was coming over to eat too."

The restaurant was crowded and a heavy cloud of cigarette smoke waved lazily over the tables. The head waiter hurried over and motioned for them to follow him upstairs. As they mounted the stairs Sam Calkin suggested they all go to the dog races after dinner.

In the second floor dining room there were fewer people and scarcely any smoke. The waiter led them to a long table by a window where someone was already busily digging into a fish dinner. The someone happened to be Dr. Serveto.

"Well, this is a pleasant surprise," said the professor, rising from his chair and catching his napkin just before it fell to the floor.

The Texans smiled politely and shook hands and said they were glad to see him. They took chairs next to him.

"How do you like the food here?" asked Cross evenly.

"Very good," said Dr. Serveto. "It's very tasty."

"Is this your first time in Juarez?" The preacher persisted in his questioning to make conversation.

"Oh, no! I've been here several times before."

"How do you like the town?"

"Well, it's all right," said Dr. Serveto. "It's a border town, of course, and it leaves much to be desired. . . . It's really a shame so many Americans get their only impression of Mexico from such towns as Juarez and Tijuana. I think they should see Mexico City to learn about real Mexico. If you fly from Juarez to the capital, you will go from one of the ugliest cities in North America to one of the most beautiful."

A dark waiter came to the table to ask for orders. Cross wanted a T-bone steak well-done and so did the Calkin couple.

Sam Calkin was eyeing Serveto sharply. "Juarez is a den of iniquity if ah ever seen one!" He pronounced *Juarez* as *war-ez*. "Why you can get pretty near any vice yuh wanna here."

"I guess you can," said Dr. Serveto, nodding. "But the Mexican authorities have begun to crack down on the narcotics traffic. They've ordered La Nacha to get out of town. She's the narcotics queen here, you know. Took over when her husband died. She lives in one of those ornate houses on 16 de Septiembre Avenue."

"Crack-downs are jest for show! Impress the American

tourist," Sam Calkin said disdainfully. Then looking curiously
at the professor he blurted out: "Where'd yuh learn ta speak
them Meskin names so good, Dr. Serveto?"

"He's been all over Latin America," volunteered Cross.

"I'm Chicano. I've always spoken Spanish."

Sam and Betty Calkin stared at the professor. The looks
were hard and the lips grim.

The waiter brought bowls of soup and salad dishes. The conversation lagged as the four people ate.

"Yuh better not eat thet salad, honey," said Sam Calkin to
his wife. "We don't wanna get the runs."

"Awright," she said.

Then Sam Calkin boldly surveyed the professor. "How
come the Meskins allow so dang much prostitution? Can yuh
tell me thet?"

"Official corruption I suppose is one reason," said Serveto.
"Besides, the poverty in Mexico is endemic, especially here in
the north. Many girls have no other way to make a living. Many
times it's actually attractive for them to spend their lives like
that—it seems better to them than the squalid life they came
from. It's not a pretty nor nice situation. But after all, we
Americans have little room to talk. I think we shouldn't point a
finger in a holier-than-thou attitude. We have prostitution in the
States. It's much more free-wheeling in our country. Here in
Mexico they have health inspectors check the brothels to watch
for disease. And of course we in the United States don't have
the excuse of hopeless poverty with which to even rationalize
our prostitution. Ours is based on affluence."

The waiter brought large T-bone steaks and placed the hot
plates on the table. He cleared away the soup bowls and salad
dishes. The three people plunged hungrily into cutting and
savoring the huge steaks. Dr. Serveto sipped at a cup of coffee.

"Ah don't know thet poverty has so dang much ta do with
their vice," insisted Sam Calkin, talking with his mouth full.
"These people are descendants of savages. Dr. Sterner tole us all
about how some of the tribes down here was cannibals and how
they skinned their dead enemy and how the Aztecs sacrificed
victims ta their gods. Don't tell me thet don't have no effect on
later generations. They don't have no real White Christian
morality."

Dr. Serveto grinned. "Well, we like to say that the Aztecs
and the other Indians of ancient Mexico were ignorant. But very

enlightened in the ways of nature. Anyway, what excuse can you give for what the Nazis did in Germany in the twentieth century? Or for what the British did in their 'glorious' empires? They were both White Christian cultures. The Germans have contributed some of the great works of literature, philosophy, and science to Western Civilization. Just think of the great cultural figures such as Goethe and Beethoven and Schiller and Thomas Mann and many others who contributed so much to White Christian culture of the West. And yet it was the Germans who perpetrated such savage atrocities in the thirties and forties. Still, the Germans alone are not at fault. The Germans are a part of White Christian Civilization and so all of Western Man is responsible for their degradations. Every White Christian is responsible because the Germans were very much a part of White Christianity. So the great Western White Civilization failed and yet you consider it superior. What excuse do you have for the savagery of the Nazis? They were not ignorant natives. They were from White Christian Civilization which prides itself on its enlightenment and humanity."

Sam Calkin was red in the face and he stuttered noticeably. "There ain't no connection between Anglo-Saxon culture and Nazi culture. Anyways, Dr. Sterner tole us all about how the most progressive countries in Latin America are those thet are most non-Indian and non-colored."

"It may be so," said Dr. Serveto evenly, "but one glaring exception then would have to be Mexico. She's mixed-blood and Indian and at the present time she has the greatest economic growth, most stable currency, and best prospects for a larger share of the pie for more of her people."

The conversation ended abruptly, as Betty Calkin changed the subject. The preacher wanted to speak out against Dr. Serveto but he thought better of it. He had sat in silence throughout the conversation but his reticence had only made him nervous and uneasy. Now he was glad the disturbing dialogue was over.

Later Cross looked at the professor and said in a toneless voice, "We're going to the race track. Like to come along?" Cross didn't know why he invited Serveto. He didn't like the man.

Dr. Serveto wondered if they really wanted him to accompany them. He hesitated and then said, "Why, yes, of course."

As they descended the stairs of the restaurant, Sam Calkin

pulled Cross aside. Dr. Serveto, who was leading the way, unaware of their stopping, continued down to the main floor.

"Gosh darn, preacher!" said Sam Calkin in dismay. "Why didja hafta invite thet goldang Meskin ta come along? I don't lak thet greaser one bit!"

"Well, I know I did wrong," said Cross, shrugging his shoulders. "I asked him without thinking. I never reckoned he'd agree to come anyway. He didn't seem too anxious."

"Well, tell him he don't hafta go, if he don't wanna," said Sam Calkin firmly. "Betty don't lak Meskins either. Ah'm sorry, Robalee, but we don't associate with folks lak him."

"Okay," said Cross. "I'll see what I can do."

Dr. Serveto was waiting near the main entrance. Cross tried to hide his embarrassment but did not succeed.

"Sorry we held you up," said the preacher, as the four people walked out of the restaurant into the street teeming with American tourists and Mexican hucksters.

The street peddlers were like fishermen angling from the banks of the sidewalks for a catch, throwing out bait of slick words and inviting manner. The four Americans ignored them.

"Sam has his car parked around the corner," the preacher said, looking sideways at Dr. Serveto. "Sure you want to come? Don't go with us just to be polite."

Serveto was confused. Did they want him to go with them or didn't they? He was unsure, but he said he was sure. Sam Calkin frowned.

They drove toward the outskirts of town where the race track was located and the traffic was heavy.

"I don't know if they'll have seats in the Jockey Club for all of us," suggested Sam Calkin. "We only made reservations for two."

The stadium was modern and impressive. Walking through the main gate, large wall murals depicting events in Mexican life and history greeted the eye. Cross was surprised at the cleanliness and good order and modern lines of the structure. This was the first time he had ever been out here to watch the hounds run.

When Cross and Serveto arrived at the door of the Jockey Club, they discovered they were alone. The doorman asked for reservations. The preacher stammered something about someone coming with them and then he looked down the long ramp below searching for Sam and Betty Calkin. Cross was speechless and embarrassed. His mouth hung open and his eyes scanned the hall in desperation. Then he caught sight of his two friends walking slowly along the massive glass facade on the ramp. They seemed unconcerned about losing their companions.

Cross said, "Wait here a minute," and ran down the stairs and along the hall to the Calkins. Serveto could see the three Texans discussing something in the distance. Then Cross came back looking rather sheepish.

"I'm sorry, Dr. Serveto," he said, "but we have to leave. Betty's feeling bad. She's pregnant, you know, and the food and the ride out here probably made her sick. I rode with them from Geneva Gap, so I think I should go back with them. They got the car! Ha! Ha!" The laugh was forced.

"Oh, that's all right," said Serveto.

"You go ahead," said the preacher. "Just tell the doorman about the reservations for the Calkins and he'll let you in. . . . You can take a taxi back into town. There are lots of 'em outside."

"Okay," said Serveto. His look was level, his lips unsmiling.

"Sorry it had to work out this way."

"That's all right. I understand."

Driving back into town, the preacher grew angry at himself for getting into a situation in which he had to lie to extricate himself and his friends. He became depressed.

"Let me out here," said Cross, as the car halted at a traffic light on Juarez Avenue.

"Don't you wanna go with us?" asked Betty Calkin. "I was thinking we might go to La Fiesta to see a good floor show. I hear Hank Thompson's appearing there now."

"No, thanks," Cross said. "That place is too steep for me."

He got out of the car, peered through the window and waved as Sam Calkin drove off.

CHAPTER ELEVEN

Cross walked leisurely along Juarez Street, taking in the sights. He slowed down at the door of a shabby night club where a hawker in a soiled jacket with epaulets motioned for him to enter. Pictures of partially clad women in various seductive poses were tacked on pasteboard beside the doorway.

"Show starting pronto, Joe! Come een! Come een! Muchas muchachas! Strip tease! Come een, Joe! Come een to El Molino Rojo!"

The preacher pushed through the swinging doors. Inside the heavy dank smell of smoke and sweat and alcohol pervaded the darkness. From the shadows emerged a waiter with tired puffy eyes and sunken cheeks who spoke to Cross close up and whose breath made the preacher wince. ·

Cross followed the ghostlike figure to a corner table that stood just off to the side of a stage with gloomy red footlights. He sat down in the dark corner and became absorbed in the dead atmosphere around him. Shadowy faces looked up from dark tables as a three-man band played a fanfare in the background of the stage.

A short Mexican sporting a mustache and a Stetson trotted onto the dusty stage and grabbed the microphone.

"Good evening, ladies and gentlemen, señores y señoritas." His English had only a trace of a Mexican accent. "We have a big show tonight. Lots of girls. . . ."

Cross drank a double shot of whiskey in one great gulp. Then he swilled down a bottle of beer. He ordered more.

A woman at the bar stopped the waiter and inquired about

"ese vivo," glancing over to the preacher as she spoke. The woman was big-boned, big-breasted, big-bottomed. She was heavily painted with deep red lipstick, black mascara defining lifeless eyes, false eyelashes sweeping forward defiantly. When she concluded her conference with the skeletal waiter, she strolled over to the preacher's table.

The brisk master of ceremonies was telling jokes, as rasping titters from the darkened audience echoed to his pornographic humor.

"You buy me drink, querido," mewed the peddler as she edged into a seat next to the preacher and curled her arm around his shoulders.

"¡No me molestes, mujer!" said Cross testily.

The gringo's Spanish startled the prostitute. She looked at him and said no more. As she got up to leave, the discordant band blared out a torrid beat.

"Princess Fatima!" shouted the master of ceremonies as he swung his arm in a gesture of introduction.

The handsome girl snaked onto the stage with a torpid expression on her face. Her body was young and firm and slim. Her hips moved sensually, rhythmically, as she thrust her hips and buttocks forward—bump-bump-bump. Cross watched her suggestive movements and drank his whiskey impassively. A giddy anaesthetic feeling enveloped his body and dizzied his brain with indescribable pleasure. A buzzing, dulling whirl of pleasure. Now a smile played on his lips and his eyes rolled grotesquely. He called carelessly for more whiskey.

Thump! thump! thump! went the drum beat. Bump! bump! bump! went the stripper's buttocks.

Robby Lee was a growing boy. He was visiting his best friend in El Paso. His friend slept naked in the heat of the city night, and in the morning Robby Lee would wake up to see the friend across the room in his bed playing with his genitals. Robby Lee felt a demanding sensuality rising in his loins, clamoring for the touch of human flesh. He conjured up pictures of round breasts and curving flesh and hairy knolls and soon his hand beat tight around himself and the creamy, sticky seed would spurt out onto the sheets and the high pitch of pure sensual pleasure would subside into a feeling of wonderful ecstatic relief flowing about his loins.

He fell into a senseless sleep again, and then late in the morning they rose and showered and fried eggs and large beef steaks and wolfed down the fluffy, yolk-running eggs and the tender, blood-running meat. They lounged about the house and would listen to recordings of Western music and tease each other and rough and tumble on the carpeted floor.

In the evening before the sun set in a blaze of color, they jumped on a streetcar and rode over the bridge into Mexico. They liked the early evening on Juarez Avenue when the night people emerged to sell their varied wares and the strip joints opened their doors and ignited their blatant lights and raucous tempo. They swaggered down the street, savoring the attention they commanded from the streetside anglers. Then when they tired of the idle strolling, they stopped to listen to the titillating tales of a procuring taxi driver and soon they were sitting in the back seat of a rattling cab, feeling their loins reviving in sensual anticipation.

The cab driver brought them to a place called Sans Souci, and the bartender served three small beers and demanded too much money. But the boys paid anyway and then took swigs of the bitter-tasting beer while ogling the fleshy women. The painted whores knew his friend and teased him affectionately in Spanish as if he were an offspring, and the friend welcomed the attention and flaunted his experience before Cross. But Robby Lee was trembling underneath his clothes and he tried desperately to appear cool. He had never had a woman and he feared and desired a whore all at once. Then a short dark girl took Robby Lee by the arm. His friend laughed at Robby Lee's look of bewilderment and fear as the girl led him away down a dimly lit hall and into a tiny back bedroom. Robby Lee's face had reddened visibly.

The back room was bathed in a yellow light from the glow of a single hanging bulb which made the room appear like a photograph that had deteriorated and yellowed with age. There was a full-length mirror standing six feet tall screwed tightly to the wall. And there was the bed.

The bedspread appeared splotched with dried drippings. The girl smiled wryly at Robby Lee's wide-open eyes. She told him to wait, as she left the room. She would be right back, she assured him. Now Robby Lee stood alone in the bedroom and wondered what he was doing here and glanced at the strange reflection in the fearful mirror. Soon a heavy-set Indian woman shuffled into the room, plumped down on the edge of the bed, and demanded to look at him down there. Robby Lee stared at the insistent figure in amazement.

"¿Qué pasa, chulito?" she said in a consoling tone with her

hand outstretched. "¡Déjame ver! No hay cuidado. . . ." Her manner embarrassed Robby Lee and he reluctantly unbuttoned the fly of his pants. She took the organ in her hand and drew back the skin from the head and inspected it carefully.

"'Stá bien," she said. "You no got no-theeng. Gimme feefty cents."

She put out her hand, palm up this time, and Robby Lee dug into his pockets for some coins. The prostitute returned as the old woman left and they whispered something and giggled.

The woman slipped out of her dress; she had nothing on underneath. Her sudden nakedness startled Robby Lee. Her skin was dark brown and her breasts hung loosely and the nipples were large and round, papular, and nearly black. Her stomach was flabby and the skin there was flaccid, and at the juncture of her stubby dark legs was a red shiny opening. No pubic hair.

She flung herself on the bed and opened her legs wide, knees up, feet on the mattress. She called to him to hurry and he fumbled nervously at the buttons. He was shocked at the lack of any modesty. But he was hard and hungry for the flesh of a woman and he climbed on her and caught a momentary glimpse of the hairless red moist opening with black-brown fringes.

It was over in seconds. He had scarcely slipped into her when he felt himself emptying his genitals of their nagging cargo. The prostitute couldn't believe it. She laughed and laughed. She laughed so hard the tears ran down her cheeks. Robby Lee was flushed with embarrassment and anger.

When they came out into the bar room, she told everyone that she had snatched away a cherry. And she laughed and laughed again and cast mischievous glances at Robby Lee Cross.

The preacher scowled, "The bitch! That Mexican bitch!"

The stripper was on her back on the floor of the stage. She was fully nude now except for a flimsy G-string which hid nothing. She writhed enticingly before the preacher's eyes. His face was grim, his jaw set tight, teeth grinding. As his mind wandered through a maze of drunken fantasies, he watched the wiggling, trembling flesh on the floor. He blinked his eyes. *Was it María Dolores?*

Cross ordered more drinks. The strippers strutted the stage one after another. They all looked the same to the preacher now, as he festered in his drunken fantasy. *The same stinking whores,* he thought.

When the strip-tease ended, the bald-headed Americans with their stern-eyed wives, cigarettes dangling from protruding underlips, wobbled in the shadows out the swinging doors. Cross sat alone and watched the club empty. The emaciated waiter stood by and eyed the departing Americans. He hawked up some mucus and spat on the floor.

Two men swaggered in, took a table across from the preacher, arrogantly demanded two margaritas with not too much salt on the lip of the glass, pulled their Stetsons cockily over their eyes, and looked around the place while making sarcastic remarks about greasers. Cross thought he had seen them somewhere before. One of the Texans glanced at the preacher, then looked at him again, this time long and hard. He mumbled something to his companion and they laughed.

The two Texans emptied their glasses quickly and ordered more. Their manner was careless, their talk loud, their laughter raucous. Again they gulped down the margaritas and waved to the waiter for more.

Cross was becoming depressed. The effects of the whiskey wearing off, he had no desire to drink more. The numbing sensation was leaving him, and the stark sinful world was descending upon him. His head ached viciously once more.

The two men began to eye Cross knowingly and then snicker in challenge. They would hum a tune in bold drunken voices and inject words to it and then look at each other and laugh at some secret witticism. They became louder and gazed at Cross more fixedly. Then in broken, drunken tones they began to wail out a song.

> "Oh, the preacher went down
> To the cellar to pray.
> He found a jug
> And he stayed all day.

> "Oh! the preacher went down to the cellar to pray,
> He found a jug an' he stayed all day.
> Ah ain't a-gonna grieve
> Ma Lord no more!

> "Ain't a-gonna grieve ma Lord no more!
> Ain't a-gonna grieve ma Lord no more!
> Ain't a-gonna grieve ma Lord no more!

"If the preacher gets ta heaven,
Before ah do.
Ah know ah'll go
Right up there too.

"Oh! the preacher went down to the cellar to pray,
He found a jug an' he stayed all day.
Ah ain't a-gonna grieve
Ma Lord no more. . . ."

Cross was up like a shot and before the overbearing Texans could stand, he overturned their table, splashing their drinks over them. As one rose to fight, Cross caught him flush in the mouth with a hard swing of his clenched fist and he heard the crack of broken teeth. Blood streamed down the man's jaw and he covered his face for a second and yelped in pain. The other man hit the preacher hard above the ear and the blow stunned him. But Cross gritted his teeth and bore into the other Texan with both fists whipping hard against the man's face. The preacher heard a bottle crash into pieces behind him and he felt a slight burning sensation on his head as he turned and struck the first Texan again so that his jaw grew bloodier and he dropped the broken bottle he had splintered on the preacher's skull. Now the second Texan hit Cross with a terrifying jolt on the line of his eyebrow just above the bridge of the nose. A deep cut opened up and gushed blood over the preacher's face. Cross lunged at his attacker tackling him hard at his midriff, knocking the air out of the Texan, and sending him sprawling on the floor, the preacher landing on top. Quickly Cross straddled his victim and clawed fiercely at the man's throat, strangling him in an insane rage. But the first Texan had regained his senses and began flailing away at the preacher's head. Cross was driven down by the blows but he reached desperately for a nearby table struggling to get to his feet. No use. He upset the table and then he felt the hard sharp toe of a boot kick him square in the pit of the stomach. He doubled up in pain, gasping for air, as the dull thud of a boot hit against his temple and everything was a painful whirl and then black.

* * * * * * *

The next day Cross remembered only flashes of what happened after the fight. He was telling Sam and Betty Calkin about it now. They were having breakfast in an El Paso hotel restaurant where they had run into each other.

Sam Calkin smiled disdainfully. "Were they Meskins?"

"Uh-uh," moaned Cross, looking haggard. "They were white guys. . . . Beat hell out of me! Now I know how it must feel to be pistol whipped."

"Well, what happened after yuh passed out?" Sam Calkin pressed.

"I don't rightly know for sure. I just remember I was staggering out the place with two Mexican cops under each arm, dragging me along. They took me to a doctor. He patched me up. . . . How do I look?"

"Yuh don't look too bad," Sam Calkin said. "Without thet bandage over your eye no one 'ud know yuh was in a real stomper. Your eyes are kinda red but thet's all!"

Cross grunted, squared his shoulders, and forced a laugh. He felt weak and shaky.

"Who paid for the damages at the Meskin hole-in-the-wall?"

"I don't know," said the preacher. "The police didn't say anything to me about it. They just let me go with a stiff warning."

They were eating slowly. Sam Calkin wanted more details about the fight. And the preacher obliged with some embarrassment.

Finally Betty Calkin interrupted. She was bored and suggested they all go on a tour of Juarez. She had heard there was a modern shopping center across the free bridge. Cross agreed to go along. He hadn't been out that way in some time.

They drove over in Sam Calkin's car. Just across the Cordova free bridge they drove past food markets, butcher shops, barber shops, and other stores catering especially to Americans from El Paso. They drove by an area where mud huts and wooden shacks served as homes for the miserably indigent who came to the border to find work and a better life and often found neither. Cross explained to Sam and Betty Calkin that many were from the countryside where they could no longer scratch a living from the barren soil of northern Mexico. Others were former braceros who were no longer allowed to migrate across the river to work the vegetable and fruit farms of the Rio Grande Valley of Texas and the Imperial Valley of California. The preacher called them "los pobres de la tierra," and in the wistful, penitent mood of the hot Sunday morning he felt a lump in his throat and a tear in his eye. It was the patronizing emotion and the tentative tears of the Christian missionary.

Now they approached a fork in the smooth-paved avenue, and directly before them stood a memorial facing southward into Mexico.

"That's a statue of Abraham Lincoln," said Cross, pointing.

"Ah thought it kinda looked lak him," said Sam Calkin. "What they so all-fired hot about thet black Republican?"

"Well, I reckon 'cause he freed the slaves and stuck up for Mexico when President Polk sent troops to the Rio Grande back in 1846."

"Well, there ain't no real difference between Meskins and niggers anyway," said Sam Calkin.

Farther on they stopped at a big parking lot, got out of the car, and locked the doors. Around the wide parking area stood many shops with sleek modern lines. They hurried across the street to a large rectangular building to get out of the blazing sun.

"This is the shopping center, isn't it?" asked Betty.

"Yep, part of it. This is the PRONAF development the Mexicans are trying to complete all along the border from the Pacific to the Gulf."

The preacher directed his friends to the main entrance of the large building and showed them a metal plaque embedded in the wall explaining that PRONAF was the project started by Adolfo López Mateos, former president of Mexico.

The heads of the three Texans jutted out, surveying the lettering on the plaque and then Sam Calkin asked: "What does PRONAF stand for, Robalee?"

"Programa Nacional Fronterizo. Means the National Border Program. The Mexicans want to beautify border towns to attract tourists and eliminate the contrast between American and Mexican border cities. . . . This is nice here, don't you think?"

"Yeah," nodded Sam Calkin. "Ain't much though. Yuh seen them shacks back there."

"What's in here?" asked Betty Calkin as they climbed the stairs inside the cool stone building.

"Arts and crafts from all over Mexico," said Cross.

The preacher was glad to be in the clean cool building, for the stinging sunshine and heavy polluted air outside had made his head spin and given him a throbbing headache. A hangover was being aroused. But inside the smells were clean and the shade was welcome. As they walked, browsing among the displays, the air smelled appealingly of worked leather and straw mats and burnished pottery. Betty Calkin bought some animal figurines made of handblown glass and she told of her joy in coming here.

Afterwards the three Texans visited the small shops across the street where everything from ornate bedroom furniture to turqoise jewelry was sold. They viewed the pre-Columbian Indian art in the small ultra-modern Museum of National History. Sam Calkin was impressed by the negroid features of massive block heads sculpted by the Indians of the Olmec culture. It convinced him of the relationship between the dark-skinned people of Mexico and those of Africa.

Cross ignored Sam's remarks and would only say, "I bet Old Cotton would like to have some of these Indian idols."

Later they drove to the big marketplace in the center of Juarez. They browsed among the stalls of souvenirs, trinkets, rugs, and baskets, and breathed in the cool air under the high-arched ceiling and smelled the sweet aromas of ripened fruit and sugary soft drinks.

Cross enjoyed watching a young Mexican trying to sell him some puppets by manipulating the hand controls to make them hop and skip and dance around. The preacher liked the puppets. It required little skill to pull the strings and make them do the director's bidding. The preacher bought one for Danny. The figure of the puppet was that of an old witch.

After making the sale of the doll, the young man directed Cross to other souvenirs made of onyx and obsidian and mother-of-pearl, ceramic vases and bowls and ash trays. He picked up one ash tray made of cheap painted clay and pointed at the Cantinflas-like figure of a man squatting and defecating under a street lamp. The young Mexican thought it humorous and snickered in a clownish way while pointing at the statuette and telling Cross to look at the funny ash tray. The preacher grimaced and turned away. The young man stood at his stall with his mouth hanging open. He was dumbfounded, wondering what was wrong. Then he shrugged his shoulders, laughed, and replaced the offending ash tray on the counter.

The preacher walked away with a disgusted look on his face. He was disturbed at the sale of such an item but more so at what it represented. The statuette of a man defecating reminded him of the essential animalism of mankind. *Man can't escape the imperfect shell that surrounds his being. Man's really an ugly brute animal with all its vulgarities. Even man's woman*

*shares that imperfection. She's even more subject to the vulgar
functions and necessities of the brute animal. As beautiful as a
woman can be, she is always grossly circumscribed by the im-
perfections of the animal shell.*

Cross walked out of the marketplace ahead of Sam and
Betty Calkin who were lagging behind, bargaining with a stall
keeper. The preacher stood in the shade along the outer edge of
the building, waiting. Small cafés and newstands and fruit drink
bars lined the outer side of the marketplace. People bustled in
and out of the doors.

As he stood and watched the comings and goings, Cross
caught sight of a squat Indian woman looking anxiously around
her. She wore no huaraches and her bare feet were black from
dirt and natural coloring and they were heavily calloused. Her
thick black hair was stringy and matted in spots as if pasted together with some kind of dried glue. Her nose was wide, her lips
heavy, her eyes epicanthic like those of an Oriental. And the
eyes burnt with anxiety and fear. Her body was wrapped in the
long skirts and heavy serapes of the Indian of northern Mexico.
One of the serapes enfolded a bulge that protruded from her
back. The preacher wondered if it was a baby or simply a load
of some kind. The bulge was completely covered by the serape
and the Indian woman paid no attention to it, as if it did not
exist. The woman was poor, miserably poor.

She was peering through the window of the café now. Then
she glanced about her and caught sight of the preacher watching. With no expression on her face, she beat a path towards
him. She stuck out a grimy hand from underneath the folds of
the serape and begged without speaking. Cross dug into his
pockets and handed her a quarter. The Indian woman made a
slight bow, then swung around and marched back to the café.
She tried to open the door. It would not budge. She looked
confused and peered helplessly in the window again. Inside the
people avoided her glances and looked away. They talked on as
if uncomfortable at the sight of her. The Indian woman gazed in
distress. She looked about her again, and then she shuffled off
around the corner of the marketplace.

The preacher shook his head. He could see the people in the
café laughing and gesturing. Above them on the wall hung the
omnipresent picture of the Indian Virgin of Guadalupe, the vir-
tual goddess of Mexico. Cross laughed wryly and shook his head
again.

CHAPTER TWELVE

At first the anonymous hate letters did not affect Dr. Serveto much. But the letters began to bother him when he received one that showed a target, the figure of a man, in the telescopic sights of a gun barrel.

For some time he had noticed the wary and hostile glances directed at him at the college since the start of the fall semester. He couldn't imagine why hostility was developing against him. He *had* suggested an invitation be sent a Marxist humanist to speak at the college as part of a series of distinguished lecturers being engaged for the new school year. Serveto had not thought anyone would mind. After all, some Birchers had been scheduled for lectures already, and the invitation to Raya Dunayevskaya would seem to balance the presentations between right and left.

Yet as he sat in his office with the hate letter crumpled in his hand, staring out the window, thinking, he realized the immense antagonism that Dr. Sterner had shown when he had raised the question of the leftist speaker at a meeting of the activities committee earlier in September. Maybe that was it, he decided. They didn't want to hear all sides. Surely he wasn't suspected of being pro-Communist. That was absurd. He had made his position clear many times in public lectures and private conversations. He believed in free will and the ability of man to control his own destiny. But had he made his position clear? He wondered. He was not sure. Anyway, Raya Dunayevskaya was not coming. She wasn't invited.

Dr. Serveto tore up the unsigned hate letter and threw it in the waste basket. He walked to the window and looked out.

Autumn was in the air. The leaves were turning yellow and pink and beginning to drop to the ground. The green of the islands of grass on the barren college hill was showing tufts of fading color, changing gradually into a pale yellow hue. And the sun was no longer as bright as it had been. The smells in the air were autumn smells hinting of cold winds to come.

Dr. Serveto breathed a long sigh. He liked the fall weather and the view from his window at this time of year. The rolling hills and round-backed buttes surrounding Geneva Gap took on a coating of golden brown, beckoning a lonely man to climb them.

Serveto's reverie was interrupted by a hesitant knock on his office door. He turned to see a shaggy unkempt figure peeking around the opened door.

"¿Qué tal?" mumbled the dusty figure, swaying into the room.

Coyote Jameson wore a buckskin jacket with leather strappings along the underside of the sleeves, and tight-fitting Levi's tucked into tan buckskin boots that were round-toed and without the high heels of the Texas cowboy kind. His face was swarthy and his hair grew over his ears like a thick mat of black bristles. His upper lip bore a heavy black mustache that was turned down at the edges, and his eyes were slightly slitted and sunk deep under bushy eyebrows. His nose was large and bulbous and his lips were thick. When he smiled he radiated an infectious friendliness and a grin that missed a tooth or two from skirmishes with gringos from this side of the tracks.

"Ola!" said Serveto, reaching out and shaking the young man's hand. "¿Qué pasa?" Dr. Serveto put his arm around the stocky youth and directed him to a chair.

"Oh, I don't know," said Coyote Jameson, shaking his head and looking downcast. The boy was innately shy and unsure of himself in front of people he liked. Perhaps it was a pose. Dr. Serveto was not sure. He did know Coyote Jameson deliberately slurred his words and used the intonations of the illiterate Mexican speaking English. Jameson knew otherwise, but he insisted on his way of talking.

"No sé," said the youth, leaning his head on his propped-up arm. "You know what they do to me, Dr. Serveto? Those gringos are giving my girl a hard time because she goes with me."

Coyote's singsong made Serveto smile, but he quickly changed his expression when he realized the seriousness of the boy's remark.

"¿Por qué? Who is your girl?" asked Dr. Serveto.

"She's that little gringita I been running around with lately. You know her. Her name's Ruth. La quiero mucho. Es muy simpática."

"Well, what's wrong?" pursued Serveto, somewhat puzzled.

"Her friends don't talk to her no more, Doc! They avoid her like she has the plague or somethin'. ¡Qué amigas! And they make sarcastic remarks when her back is turned about her screwing around with Mexicans. Cabrones!"

"How does she take it?"

"She's a dang good sport, Doc. Jest laughs it off, but I know she don't like it none! It's gettin' to her. Pobrecita! She's real simpática, Doc. You ought to see her. . . . Prettiest long hair you ever saw!"

The young man shifted restlessly in his chair and tugged absent-mindedly at his boot straps. Dr. Serveto said nothing. He knew the boy simply wanted to speak out about things that bothered him. There was a long pause.

"I hate phonies," said the sturdy young man finally. "I am what I am and that's all that I am, like Popeye says. If they don't like me, pueden besar my rear end!"

"Well, don't feel badly about it, Coyote," Serveto said. "You've got to realize that Texans refuse to recognize that it isn't where you come from or what your origins are that counts, but rather what a person makes of himself! That's what really matters! What you make of yourself. Anyway, when it comes to minority groups, religious questions, economic matters, and whatever, some people will believe what they want to believe in spite of the facts! So don't worry about it. Just go your merry way and live your own life and develop all the good you've been born with."

There was a long pause as both men thought about it all.

Finally Coyote Jameson said, "You know, Doc, I used to know a prof out at this little college in Corpus. Queerest dang dude you ever saw! Taught Spanish and Portuguese. Name was Gomes. Liked to make out like he knew pretty dang near everything. Had Portuguese blood in 'im. But caramba! did he try to be something other than he was! Always handed us this garbage about the Portuguese not being fanatical like the Spanish. Brazil he said was real different—you know, that 'Christ hangs easier on the Cross' jazz. He was a real fruitcake, Doc. Tried to be something different! Hung around with gabachos all the time— never gave un Chicano half a chance in class, or anywhere.

Always ass-kissing gringos. Wouldn't dare be seen with Chicanos. Was a homo, too. Had affairs with all the yellow-headed gabachos he could seduce from his classes. He didn't drive a car. I don't know if he was too scared or jest incompetent. I used to see him standing under a Pay Less Drugstore sign every Sunday morning waiting for a bus after spending the night with one of his lovers.

"Man! He was real sissified! ¡Pinche joto! Used to put some kind of stuff on his lips to make them shine. Always smacked his lips when he was eatin' too! He used to polish his nails with clear white polish all the time so they'd sparkle and he always smelled like a French whore—splashed on so much danged perfume or somethin'! Yeah, ol' Gomes was real Coca-Colisado, if I ever seen someone like that! He wanted to be a dead-ringer gringo!"

There was a long pause again. Coyote Jameson stared downward as if boring right through the floor.

"You know, Doc, I used to play with gabachos when I was growin' up in Laredo. I remember I had a friend who had yellow hair and blue eyes. We were good friends, all right. We were only about eight or nine then. But one day he says to me, he says, 'Coyote, ah like yuh so much, but ah wish yuh wasn't so Mexican-looking!' "

Coyote bowed his head. "That hurt, Doc! That hurt real bad!" A momentary silence. The young man changed the subject quickly.

"You going to the football game tonight, Doc?" His eyes focused on Dr. Serveto and lost their blank stare now as if a catch had been suddenly released.

"I guess I will."

"Wanna go with me? Ruth ain't goin'."

"Sure. What time shall I pick you up?"

"Las siete y media. That all right, Doc?"

"Sure," nodded Serveto.

Coyote Jameson got up from the chair and swung lazily out of the office. He didn't look back.

Serveto sat thinking about the young man who had just left. The boy feels lost, he thought. Dr. Serveto knew that Coyote Jameson was not accepted by the people across the tracks even though he lived on that side. They suspected his name and his manner and they wondered about his fooling around with gringas. His language was a little too forced whether he was speaking Spanish or English. The truth was that Coyote Jameson was an outsider, welcomed neither by one or the other of the blood lines from which he sprang. This caused him to be rebellious and belligerent and eccentric when viewed by the conventional people on both sides of the tracks. Consequently, he was a loner.

Serveto rose from his chair and stretched his stiff limbs, yawning widely. He decided to go to his apartment and prepare for a cool evening out in the open.

* * * * * * *

It was just getting dark when Dr. Serveto slid into his foreign sportscar and drove across the tracks to the little adobe house where Coyote Jameson rented a room. The family, all with thick black hair and skin of copper brown, stood or sat around the doorstep of the sodhouse. The head of the household lounged against the wall of the house, talking casually with Coyote Jameson, and as Dr. Serveto drove up to the tottering, unpainted fence enclosing the property, the children quit their frisking and stared at the newcomer while the adults nodded slightly, greeting him suspiciously. Dr. Serveto nodded back and said, "Cómo 'stán," and waited for Coyote Jameson to run in his room to fetch his buckskin jacket and come running out again. They all waved goodbye, and Serveto and the strange young man were off to the stadium.

Cars and trucks packed the parking lots around Odie Field near the radio station. This was the first football game of the season for Cal Davis and the air was buzzing with talk of an undefeated campaign for the cherry and white. The Cal Davis Saints were said to have the strongest team in years. Chi Chi Santiago was back for his senior year and he was "the best gol-danged quarterback in these here parts." Besides, the coach wrestled up some "colored boys" from the Gulf coast and they were like "greased pigs running with that ball," so said some of the crowd as they made their way through the hurrying groups of fans toward the stadium.

The atmosphere was electric with anticipation in the gathering dusk. Folks took their football seriously in Geneva Gap. An earnestness that Serveto had seldom seen was being shown that evening.

The two men clambered up the wooden bleachers and took seats above the forty-yard line. The stands were filling up as the opposing teams ran onto the grassy field and started to work out under each goal post. The excitement of the first big game was mounting.

Dr. Serveto and Coyote Jameson watched the vibrant proceedings in rapt silence. The band was playing a rousing fight song, the seats were filling up rapidly, and the heavy twang of West Texas speech permeated the air. Everybody seemed to be there. No one missed the big game in Geneva Gap.

Dr. Sterner and Cotton Zarler arrived. They met in the aisle at the edge of the bleachers and then took seats just in front and below Serveto and his young friend. Their wives squeezed into a space behind and above, two rows up. They were immediately behind Dr. Serveto and Coyote Jameson.

The place was packed. Dr. Sterner looked back over his shoulder and waved to his corpulent wife and the slight figure of Hanna Zarler. Then he saw Dr. Serveto and exchanged cursory greetings with him, as did Cotton Zarler. Dr. Sterner whispered something into Old Man Zarler's ear and then glanced back again at Serveto.

Meanwhile, Serveto could hear the frothy conversation of the two women seated behind him.

Mrs. Sterner was speaking loudly. "Yuh know, Hanna, we got four or five of the new faculty this year for our church. Some wasn't too anxious to join but we twisted their arms a mite and they came around. Some are Baptists and Methodists but we corraled them all for our church!" Mrs. Sterner was very pleased. She laughed heartily and her big breasts shook with joy.

Hanna Zarler chuckled quietly. In dry nasal tones, she told Mrs. Sterner that she and her committee had wrangled some of the newcomers for the First Christian Church. She was mighty happy, she said, because now they could get their church socials going good right away. Mrs. Sterner agreed it was all very nice and the two women smiled and laughed and chatted endlessly about the church socials they were planning this year and how many new people they had snared for their churches.

When the game began, the crowd became more excited. The first kickoff of the season sent swells of murmuring shouts through the crowd, and the nervous feelings caused people to belch up their dinners.

The game went badly for Cal Davis. The crowd grew angry and disgruntled. The visiting team was from the Gulf Coast and the players seemed anxious to maul the young Blacks from their area who had spurned their school for Cal Davis. They seemed intent on getting the Black halfback because he was fast and hard to tackle, and he gained most of the yardage for Cal Davis.

The two teams fought their way up and down the field like two gargantuan armies struggling for survival. The air was split with the crunch and cracking impact of hurled bodies and falling men. Sharp warlike yells rent the air. The field was one of battle.

Play after play, the Black halfback for Cal Davis danced and skipped and feinted his way gracefully through the hulking figures. The crowd cheered him on. Then suddenly in the second quarter after making a long gain, he was thrown hard to the ground and he landed "crack!" on the cement curb encircling the grass infield. The crowd jumped to its feet and shouted obscenities at the opposing players.

Cotton Zarler boomed out his feelings above the roar of the crowd: "What are those dirty niggers doin' ta our colored boy? Throw them God-damned niggers outa there!" Then facing Dr. Sterner he mumbled grimly, "Ah lak ta jump on them coons!"

Players from both benches had already swarmed onto the field and there were fists flying and helmets being swung for several frantic minutes. Finally the coaches calmed the players down and the referees ejected one Black from the other team. The crowd for Cal Davis cheered.

Dr. Sterner yelled out to the field with his hands cupped around his mouth like a megaphone, "Bye, bye blackbird!" And those nearby roared with laughter and Old Man Zarler patted Dr. Sterner on the back and laughed mightily.

At half-time the score was 14—7 in favor of the visitors. Now the crowd relaxed a bit, but many still argued long and loud, while drinking from paper cups of steaming coffee, about what the coaches should do or should have done and what was wrong with Chi Chi Santiago. The Chicano quarterback was not having a good night.

Dr. Serveto and Coyote Jameson walked around the dirt track surrounding the football field. Above them the large klieg lamps drew moths and other flying insects and threw wide beams of artificial light downward, floodlighting the field. Dr. Serveto walked slowly, taking in the action around him. The Cal Davis band was strutting onto the field now, blaring out brassy sounds as the two men sauntered over to the snack bar and bought paper cups filled with bitter coffee to help drive out the chill of the damp fall evening. People were milling all around them.

Serveto caught sight of a young Chicano walking with his friends. The boy saw Dr. Serveto and nodded with large sad eyes. Serveto felt sorry for the boy. He was a good athlete but he had failed his course during the summer and had been declared ineligible.

Serveto remembered now what had happened after the final grades were posted during the summer. The football coach had come to his office bemoaning the misfortune of losing his right end because of academic problems. He pleaded with Dr. Serveto to change the failing grade, but the latter was unmoved. He told the coach that he could do nothing. He was sorry he had to fail the boy, but it was wrong to do otherwise.

The coach then shifted his tactics. In appropriate heart-rending, Texas-twang fashion, he informed Dr. Serveto about the boy coming from a deprived background on the Mexican border. He told how Cal Davis couldn't recruit the top athletes with good academic potential here, because Texas and Texas Tech and the other big schools drew them away. So poor old Cal Davis had to take the athletes with the poor school records. This boy was one of them. He needed a chance and a break, the grieving coach declared. Just a chance. Just one break. Why, the boy knew his handicaps himself! He was a good boy. Why, he told the coach in so many words: "I'm just a poor dumb Mexican!" Now, wouldn't he help this poor downtrodden boy to get a start in the right direction?

The answer was no.

The coach looked unbelievingly at the professor. His sobbing tactic very seldom misfired. He was crestfallen, but only for a moment. He snapped out of his temporary speechlessness, his face a glowing crimson, and he cursed angrily at Serveto for what he was doing to Cal Davis football. Then he stormed out of the office, banging the door so that the glass panes rattled.

Now, during half-time at the football game, Serveto told Coyote Jameson of the incident. The sturdy young man shook his head as he listened soberly.

Back at the bleachers, Serveto found Robby Lee Cross and his wife sitting nearby. The professor took a place next to Marie, who showed no signs of her advancing pregnancy, and struck up a lively conversation with her and the preacher.

Cross looked warily at Dr. Serveto but talked in a friendly manner all the same. Still he kept his eye on Marie to see that she was not enamored with the handsome professor.

Marie spoke amiably but maintained a certain reserve lest her husband become jealous. Their relationship was still not going well, but he had brought her to the football game which she hoped meant a change of heart. Especially now, with the baby on the way.

The second half began and the Saints continued to play badly. Chi Chi Santiago fumbled away the ball during a drive down the field to the enemy's thirty-yard line. Santiago's mistake was too much for some of the fans. They screamed unmercifully for the Mexican's removal from the game. And the sharp-eared coach complied.

During the excitement caused by the fumble, Cross thought he caught Marie and Serveto exchanging intimate glances. A grim jealousy swelled within him. He watched their every move now.

Late in the fourth quarter Cal Davis had slashed and clawed its way down to the two-yard line in enemy territory. The coach sent Chi Chi Santiago back into the game. If Cal Davis could push across a touchdown, it would have a chance to tie or win the game with a conversion.

Chi Chi came up to the scrimmage line and barked out the signals behind the center. He took the ball and plunged headlong over the goal line. Touchdown! The crowd jumped to its feet and whooped and hollered and emitted ear-piercing rebel yells. That Chi Chi Santiago was a great football player! Yessiree!

But the game was not yet over. Less than thirty seconds remained on the scoreboard clock and Cal Davis called a time-out. The coach sent in instructions. The crowd stared anxiously. The coach would certainly go for a win—he wouldn't dare do otherwise. The pressure of the crowd demanded victory. The team had to try to work the ball over for two points. There would be no kick.

Chi Chi Santiago brought the team out of the huddle. He looked over the opponent's defenses and decided to change the play at the line of scrimmage. He screamed out the signals over the roar of the feverish crowd. He took the ball as it slapped into his hands at the crotch of the bulky center and for an instant it seemed he would go over easily for the victory. But the boy was hit hard by a vicious tackler and the ball squirted out of his hands and out of bounds. The crowd groaned in disbelief. A first fight broke out between the opposing players on the field. Then men and boys from the bleachers, seething with pent-up anger at the frustration of the game, stormed onto the field and a wild melee ensued. Cross jumped down the bleacher seats to help restore order. Serveto restrained Coyote Jameson from following.

Serveto could hardly believe the savage emotion he saw in the faces of the Cal Davis crowd. Even women screamed out fervid vulgarisms in the uproar. The crowd wanted blood.

Suddenly, as more husky students jumped down the bleacher seats past them, one anxious cowboy bumped Marie Cross and sent her reeling down to the next row of benches and she landed hard on the wooden planks. Serveto jumped down to where she lay and lifted the groggy woman onto the long bench. He sent Coyote Jameson to wet a handkerchief and the boy ran among the milling mob to a water faucet along the edge of the field. He came hurrying back and Dr. Serveto applied the wet cloth to Marie's head.

When Cross came back to the stands after the fight, he saw Serveto with his arm around his wife just regaining her senses. He cast a darting look at the professor as Coyote Jameson explained the accident.

Driving home on the highway that night Cross would not speak to Marie. His face mirrored his grim sulking anger. He remembered the words Ol' Dan'l Cross uttered so long ago.

"A Mexican's a Mexican!" he had warned. "Yuh can't trust 'em! They'll stab yuh in the back! Yuh mark ma words, boy!"

CHAPTER THIRTEEN

"Doggonit!" Lee grumbled. "Why don't you take care of things around here? You've gotten so God-blessed helpless here of lates! What do you do all day?"

It was daybreak, and Lee was standing at the kitchen sink washing a spoon which he had fished out of a smelly pile of dishes. Marie sat at the table, looking haggard and worn.

"I'm sorry, Lee. I haven't been feeling well. I feel so tired and weak. I don't know what's wrong with me. . . ." Her voice trailed off into a sob. She sniffled and dabbed a handkerchief at her swollen, red eyes.

"Stop sniveling, for God's sake!" Lee grunted.

The miscarriage and its message had hardened the preacher. *The bible says. . . .*

He finished rinsing the spoon and plopped it into a cup of steaming coffee, stirred it, then raised the cup to his lips and sucked at it softly between his biting words.

"Just look at yourself! Why, you look like the last rose of summer, I guess! I'll be damned if you aren't acting like one of those lazy Mexican sluts. Get hold of yourself, woman!"

"Please, Lee, don't be mean," she pleaded. "I can't stand it anymore."

Marie covered her face with her hands and broke into tears. But Lee stood apart.

A sickly loneliness gripped her. She was losing weight. Her body seemed to age by the day; her shoulders hunched forward, her breasts hung barren and limp. Her gaunt, rawboned face framed large frightened eyes, now bulging and circled with grim black shadows. She ate little, brooded much, and dragged herself listlessly about the house.

Even Danny was unable to cheer her. He played little tricks
on her hoping to strike some laughter. At night the boy cried in
the large crib, wondering what was happening to his mother.
Marie would hear the boy whimpering at times, for she seldom
slept now, and she would rise from bed, stroke his head with
the full palm of her hand, and whisper soothing words in his
ear. When Danny fell off to sleep, she would return to her bed
and lie wide awake.

She couldn't understand. She was in an alien land, alone,
despised, friendless. And the miscarriage. It had only deepened
her despair.

She was never warm anymore. Icy chills coursed through
her body no matter how many clothes she wore. And the pains.
Sharp, piercing pains. All over her body. At times she felt she
would go mad.

Marie knew how neglectful she had been lately. *Poor Lee,*
she thought. She couldn't work like she used to. So weak. So
tired. She knew the house was in total disarray. She tried. But it
all seemed too much. Her world was overwhelming her with its
demands. I can't cope with it all, she thought, I can't, I can't.
She would weep bitter tears. And wrapped in blankets she
would huddle in a dark corner of the house, trembling.

A cold wave had hit the Big Bend. The stinging winds wailed
through the eaves of the faraway house. On such days Marie
would edge close to the window facing Sun Mountain and peek
out, hoping to glimpse some resurrecting sign on the windswept
landscape. But a gray gloom hovered and swirled about her
mountain and the cold lonely house. She saw her gardens lying
forlorn and deserted. Pale dry corn stalks rustling in the wind;
yellowing plants of squash and tomato and melon blowing limp-
ly, drooping, drying, dying; crisp dry leaves dancing around the
yard driven by small wind devils. And in the distance across the
arroyo the trees of the woods swaying stark and naked and
sticklike against the bleached blue of the sky and the flat elon-
gated wind-whipped clouds.

Marie would shiver and shuffle quickly away from the window, the desolate scene plunging her into deeper depression.

At times Marie would cease her aimless haunting about the
house and plant herself before a wall mirror and stare. The reflection always shocked her. Her long jetblack hair fell about
her shoulders in tangled knots, dull, dry, wiry. Her face wore a
mask of deathly pallor, her eyes ringed by shadow, her lips pale,

bloodless. She would shriek at the sight of the ghost in the mirror and turn away quickly, gasping for breath. She cried for God's mercy.

One day, all at once, she knew. It was all very clear. She wondered why she hadn't thought of it before. Yes, that was it. God was punishing her for marrying outside the Church. God was rebuking her for allowing Lee to baptize Danny when he should have had a formal christening in the Catholic Church. Yes, that was it. Lee no longer loved her and tormented her constantly with his suspicious questions because God had ordained it all. She was deserted by her husband because God was demanding penance for her sinful negligence. The loss of the baby confirmed it. Yes, that was it. It was her own fault. She had brought her fate upon herself. She had neglected her religious duties and God was now demanding retribution.

But must she simply endure the pain and the guilt until the end? No. She could leave Lee and return to the Church. Baptize Danny. Yes. And perhaps some day marry her man within the Church. But Lee would never do that! "Oh God!" she cried, "then I must leave him." Marie sobbed bitterly and alone. Day after day. Yet she knew she must tell him. But how?

Lee had been suspicious in the past. Recently, that part of his nature had resurfaced to plague them both. How would he ever understand why she had to leave him? Would he chastize her with his self-righteous moralizing? Would he accuse her of committing adultery?

In the early years of their marriage they had used the Rhythm Method to avoid a pregnancy. Lee had been afraid that Marie would bear a child while Ol' Dan'l was still alive. So they used the Rhythm Method, because it soothed Marie's conscience to practice the kind of birth control her church approved and it pleased Lee since it fostered the kind of sexual abstinence he believed in. But it had also created problems.

Lee had become terribly cynical during those years. Whenever her menstrual period did not occur on time, Lee would grow worried, argumentative, and suspicious. Sometimes he even insinuated things. The ceremony in the barn had not been the first time he had shown such suspicion. It had hurt her so deeply that for days she had been completely enervated, losing the very will to live. But Lee refused to stop. He nagged and taunted and chided her. At such times he repeated the story of the young soldier from Geneva Gap who had married a Mexican girl just before leaving for war in a distant Asian land. He later learned from his angry parents that the girl had given birth to a child—twelve months after he had gone away. The young Texan shot himself because of that woman. "That Mexican bitch!" Lee would snarl.

That is what Marie thought about during those cold days of early autumn. The sun deigned to reappear at intervals and warm the Texas hills and only then did she seem to regain her lost energy. But only for a time. She sank into her depression again and again, thinking, always thinking. About Lee and about her decision to leave him.

She remembered how Lee had spoken of his mother years ago. He idolized his mother. She had died when Lee was only five. He had scarcely known her. Yet in their long talks when they were both teenagers, he had almost pictured his mother as some kind of saint who never would have stooped to sex to bear her children. He couldn't imagine his mother opening her legs to any man, even his father, and slapping herself sensually upward against his hairy trunk. Her thighs would flare for no man, he seemed to say. Her womb would never crave for the shuddering impact of any man's sex. Indeed it seemed at times that Lee believed his mother had never been subject to all the usual natural functions of mere human beings. She was someone apart, pure white lovely, and untainted.

Now in the lonely faraway house Marie thought of Lee's mother and an unwilling hate welled up within her. She tried hard to suppress it and turn her mind to other things. Then, thinking of her duty and her penance, she determined to tell Lee soon. I must tell him, she thought. I must leave Lee.

*   *   *   *   *   *   *

"¡Viva la huelga!" For weeks the campesinos had been striking Old Man Zarler's cotton fields, and now some stood at the edge of the highway pancaking their cold stiff hands over a large oil barrel from which a warming fire bellowed in the chill fall wind. Other pickers were pacing slowly along the fringes of the cotton fields, picketing with placards on which militant slogans exlaimed: "Viva la Raza" and "Venceremos"; and others with a large picture of Zapata, the Mexican revolutionary populist with bandoleers crisscrossing his chest, a rifle in his right hand, and a swelling sombrero on his head. "Tierra y libertad" Farther down the highway along the fields stood a makeshift

altar where two of the destitute migrant workers were wor-
shipping an image of the Virgin of Guadalupe. Robby Lee
Cross caught glimpses of this bedraggled army in its initial workings as he turned the little pickup off the highway onto the
washboard dirt road that led to Cotton Zarler's big house in the
distance.

Cotton had invited the preacher to see for himself what
"them dadgum Mexicans" were doing to him. Cross sympa-
thized with Old Man Zarler when he told him on the telephone
what a ruckus Dr. Serveto was stirring up, and so the preacher
felt obliged to stop by the ranch and console Old Cotton in
person.

Cross steered the pickup alongside the ranch house under a
huge gray cottonwood. The preacher recognized the Volkswagen bus parked in front of the house and knew Old Cotton
was in. As he climbed out of the pickup two large wolf-like
hounds loped out of the veranda and barked menacingly at him.

"Schatzie! Schnakie! Stop that! Hold your horses!" yelled
Old Man Zarler as he stepped down from the front porch and
walked toward the preacher to greet him. The dogs yowled tear-
fully at their master's reprimand but still sniffed suspiciously at
the preacher's legs.

"Don't be scareda them bozos," said Old Man Zarler as he
approached with his arm outstretched, hand unclenched, searching for a handshake. "Yuh remember ma little ol' Shepherds,
don'tcha preacher? Ha-ha!"

"How'reyu, Cotton," said Cross, shaking hands. "Sure do.
Mighty fine looking animals!" The preacher shot a wary sideways glance at the moaning, sniffing dogs.

"Ah was jest goin' over ta the store," said Cotton. "Wanna
come along?"

"Sure."

The two men walked over to a small oblong adobe building
which served as the commissary. The wind blew through the
seams of their light jackets and caused them to hunch over in
reaction to the chill.

"Hanna's at the town house, today," said Cotton, "so ah
gotta grub up ma own vittles. Got lots of stuff over here."

Zarler pushed open the bell-tingling door and the two men
walked into the dark, low-ceilinged room, where cans and sacks
and jars of foodstuffs sat on unpainted wooden shelves. A short,
stocky shadow behind a counter at the far corner snapped off a

radio playing loud ranchera music and moved into the light beaming through a high window. Cross recognized the man.

"¿Qué tal? Pepe," roared Old Man Zarler, as he reached the counter. "Yuh know ol' Pepe, don'tcha preacher?"

"Uh-huh," nodded Cross. "He used to work for Jake, didn't he?"

"Yep, sure did." Now turning to the Mexican, Zarler said: "Say howdy ta the preacher, Pepe!"

"Buenos días."

Cross stared vacantly at the Mexican.

Cotton Zarler began collecting food items from the shelves, ordering Pepe to come along and carry them for him. Cross stayed at the counter, observing.

The commissary was like most general stores. It sold everything from bridles to bread, and the merchandise seemed to cover every bit of wall and floor space. An old potbelly stove stood in a corner, its black smoke pipe reaching through the ceiling. An old rocking chair, its paint chipping off, sat glumly nearby. And on a post support was nailed a cardboard sign on which was scrawled: "Shoplifters will be shot. Try me!"

This was Old Man Zarler's store that he kept to provide his workers with all necessities so that they wouldn't have to go the long way into town. Scarcely any of the campesinos owned a car anyway. "So that's that!" Cotton often said. "No fuss, no bother, no heartache. Ma Mexicans have ever'thing they need rightchere. An' they better damned well appreciate what ah'm doin' for 'em!"

Cotton marched back to the counter now, with Pepe trailing behind loaded down with bread and bologna and milk and canned beans. Pepe dropped the items on the counter and began placing them in a brown paper bag.

"Yuh stay and set a spell with me, preacher. We'll go over ta the big house and chaw a bit on these here goodies."

They walked out the door, Cotton carrying the sack of groceries, and they heard Pepe snap on the radio and the husky voice of a mariachi sing out again.

"Them Mexicans have it too danged good!" said Cotton, as the two men sauntered toward the big house. "Yuh know what they're bellyaching about, preacher? They want $1.25 minimum wage per hour. Can yuh imagine thet—fer nothin' but stoop labor? Thet Serveto's behind all this ruckus! Ah seen him around the highway talkin' ta the Mexicans. Ah know what he's thinkin'. Ever since the government stopped the bracero program, Red agitators lak him have been rilin' up our domestic Mexicans ta strike. They figger they got us by the balls now. They ain't goin' ta get ta me though. It'll be a danged cold day in hell afore them Commies make me crawl, yuh better believe it!"

The dogs greeted them at the doorstep with leaps and yelps and the two men walked in the house, followed by the two frisking dogs. Cotton pulled up a chair for Cross in the kitchen and began preparing a light lunch. He sliced the bologna and threw some pieces at the dogs who wolfed them down in quick gulps. Then he set two places at the table and stirred the canned barbecued beans heating on the butane gas stove. All the while Cotton was talking about the troubles he was having with his Mexicans.

After they had eaten, the two men slouched in the straight-backed wooden chairs and continued talking and sipping coffee.

"They don't lak ma credit system at the store. Ah reckon it's Serveto's been tellin' 'em thet the interest ah charge on unpaid grocery bills ever' month is an instance o' debt peonage. O' course, some of ma Mexicans jest don't pay their bills on time, so ah gotta charge somethin'. The longer the bills go unpaid, the higher the interest! Ah ain't runnin' no philanthropic society around here! What does Serveto expect me ta do? Give it all ta them free? Thet's socialism, boy! But ah reckon he does want thet! Thet goldanged Commie!"

Later Old Man Zarler took the preacher on an inspection tour of his cotton spread. He showed him the cold clapboard barracks building with its bare walls and exposed beams and austere bunk beds on which urine-stained mattresses were rolled up at each end. Two or three of the bunks were laid out with fresh mattresses and blankets and sheets and pillows indicating that some of Cotton's workers were defying the strike. The footlockers at these beds were padlocked, while the others at the foot of each vacant bed lay open and dusty and empty. A potbelly stove stood in the middle of the long room. Fresh wood was piled in a box nearby for a fire when the strike-breakers came in from work.

Old Man Zarler kept mumbling, "Ah do right well by ma workers. Ah'm real proud of ma conveniences. Ah even got indoor toilets! What more they want?"

Afterwards Cotton and the preacher climbed in the Volkswagen and drove around the fields. Large dust clouds billowed from the churning wheels of the bus and were blown across the fields of dying cotton by the whipping wind.

"This was good middling cotton when it was ready for pickin' some time back," said Old Man Zarler as he drove. "But look at it now. Lint and fuzz blowin' ever' which way and the bolls fallin' off. It was good grade Pima cotton oncet, but not now. Them huelga people have pretty near ruined this year's crop. Ah lak ta lynch Serveto with ma bare hands and hang him high! Thet Commie bastard!"

Cotton drove onto the highway to show Cross how "high and mighty" the campesinos had become. The pickets recognized Zarler and shouted "¡Huelga! ¡Huelga! ¡Huelga!" Cross caught sight of Coyote Jameson in the crowd, shaking his fist and yelling at Cotton Zarler. Zarler shifted gears and sped the bus away from the noisy workers.

"See what ah mean!" Angrily he checked the rear view mirror to make sure no one had climbed on the rear bumper. "Them sons-o'-bitches are askin' for it! Ah been talkin' ta the sheriff about it an' he's on ma side. Ah'll get 'em soon, even if ah hafta run 'em off maself!"

Farther down the highway Old Man Zarler turned right onto another access road leading back to the ranch. He raced the bus on the bumpy, dusty road, mumbling obscenities as he drove. He was still cursing violently when he stopped the dusty Volkswagen before the big house.

Indoors Cotton made another pot of coffee. It was chilly in the house, so he turned on the large butane gas heater in the living room. Soon it was uncomfortably warm and Cross took off his windbreaker.

"Well, now yuh seen it all yourself," said Cotton, settling into an accustomed groove on the old dusty couch and sputtering with his lips at the hot cup of coffee. "What do yuh thinka all thet foolishness?"

Cross leaned back in an old rocking chair and scratched his head. "They're asking for it, all right," he said lamely.

The preacher was trying hard to think of something encouraging, something inspiring, to say to Old Man Zarler. There was a momentary pause. Cross reached down to the coffee table to pick up his cup. In that instant the preacher claimed his theme. It was something he believed in deeply.

"You know, Cotton, I have great faith in the omnipotence

of the Lord. I believe that God knows all things, past, present, and future. He is truly omniscient. He must be so, otherwise He wouldn't be the all-powerful Being. He knows the fate, the destiny, of each human soul. He must know that! Therefore, I believe in divine fate, divine destiny, divine predestination, or whatever else you want to call it. It doesn't make any difference what you call it! The truth is that God knows what's going to happen! But that makes no man less responsible for his actions! Men act certain ways, because they want to do those things. God doesn't ordain how they should act, but He does know that they will do certain things because of their basically evil nature. Most men are inherently bad. They are predestined to live in evil and they are responsible to God for their sins.

However, there are others in this world who are predestined to lead, to conquer, to dominate because they are inherently good and virtuous. And they will prosper—that is their fate, their destiny. It's no wonder that a nineteenth-century preacher once wrote: 'Godliness is in league with riches.' Such people—much like yourself, Cotton—are destined to dominate to assure the survival of the fittest, the survival of the Elect, the survival of White Anglo-Saxon Protestants, the chosen people.

Our mission is global, Cotton! Why do you think we're sending our boys to Asia to fight atheistic Communism? It's our fate, our destiny, to police the world in the name of White Christian Civilization. It's our peculiar burden—a burden that must be borne by White Anglo-Saxon Protestants. It's our manifest duty to bring our superior ways to inferior, less fortunate races all over the world.

And the same is true here in Texas! Men like you, Cotton, are predestined to control the rabble, the inferior classes and races. We can uplift them as much as we can, as much as their degenerate nature will allow, at the same time as we control them and police them. These people are responsible for their actions. But at the same time, we must pity them and pamper them to a certain extent—you know, Cotton, like children must be coddled. For they are basically inferior, basically dependent on stronger natures. These people are predestined to occupy certain lower positions in society.

In Leviticus God ordered the Israelites to enslave the nations around them as they moved into the Promised Land. Thus the Israelites did not drive out the Canaanites and Gibeonites but put them to work under their power. For as Joshua declared to the conquered peoples: 'Now therefore ye are cursed, and there shall none of you be freed from being bondsmen, and hewers of wood and drawers of water for the house of my God.'

There must be a mudsill of society! The mudsills of society do the menial tasks and allow us and our progeny to pursue the finer things in life. So they are necessary and the Lord God has predestined them for such simple, manual labor for our ultimate benefit. But we must coddle them occasionally when they throw fits like helpless children, and at other times we must break them when they push too far! There is a limit to everything and those who are superior in power, intelligence, and riches, must occasionally break the mischievous will of the lowly mob. So, Cotton, I would say for you to gird your loins and do what you must do and then sleep with a clear and easy conscience."

Cotton Zarler stirred uncomfortably on the couch. He lifted the cup to his lips and drank down the cooled coffee. During the personalized sermon he had sat very still with eyes cast to the floor, savoring the pleasant and reassuring words of the preacher. But now he was fidgety, as if anxious to take action. He stood up and threw his arm around Cross, who was putting on his jacket preparing to leave. He thanked the preacher for lifting his spirits and told him he now knew what he must do.

"Thankyee kindly, Robalee!" repeated Old Man Zarler outside, as Cross started the engine of the old Ford pickup. "Ah sure appreciate your message. It was down-right inspirin'. An' ah mean it, preacher!"

*   *   *   *   *   *   *

Two days later Speedy Carpenter told Cross all about it, while he was at the radio station taping a sermon.

"The strike's been broke," he said.

The preacher was elated. "Good," he said. "I knew ol' Cotton wouldn't stand for that nonsense much longer. How did he do it?"

"He got the sheriff ta arrest them Mexicans for trespassin' last evenin'. Most done spent the night in jail. Ah hear tell some's got out this mornin' on $250 bail."

"Were the ringleaders caught?" asked Cross anxiously.

"No, ah don't reckon so. Unless yuh call Coyote Jameson a ringleader. He refused ta post bail. Says he's stayin' in ta protest PO-lice brutality. The workers, ah hear tell, are high-tailin' it outa town. They got their lumps last night!"

"Good," said the preacher evenly. "Good."

CHAPTER FOURTEEN

On a moonlit night in late October, Dr. Serveto was burned at the stake. It was homecoming for Cal Davis College and the effigy hanging over the bonfire bore the name of the blasphemous Chicano.

The preacher watched the proceedings that night. He said nothing nor did he interfere. He simply observed the immolation. Cross thought Dr. Serveto deserved it. An outsider just couldn't come into Geneva Gap and start criticizing everything and stirring up trouble and expect to be honored. Besides, it had been an eventful homecoming week and Dr. Serveto had brought much of the indignation and trouble on himself.

The difficulties had begun early that week when Dr. Serveto had been invited to speak at the annual banquet of the Geneva Gap Chamber of Commerce. The chamber members suspected the man and they wanted reassurances from his own mouth that he was no danger to Geneva Gap. Most everyone there that evening was a Cal Davis alumnus or a Cal Davis professor, and what was good for Geneva Gap was good for the college. Cross had not attended, but he heard all about it at the barber shop.

"Thet goldanged greaser called his talk 'The Sacred Cows of Texas,' " Jake Greenfeld had told the preacher. Cross was sitting in the barber shop waiting his turn and scanning the *Geneva Gap Echo* when Jake brought up the whole matter while trimming Old Man Zarler's tonsured crown. Rex Austin was at the first barber chair cutting Will Busbee's thinning hair and they all nodded and grunted their approval of what Jake was saying.

"Why, he attacked ever'thing near and dear ta the hearts of Texans!" Jake continued, addressing the preacher with obvious bitterness.

Cotton Zarler interrupted with a sneer, "He said the sacred cows got started with the 'revered longhorn,' as he put it. The sonuvabitch mentioned the Bevo mascots of the University of Texas as the best example of such misguided reverence. Thet goldanged greaser!" Old Cotton shook his head so indignantly that Jake backed away with his clippers.

The barber was perturbed. He was not to be waylaid by anyone when he considered a story his own. He looked truculently at Old Man Zarler and then continued.

"Yuh know what he said, Robalee? He accused Texans of livin' under the delusion of bein' the chosen people of God Almighty. Can yuh imagine thet, preacher? What gall! He went right on ta say thet we's living under the delusion thet nothin' matters much in this world but Texas."

"He's right there," said Old Cotton, shaking his forefinger for emphasis. "But it ain't no delusion! Thet Serveto's jest allfired jealous o' what he seen rightchere."

Jake Greenfeld shot a hostile glance at Cotton Zarler. Didn't he realize this was his story?

"Yuh know what else he done lectured on?" asked the frustrated barber. He answered his own question: "The Alamo. He said the Alamo was another sacred cow. He said it was a memorial ta men who was stealing away a country from its rightful owner. Can yuh imagine thet, Robalee? Them's the words of a traitor, ah say!"

While Jake looked at Cross and waited momentarily for the appropriate response of disgust, Old Man Zarler took up the slack.

"Serveto also said the doin's precedin' the Mexican War was not the most admirable pages in American history. . . . How did he string them incendiary words tagether now? Do yuh remember, Will?"

Busbee grinned wryly. "He said something like Texans remember the Alamo—and remember the Alamo—and remember the Alamo—when it should have been cut down long ago and forgotten. It was a play on words. Alamo means a tree in Spanish. He compared it to the barbarous idols of the Teutonic tribes during the period of the Roman Empire. He said Texans revered the Alamo and praised it and nearly prayed to it."

"What else did he say, Jake?" asked Old Man Zarler. He knew he would not get the best haircut if he monopolized the conversation.

Jake was placated a bit. "Well, he said thet another sacred cow was the Texan doctrine of keepin' them Mexicans in their place. He said it was racism and somethin' else ah couldn't understand."

"Chauvinism," interjected Will Busbee. "He said Texans have a chauvinistic doctrine akin to that of Manifest Destiny which, he said, Texans never really discarded. Ultra-nationalism was what he was talking about, Jake."

"He said we ain't forgot we was the Lone Star Republic for quite a spell back there in the nineteenth century," remarked Cotton Zarler.

Busbee continued. "He said Texans see only what they want to see and recognize only what they want to recognize. You know, Jake, like a Venetian blind. You can let in just as much light as you want. That's what Dr. Serveto said, all right."

During the discussion Rex Austin remained silent, working steadily on Will Busbee's hair, but stopping occasionally to listen more closely. He felt extremely sheepish around the preacher since the beating he had taken some time ago. His nose still had not healed completely.

Jake had finished cutting Cotton Zarler's hair. As he brushed him off with a whisk broom, he carried on the conversation.

"The thing thet riled me the most," said the barber, "was the way Serveto made fun o' Texas. He said this here country ain't no Promised Land. He said it ain't no land of milk and honey. What do yuh thinka thet, preacher? Ain't thet downright irreverent?"

"Did he really have the nerve to say all that?" Cross asked in disbelief.

"Sure did," thrust in Old Man Zarler, as he handed the barber some money. "Why, Dr. Sterner and me got so danged insulted we jumped ta our feet and demanded Serveto leave the rostrum. And he did too, an' he was hooted outa the hall. Thet sonuvabitch! He's a goldanged Commie, Reverend!"

At this point Cross had climbed into the barber chair. Jake covered him with an apron and started the clippers around the ears. The preacher asked for a head massage first, so Jake reached for the hand vibrator to oblige. Meanwhile, Old Man Zarler sat down near the door. He wasn't through with this bit of scandal.

Jake was not finished with dissecting Serveto either. He

plunged into his denunciation again as he ran the vibrator on the preacher's skull. Cross listened more closely now as the massage relieved the piercing pains in his head.

"Thet greaser made a second mistake this week, too. When he posted his mid-semester grades, he done failed pretty near a third of his class. Ain't thet right, Will?"

"Sure is, Jake. Man! the students were real mad! They been boycotting Serveto's classes the rest of the week and displaying signs all around campus demanding he be fired."

For the first and only time Rex Austin joined in: "One student's been writin' 'Serveto Sucks' on all the blackboards in ever' classroom. Even wrote it on Serveto's door! Ha ha ha!"

Cross stared with disgust at Rex Austin and the latter lapsed into sheepishness again. Cross then said, "I know those things have been scribbled all over the campus about him. I can't say I approve of it. At the same time, I can't help feeling Serveto was clearly asking for trouble."

"He sure was," chimed in Old Man Zarler. "He's been booted out too."

Everyone nodded and mumbled his approval. There was a short lull in the conversation.

Beware the Mexican troublemaker, thought Cross.

"Yeah," said Jake. "He's still frisky as a horned toad and hell-bent as ever! Folks sure are anxious for him ta clear outa town."

That is the way Cross had heard the story of Dr. Serveto's removal. Cross felt that Jake Greenfeld and the others knew what they were talking about. But that was yesterday. Tonight the students were merely letting off steam before the big football game.

The bonfire on the sloping hill in front of the administration building was huge and bellowing. Sparks cracked occasionally over the heads of the spectators and the band played rousing marches and the cheer leaders screamed out their commands to the excited crowd to do the locomotive or do the Cal Davis fight song. The team, undefeated since the opening-day loss, was determined to emerge victorious tomorrow.

One of the husky athletes swung the effigy over the fire by dangling it from a long pole by its neck. The flames licked up at the grotesque figure and consumed it quickly. The crowd cheered. It was a tradition at Cal Davis to burn an image of Old Man Gloom at homecoming, but tonight the mischievous students had hung the label "Dr. Serveto" around the effigy. The cheers had been deafening and the laughter raucous. The students liked the switch.

The restless celebrants, with a certain glint in their eyes, moved back and forth among the willowy dancing shadows choreographed by the crackling, high-rising bonfire. The heat of the fire warmed the faces of the bystanders to such a degree at times that they had to turn away lest they be scorched. And the band blared on. The fight songs stirred the students to bursts of school spirit and near frenzy.

Then someone had an idea. Cross saw several young cowboys trot to an old car, jump in, and drive off with the squeal of spinning tires and great billows of clinging dust. They returned in minutes and emerged from the car with armloads of books and then hurried to the dissipating fire. To the preacher's astonishment, the young cowboys began to toss book after book into the waving, twisting inferno. The students roared their approval. Rebel yells rang in the eardrums. A man flickered from the shadows and turned away in disgust. Cross swore it looked like Dr. Serveto.

But the preacher was tired and his head ached badly. It had been a long hard day. He had attended one class this morning and then spent the rest of the day selling his knives in the area around Geneva Gap. He hadn't sold much. He had decided to stay over for the pep rally, but now he was bone-tired, the pains in his head leaving him weak and trembling. He slipped away from the frenzied crowd and walked to his pickup.

Driving home on the highway, the preacher began to relax. It was quiet and peaceful. All he could hear was the tapping purring monotone of the engine. It felt good now after the cacophonous noise of the Cal Davis rally. And it felt good to let his muscles go limp after the long fatiguing day. Even his headache seemed to fade.

The great pale yellow moon, its face full, reflected a warm light on the landscape, illuminating desert objects that seldom enjoyed the pleasure of a nocturnal light that cast giant shadows across the lonely prairie. The night was warm. A holy night. Or so it seemed to the preacher. And the great round moon shone like the eye of God. The preacher felt at peace with the world. At peace like seldom before. The sacred night embraced him with its warm light and soothed his tattered nerves.

He approached the hills that rose like ancient battlements

around the little valley that was his home. Soon he was swinging the truck off the highway and bumping over the cattle guard and churning up dust on the dirt road by the woods on his way to the sturdy rock-bound house where Marie and the boy lay fast asleep. Cross thought of his wife as he came to a stop at the side of the house. A mixed feeling of hate and love for the woman rose in his breast. He had not loved her for so long now.

Cross got out of the pickup and reached back for his black valise. He slammed the door of the truck and walked wearily around the back side of the house. He hesitated for a minute at the door, searching field and corral and the imposing shadow of Sun Mountain for something, he knew not what. It was as if the hand of God, reaching invisibly from the great round eye of the moon, compelled him to survey his land before he retired.

Then he saw it. It made his heart pound madly. Slinking menacingly along the lower ridges of Sun Mountain was the great black wolf. The black lobo. Its eyes shone slanted and yellowish in the bright light of the full moon. The preacher froze. He watched its silent slinking movements along the slopes. He watched in terror. Cross did not know how long he stood there by the back door of his home and followed the great black shadow with its burning frightful eyes. But the black lobo seemed only to be reconnoitering the sleepy ranch. It howled chillingly and then disappeared into the shadows on the far side of Sun Mountain. Cross relaxed. His nerves tingled with subsiding fear. He glanced once more at the mountain and then entered the sanctuary of his home.

Cross tiptoed through the darkness into the back bedroom. He checked the big crib and felt the warmth and heard the even breathing of the boy. He removed his clothes and rolled into bed. It had been a long time since he had shared this bed with Marie. The sheets smelled clean and fresh and he reached over and felt the curves of the sleeping woman. Then he drew away lest he wake her. He turned on his side and in a twinkling was sound asleep.

During the long night the preacher dreamed. He saw himself in bed. A shadowy, deathlike figure approached slowly and then stopped and touched him on the forearm with a finger as cold as ice. Cross awoke with a jerking guttural moan and wide terror-stricken eyes. He was sitting up. Intense chills washed down his back and up again and flooded his head. The blood itself seemed congealed in his veins and his heart palpitated wildly and sent sharp cutting pains through his chest. The chills enveloped his whole body now and he trembled violently and gasped for breath. He looked about the dark room with wide-open eyes and saw only the usual shapes and forms of the back bedroom and saw the warm light of the full moon gleaming through the unshuttered windows. He breathed more easily. He inhaled deeply and sighed with relief. The chills bathed his body more infrequently and less intensely now. The fear was leaving him. He sighed again and lay back on the pillow.

The preacher lay awake for a time, thinking. He listened to the lonely sounds of the night . . . the crickets chirping, the leaves rustling, the singing hum of empty silence on the great plains.

Cross ached for the warm touch and feel of a woman. He remembered how it was to penetrate the hot sweet passage. His penis throbbed, and he took it in his hand and massaged it gently. His flesh nearly glowed with sexual desire; his mind seethed with visions of beautiful naked bodies, prostrate, grasping, gasping in wild animal orgy. He imagined a huge brute of a man, dark as a Mexican, thrust his bull-like phallus into the voracious hair-fringed orifice between the thighs of a writhing sex-crazed woman. He imagined the insatiable woman was Marie! And the fantasy aroused a delightful blending of jealousy and passion and caused his hand to beat hard around himself so that a pleasurably jarring orgasm convulsed his body.

Cross lay stock-still now, except for his heavy breathing. He was afraid he had disturbed Marie, for she stirred in her sleep. But it was all right. The woman did not awaken. Cross breathed a sigh of relief as he turned on his side. About his loins he felt the warm wet sperm he had ejaculated. A morbid shame overcame him and he covered his head with the comforting blanket.

CHAPTER FIFTEEN

He was in a sullen mood as he raced the old Ford on the highway away from Geneva Gap. Cal Davis was losing its homecoming game and that misfortune had thrown Robby Lee Cross into an even deeper depression. Already, this morning, Marie had revealed her decision to leave him. That had stunned Cross. But he hadn't argued with her. He simply left the house and went to the football game to divert his mind from his troubles.

But the game had not gone well either, and the piercing headaches had begun to throb again. Cross was distraught and fidgety. He longed for some relief from the pressures of his life. He could endure the pain no longer. Seeing the depressing fate of the Saints, he decided to leave the stadium and drive to the isolated water hole he had discovered some time ago.

Beer was a welcome sight. Cross could see the tiny oasis in the faraway distance as he rocked and bumped precariously in the cab of the rickety pickup speeding on the potholed, dusty road. It was a cool autumn day in the desert with the sun's rays no longer sapping the sweat and the strength from a man's body. And the desert stretches seemed much less forbidding now.

Cross pulled up at the general store where a lonely gray pickup stood alongside. The preacher saw no one as he slid out of the truck. The huddling nest of buildings seemed deserted and lifeless, the preacher hearing only the incessant buzzing monotone of winged insects. At the door of the store, he looked around before entering. No trace of movement. The town seemed dead.

He entered and walked into the back barroom.

"Anybody home?" he yelled.

No one answered. A calmnness, a stillness, pervaded the shadowy barroom. Cross surveyed the rows of bottles along the wall and then caught sight of Eve Eternal. His eyes riveted on the sensual woman of careless abandon. His heart pounded as he felt a hungry passion revive in his loins. He watched the woman warily, then hesitantly he stepped around and behind the bar to gaze at her more fixedly. A curious expression played on the preacher's face. Either an expression of desire or hate.

The preacher reached for a bottle, taking his eye from Eve Eternal just enough to notice the scrawled note on the counter by the cash register. Cross could barely decipher the pencil scratchings. "Be back later. Help yourself, but leave your money on the bar. We ain't charity."

The preacher wondered if Jael had left the note. He remembered her as if she had been in a dream a long time ago. He couldn't imagine her a real person, flesh and blood. She appeared so amorphous and hazy in his mind. Why, at this moment Eve Eternal was more real to him.

The preacher poured a tall glass, lifted himself onto the bar, and proceeded to drink carelessly and stare intensively at Eve Eternal.

The words of the book of Judges played in his brain: "*And Jael went out to meet Sisera, and said unto him, Turn in, my lord, turn in to me; fear not. And when he had turned in unto her into the tent, she covered him with a mantle.*

"*And he said unto her, Give me, I pray thee, a little water to drink; for I am thirsty. And she opened a bottle of milk, and gave him drink, and covered him.*"

The preacher shook his head as the liquor worked its spell. Cross lapsed into a buzzing anaesthetic state of non-thinking.

After several hours of pleasant intoxication, the preacher slapped some money on the counter and maneuvered a weaving path to the old Ford pickup. No one had come into the store, the saloon, all afternoon. He couldn't understand it. The place was dead. "Well, who cares?" He revved up the engine of the pickup, spun rubber on the loose gravel, and raced out onto the dirt road leading back to the highway.

He brooded over his life now as he drove carelessly on the black asphalt highway. He got up at dawn each day, drove miles to Geneva Gap, went to college, worked hard at selling and preaching, ate three routine meals a day, and drove the long highway back to the ranch at night only to sleep fitfully and alone. The same old grind. And what did it all matter? Everything seemed tasteless, colorless, and flat. And he seemed always tired lately. Life seemed a mad merry-go-round of senseless comings and goings. Nothing seemed worth striving for. Everything he saw, everything he felt, everything he did, seemed as nothing to him now. Everything was nothing. NOTHING. He wondered if he should simply drive as hard and fast as he could and then swing off a cliff somewhere into painless oblivion. End it all. That was one answer to the nagging ache of emptiness he felt deep in his bowels.

No. That was no answer. He must get hold of himself. "Gird yourself with the strength of the Lord," he told himself. He must not despair. He must not give up. He must not. He shook his head violently several times as if he were trying to shake loose from his drunken morbidity. He focused on the road ahead.

The highway was hard and smooth in late October. The slanting rays of the sun had eased the heat since the beginning of autumn, and the black asphalt highway no longer became sticky and oily.

Dusk was approaching and the dark mesas in the distance were casting long shadows across the wide open plain. Cross surveyed the landscape trying to take his mind off his troubles. In the skyline ahead he could see great thunder clouds gathering. Soon it would rain.

In a twinkling the sun disappeared behind the mushrooming thunderheads on the western horizon. A cool shadow crept over the land. And in the onrushing distance Cross saw a tiny black figure bobbing on the highway moving towards his speeding vehicle.

The black figure grew larger and larger in the onrushing distance as the little pickup sped onward. Then he recognized the black robes and old wicked features of Brigitta Obispo. Cross kept an eye on her as he sped forward. She grew larger and more distinct, and then in an instant he had whizzed by her. The preacher looked in the rear view mirror and saw her stop and gaze after him in the gloom of the approaching storm. Her black figure shrunk rapidly now as he sped away in the old Ford pickup. The preacher shuddered. He wondered what she could be doing in the middle of nowhere at this hour of the expiring

day. He shuddered again and tried to forget her deathly ky-
photic silhouette.

Cross began to sing. He sang so forcefully that his vocal
chords ached with the strain, but he continued to bellow forth
the song.

> "You'll take the high road
> And I'll take the low road.
> And I'll be in Scotland afore yuh.
> But me and my true love
> We'll never meet again
> On the bonnie, bonnie banks
> Of Loch Lomond."

Over and over again the preacher cried out the words of the
mournful dirge. Over and over again so that his throat became
rasping raw with the shouting. Then when he could bear the
pain no longer, he swallowed and began to whistle the sad re-
frain.

The threatening storm was upon him. Cross could see above
a whole convoy of huge cotton clouds escorting ships of purple
thunderheads, bearing precious cargos of rain in their holds.
They moved silently across the great ocean of gloomy heaven.
He heard the first warning rumbles of thunder like the muffled
guns of great warships. Then came salvos of clapping thunder
and instantaneous flashes of jagged lightning. The rain came in a
sudden downpour. And all about the highway there lay a deep
dark gloom.

Cross slowed the truck to a crawl. He switched on the headlights and turned on the windshield wipers . . . working back
and forth . . . back and forth. Between the clearing swipes Cross
could see the gray sheets of rain plummeting downward and
forming puddles on the bald thirsty earth of the desert
stretches. He drove over a narrow bridge spanning an arroyo
that was straining its banks to contain the flash flood of rainwater. Branches of mesquite and sagebrush raced under the
bridge, caught in the swift current.

A little beyond the bridge Cross caught a glimpse of a big
yellow coyote scampering across a field of scrub brush, seeking
refuge from the sudden downpour. The fur of the animal was
pasted down with rain so that its body appeared skeletal and
scrawny. The preacher snorted at the skittish down-tailed lope
of the desert predator.

It was a long while before Cross steered the little pickup off the highway and onto the access road leading to the ranch. It was still raining, less intensely now, but the downpour made the early evening even darker than usual. Cross swung the truck alongside the ranch house, killed the engine, and dragged his black valise along the seat as he slid out the door from the cab of the truck. He could see a dim light in the living room window as he walked dejectedly in the rain toward the front entrance. He still had a dizzy drunken feeling as he wearily mounted the rock steps and entered the porch. But the stupor of the long drive had dissipated. The short walk through the rain shower seemed to sharpen his senses.

Cross hesitated a minute before entering the house. He felt a sudden premonition of danger. He wondered at the fear welling up within him.

As he entered the dimly lit living room, his heart leaped and a painful throbbing clutched at his throat taking his breath away. A shadow of a man stumbled through the swinging door of the kitchen. For an instant Cross froze in terrible bewilderment. He heard the squeak-squeak-squeak of the kitchen door swinging back and forth on its hinges and then the ka-bam! of the rear door being slammed and the sound of running footsteps outside.

Cross overcame his fearful inertia and ran to the window facing the far side of the ranch. In the misty rain he saw the shadow of the man again, fumbling with something in the front seat of a low-slung foreign sportscar. Then Cross heard the sputter of the engine and the slosh of racing wheels in muddy puddles and saw arms lashing wildly to turn the speeding vehicle, as the car sped away into the blackness and mist of the rainy night.

Cross stood at the window, staring with disbelief and terror into the dark night. Hideous thoughts crossed and recrossed his mind. Marie! Oh, Marie, Marie! She did have a lover! He had caught them together at last! He should've known all along. He had suspected her before. She had always been a weak sensual woman. She had to feel the savage impact of a man's body. A lecher's body! She had always lusted! Like every woman, half whore and half mother. A steaming bitch! Eve Eternal, no Virgin Mary. She couldn't control her evil lust. He covered his eyes with his arms as if for protection. His head whirled in a mad merry-go-round of pain and anger and despair. And his anger grew to insane rage at the sickening plot he had uncovered. The shadow! The evil shadow of the man. That Mexican lecher! It must be him!

The preacher walked about the room in great agitation, his eyes red with rage, wet with tears, his hands fidgeting, squirming, as if searching for an answer, a judgment.

Suddenly he stopped his frenzied pacing. His eyes, filled with hate and rage, held firm on the black valise lying on the coffee table before the couch. The preacher gazed intently. Then slowly, deliberately, he walked to it. He knelt down before the low table and opened the lid of the black valise. He did it all with great care, as if performing a ritual that allowed no deviation. The maddened preacher recalled the words of Leviticus: *"And the man that committeth adultery with another man's wife . . . the adulterer and the adulteress shall surely be put to death."* His wild eyes inspected each knife carefully, as hands slid caressingly over sharp shiny weapons. His hands trembled. The right hand enfolded the grooved handle of a heavy butcher knife. It was his biggest and most expensive instrument. Its cut was swift and sure like that of a machete. Cross brandished it unconsciously. His eyes burned.

The preacher rose to his feet and stepped slowly toward the back bedroom, the butcher knife glinting in the dim light. His walk was deliberate, almost reverent, as if approaching the altar of God. He moved silently into the room and stopped inside the doorway.

On the bed against the wall the woman lay huddled. Her body was bare and her fine naked legs twitched convulsively. The room was dim, lit only by a small bed lamp, and the shadows in the room of sin were ominous and expectant. Cross discerned all of this in an instant. *The woman is awaiting her fate, her punishment.*

She whimpered as if in shock, and he saw her body shake with terror in the shadows along the wall. The painful throbbing clutched at the preacher's throat again as he moved slowly towards the bed.

The fearful butcher knife fell like an axe on the woman. A fierce soulful scream shook the house. The butcher knife fell again and again and again. It chopped, it sliced, in a savage rush of swings from heaven to hell. Every limb, every curve, all her beauty hacked to bloody pieces. And the butcher's knife sank like a cleaver again and again and again into María Dolores.

Suddenly the chopping frenzy stopped. The preacher's right

arm dropped to his side and the bloody cleaver clanked to the floor. The breathless man stood motionless for a long time at the edge and end of his marriage bed. Blood flowed and trickled over the edge, forming little lakes of life on the floor. And on the bed human flesh and bone lay broken and still oozing.

The figure at the edge of the bed seemed to sink into the ground. His shoulders hunched over, his head bowed low, his whole frame hanging loosely. Then his head moved slightly and the eyes and brain began to focus. He felt a weak hollow sensation in his loins and a hot sticky wetness down his pant leg. He felt freed of all passion, completely satiated.

He looked at the gore on the bed as if in wonderment. His gaze filled with horror. He turned away, his hands to his face. He screamed to wake up! He must be dreaming! He must be dreaming!

A sharp, jangling wail like a faraway siren began to pierce deeply into his nerve-wracked brain. It grew louder and more piercing as if it were going to burst his head asunder. The preacher grimaced in pain, slapped his hands over his ears, and groaned in agony. He turned toward the crib and saw Danny standing in the fenced-in bed, screaming and sobbing uncontrollably.

"Stop it!" barked the preacher. "Stop it!"

But the boy only screamed louder in his terror. Cross sprang to the crib and cuffed the boy hard on the side of the head. The boy fell unconscious to the mattress.

Then a deathly silence.

The preacher felt suddenly ill. He ran staggering out of the bedroom, through the living room, and out the porch. He scarcely made it out the screen door when he became violently sick. Over and over he vomited against the front wall of the house, until he thought he would vomit his life away. The liquified half-digested food ran down the solid rocks of his home. The preacher vomited even more till there was nothing left. But, leaning his head against the wall of rocks, the man continued to retch so that his head seemed on the verge of bursting. When the retching ended, then a grim limpness and nausea. He coughed hard and spat on the ground.

Cross staggered to the pickup and clambered in. He was soaked with the rain, but the cold moisture had revived him. He started the engine, switched on the headlights, and wheeled the truck around and drove madly up the muddy splashing road and onto the lonely highway.

The painful throbbing clutched at his throat again. He could barely breathe. His body pulsated violently. He couldn't believe what was happening.

He felt as if his essence were apart from his body, watching from a distance. Fearful thoughts shot through his mind. It had all happened before and he was just now acting out the fearful tragedy. He craved belief in some personal predestination. But his will was not involved! His conscience was not involved. Surely not that! His body was speeding toward its fate impelled by forces for which Robby Lee Cross was not responsible. He could change nothing! NOTHING. It was all beyond his power. And the more he wished he could change his fate, the more he knew he could not. The horrible deed was done.

Cross cried out in anguish. Why was this happening to him? The painful throbbing clutched at his throat. He felt doomed. There was no turning back. He screamed against the fate that had captured him. Tears filled his eyes and ran down his cheeks, as he wailed in agony.

"God! Oh, my God!" he cried.

Cross was driving at a deadly speed. Tears flowed from his eyes and the rains poured from the heavens and the little pickup skidded on the wet pavement of the highway.

CHAPTER SIXTEEN

"Them black vultures got ta him, yuh know," Jake Greenfeld said in a lowered voice, his eyes furtive, fearful someone passing by the barber shop might hear this terrible judgment.

"Ah heard 'bout thet," boomed Cotton Zarler in response, caring not at all who might be listening. "Ah'm mighty sorry the highway patrol didn't find the wreck quicker. Leastaways he wouldn'ta had his body pecked at so bad. Ah hear tell them vultures got ta his eyes and his balls. Poor ol' Robalee!"

Jake, Rex Austin, and Dr. Sterner nodded soberly at Cotton Zarler's words. The four men meditated sadly for a few moments. Then Rex Austin resumed cutting Dr. Sterner's hair, while Jake Greenfeld remained immobile behind Cotton Zarler sitting in the first chair.

"Ah'm feelin' awful sorry for Will Busbee maself," moaned Rex Austin. "Ah don't reckon he had nuthin' ta do with the murder o' Robalee's wife, much less anythin' else. The fingerprints on the butcher knife was Robalee's own fingerprints!"

"Well, they ain't holdin' him for murder, Rex," said Cotton Zarler. "Ah talked ta ma ol' buddy at the sheriff's office an' he tole me they got him for rape. Seems lak little Danny done testified ta Will Busbee's part ina whole affair. Hear tell the boy saw the rape."

"Did he see the murder?" asked Dr. Sterner expectantly.

"Nope. Not as ah know of anyways. There's a lot o' details ain't out yet. Hear tell Danny was in shock for a long time afterwards."

"There ain't no way Will Busbee can be convicted," said

Jake Greenfeld firmly. "Ah feel lak thet Mexican family o'
Marie's is puttin' him up ta all this nonsense. Mebbe Serveto's
involved too!"

"You're dang right!" jabbed Cotton Zarler. "We ain't gonna
be fooled by them agitators from Mexican Town, yuh can bet
your bottom dollah! No jury made up o' good Christian Texans
is gonna send 'im downa river for some Mexican troubles!"

"Won't dare, sure as shootin'," said Dr. Sterner.

A pause to reflect.

"Too bad about Danny."

"Well, what yuh expect, Jake?" bellowed Cotton Zarler.
"Robalee had no business marryin' inta a Mexican family. Ol'
Dan'l used ta piss an' moan about Robalee marryin' up with a
Mexican. Used ta come up for supper sometimes an' tell me an'
Hanna all about the trouble he was havin' with Robalee. Ol'
Dan'l died of a broken heart, and yuh better believe it!"

"Ah feel sorry for young Danny, though," insisted Jake
Greenfeld. "He's livin' with the Obregons in Mexican Town."

"Yeah," growled Cotton Zarler. "Bein' raised lak a Mexican."

0207